THE
LOON'S
SONG

THE LOON'S SONG

A Wynter Island Mystery

KIM HERDMAN SHAPIRO

LEVEL
BEST BOOKS

First published by Level Best Books 2024

This novel is entirely a work of fiction. The names, characters and incidents portrayed in it are the work of the author's imagination. Any resemblance to actual persons, living or dead, events or localities is entirely coincidental.

Kim Herdman Shapiro asserts the moral right to be identified as the author of this work.

Author Photo Credit: Ben Shapiro

First edition

ISBN: 978-1-68512-603-2

Cover art by Kim Herdman Shapiro

This book was professionally typeset on Reedsy.
Find out more at reedsy.com

For Arlene,
with love and gratitude
for all the years of sisterhood

Reviews for The Raven's Cry, Book I of The Wynter Island Mysteries

"Readers who enjoy skewed, twisty plots will appreciate the threads of quirky characters and doubt Shapiro has carefully woven together. Fans of small-town cozy mysteries will enjoy this action-packed yet character-driven story."—BookLife/Publishers Weekly

"Shapiro, a former print and broadcast journalist in Canada, creates a vivid world on Wynter Island, and it's one that's full of quirky characters—from bitter hotel manager Bob Corker, who's certain that his daughter should have gotten Kate's job, to kind Shea Porter, an animal rescuer and librarian, and elderly Vera Schmidt, whose reputation for the best eggs on the island starts events in motion that put Kate's life in danger. Although the novel can't accurately be called a cozy mystery—certain details are simply too graphic and frightening for that subgenre—the small-town environment is inherently comforting, with enough genuine goodwill that readers will be able to see Kate's future as a happy one—provided she gets through the next few weeks alive. A suspenseful blend of cozy and thrilling mystery elements."—Kirkus Reviews

"Kim Herdman Shapiro tells a deeply immersive, evocative tale against an enticing backdrop of characters and plot threads that will leave cozy mystery fans eager to explore in future installments."—IndieReader

"*The Raven's Cry* will have you on your toes after encountering cleverly imagined stakes, surprises, and tidbits by the experienced journalist and author, Kim Herdman Shapiro. It is a must-read mystery that brims with exciting cliffhangers which will adeptly build anticipation for the second part of this new series."—The Feathered Quill

Characters

Main

- Kate Zöe Thomas - Manager of CWYN - Wynter Island's Community TV station
- Jupiter - Kate's Australian Shepherd mix and constant companion
- Gwen Wynter - Matriarch of island and owner of CWYN
- Shea Porter - Kate's best friend. Island librarian and animal rescuer
- Ben Navaerez - Local veterinarian who is romantically interested in Kate
- Michael Rossino - Island Trustee and lawyer, married and unaware of Kate's crush on him

Police

- Sgt. Stewart MacLeod - Chief RCMP officer on island
- Const. Lesley Akiyama - Other full time RCMP officer on island, in a relationship with Shea Porter
- Staff Sgt. Ian Singh - RCMP officer brought in to deal with homicide investigations

Islanders

- Vera Schmidt - Retired pharmacist who specializes in herbal medicines
- Bob Corker - Co-owner of the Lind Hotel and volunteer at the TV station
- Doreen Corker - Co-owner of the Lind Hotel, married to Bob

- Dougie Whitestone - Local jack-of-all trades and volunteer at the TV station
- Anna Rossino - Lawyer and Green Party politician, in a troubled marriage to Michael Rossino
- Nate Rossino - Son of Anna and Michael and volunteer at the TV Station
- Fisherman Phil - Grumpy elderly fisherman
- Kurt - Co-manager of The Legion Bar
- Harald - Co-manager of the Legion Bar, married to Kurt

T'sawout Band - Wynter Island Reserve #9

- Sam Hanks - Unofficial leader of the Reserve, consultant for businesses working with Indigenous peoples
- Selesia Sixto - Sam's sister and social worker. Divorced with two sons
- Brad Sixto - Selesia's son - 16 years old
- Will Sixto - Selesia's son - 18 years old

Newcomers to the island

- Rosalie/Rose Morgan - Wynter Island native who ran away to Hollywood and became a TV star. Retires and returns to island to write her autobiography.
- Jason Bálachet - Rosalie's manager/boyfriend
- Scott Quillimento - Personal assistant to Rosalie
- Betty Wu - retiree who has bought the house next door to Rosalie's
- Gordon Wu - husband of Betty

Maps

SALISH SEA BASIN

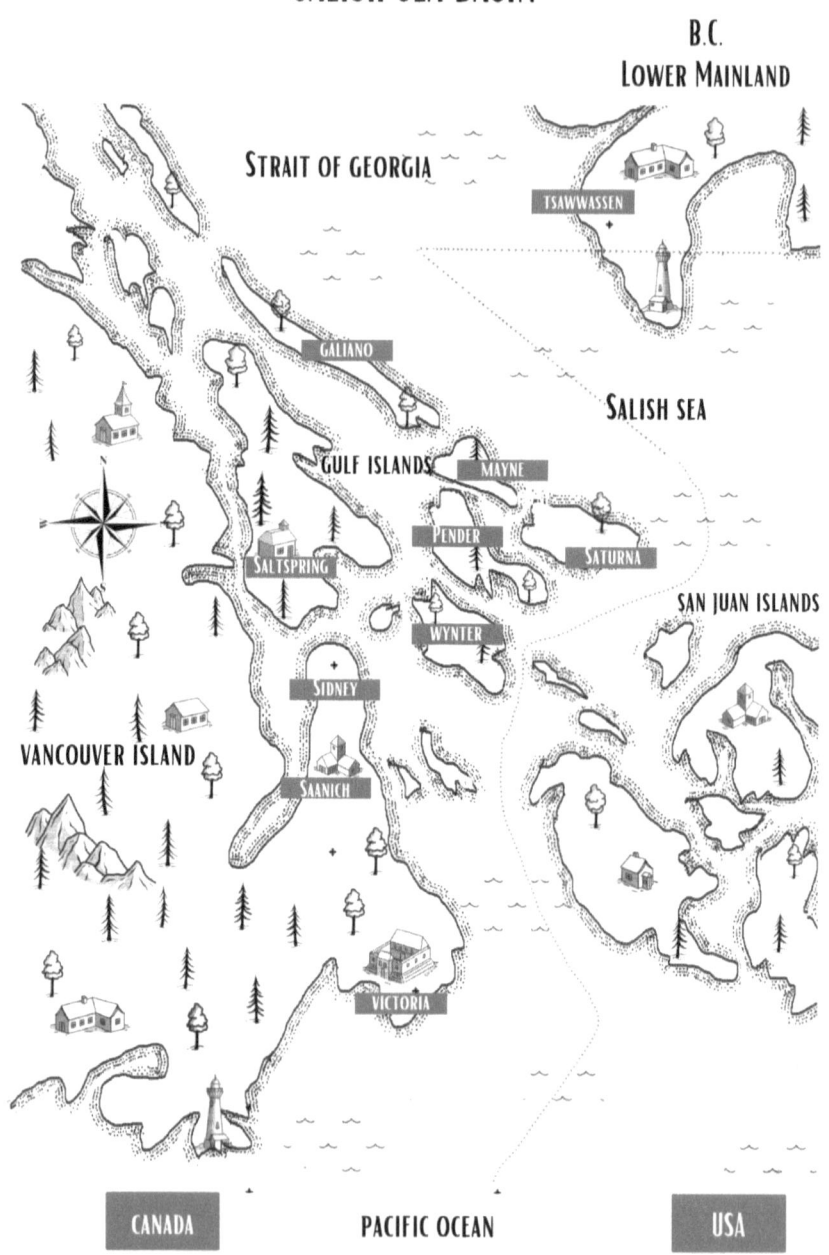

B.C.
Lower Mainland

Strait of georgia

TSAWWASSEN

Salish sea

GALIANO

Gulf islands

MAYNE

Pender

Saturna

San juan islands

Saltspring

Wynter

Sidney

Saanich

VANCOUVER ISLAND

Victoria

CANADA

PACIFIC OCEAN

USA

★ THIS IS A FICTIONAL MAP

WYNTER ISLAND, B.C.

POP. 2,452

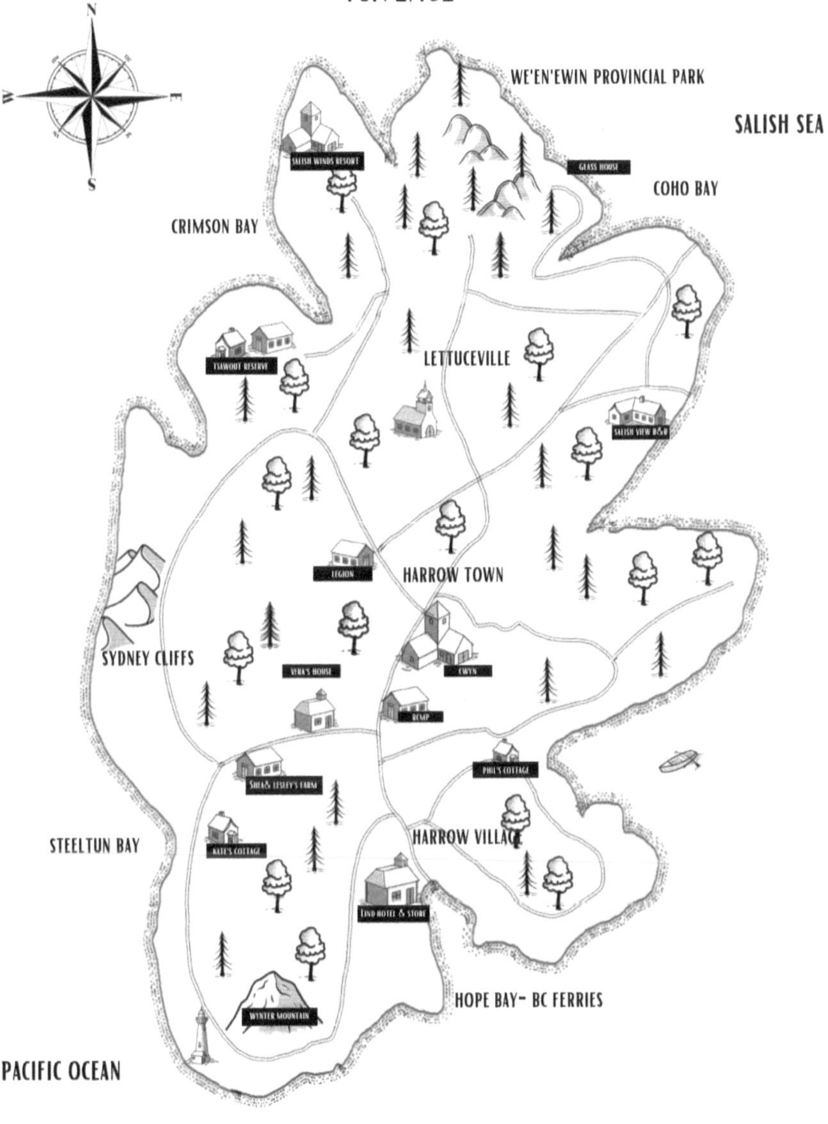

WE'EN'EWIN PROVINCIAL PARK

SALISH SEA

GLASS HOUSE

COHO BAY

CRIMSON BAY

SALISH WINDS RESORT

TSAWOUT RESERVE

LETTUCEVILLE

SALISH VIEW B&B

LEGION

HARROW TOWN

SYDNEY CLIFFS

VERA'S HOUSE

CWYN

RCMP

SHEA & LESLEY'S FARM

PHIL'S COTTAGE

KATE'S COTTAGE

HARROW VILLAGE

LIND HOTEL & STORE

STEELTUN BAY

WYNTER MOUNTAIN

HOPE BAY— BC FERRIES

PACIFIC OCEAN

Chapter One

"I can't believe that bitch actually came back."

I took a sip from my paper coffee cup and walked toward the two women chatting beside the cash register. The rain thundered outside the steamy windows of the Lind General Store, a sluice of water racing downhill toward the ferry dock. In bright sunshine, the grand Victorian-style Lind Hotel beckoned tourists to its bed & breakfast, restaurant, and cozy General store. But it had been a horrible summer on Wynter Island, weather-wise. Nothing but rain, rain, and then more rain. We'd barely seen the sun since June. And it wasn't just us. The entire southwest coast of British Columbia was as soaked as we were. Was it possible for people to mildew? If we didn't get some sunshine soon, I might have to start worrying about that.

"Which bitch came back?"

Vera turned from Doreen to see who had spoken. "Oh, it's you, Kate." Her brow softened as she smiled over at me. "I wasn't sure who it was."

I walked over to the two women. Vera, the island's retired pharmacist, wore her gray hair swept up into a bun topped with an abalone hair clip, her body dressed in a paisley smock dress that looked large enough to hide two Vera's within it. Vera's style was questionable—to say the least—but she sold it with her typical verve and conviction. Doreen, who ran the hotel and General Store with her husband, appeared much more down to earth in her jeans and blue fleece top. It would have been easy to place both of them in two white t-shirts with the words "Extrovert" written on one and "Introvert" written on the other.

"Does it matter who it was?"

Vera and Doreen exchanged a look that said, you better believe it does, before shaking their heads no.

"Oh no. We were just gossiping."

"I know, that's why I asked. Oh, before I forget." I slid my toonies across the counter towards Doreen, who picked it up and placed it in the drawer. "For the coffee."

"Thanks, Kate."

Jupiter, my Australian shepherd mix, skittered around my feet, anxious for the treat he knew was in my pocket. "Okay, Jupiter. Settle."

He lay down on the floor beside me, his nose pointed upwards, mouth open and ready to receive. He radiated self-satisfaction like a child awaiting a lollipop. I bent down and placed a treat in his mouth, which vanished immediately with a rosy tongue slurp.

"He's getting better, isn't he?" Vera asked, looking down at his distinctive white, black, and grey coat, which gave him the look of a small silver wolf.

"I've been working with him. Reading books on dog training and dog behavior. He'll let you pet him now if you want to, Vera."

"Really?" Vera placed one quick pat on his silky back and immediately lifted her hand away. She remembered only too well the stray I had adopted a few months earlier. Anti-social was an appropriate term to describe him. "He's getting friendlier."

"How long have you had him now? Four months or so?" Doreen asked.

"Yup. We're partners in crime, aren't we, Jupe?" He glanced up at the sound of his name, hoping for another treat. "No, that's it for now, mister. You settle while I find out who Vera and Doreen are gossiping about."

Doreen sighed. "It's Rose. Rose Morgan."

I hesitated, waiting for more information, but none was forthcoming. "Okay, who is Rose Morgan?"

"You don't know who Rose Morgan is?" Vera asked, stunned.

"Of course, Kate doesn't know who she is." Doreen turned back toward me. "She goes by her stage name now: Rosalie Morgann."

"Rosalie Morgann? The actress? The one in that evening soap?"

Both women nodded their heads.

"She's from here? Wynter Island?"

"Yes, not that you'd know it from her interviews. I don't think she's ever even mentioned that she's Canadian. She probably wanted to cover her tracks. Didn't want the press finding out about the mess she left when she ran away."

"Ran away? Hold on, go back to the beginning, Doreen."

Doreen sighed. "Okay. Rose, sorry Rosalie, grew up here on Wynter. Her father was a fisherman. I can't remember what her mom did."

"Nurse," Vera supplied.

"Yes, her mother was a nurse. She was killed in a car accident when Rose was about nine. Her father never got over it, started to drink, and stopped fishing regularly. He sold his boat when the bills started to pile up, and they lived off that money until it ran out."

"It was unfortunate," Vera said. "People tried to help. I know Phil tried to get him to see the doctor, but he wasn't having any of it."

"So what happened to Rosalie?"

"Well, all of their money went to booze and then, if she was lucky, food," Doreen answered, her face betraying a brief moment of sadness. "The minister saw to it that regular meals came to the house. He finally called Social Services, and they came out from Victoria and read her father the riot act."

"Did that help?"

"Sorta. He went on welfare and ensured Rose had enough to eat."

"Well, she might've had a full belly, but she didn't have a stitch of decent clothing to cover it," Vera said. "She ended up living in hand-me-downs."

Doreen added, "So she looked a mess: dirty hair, unwashed, shabby clothes. The kids started to tease her."

"So far," I said, "I'm not seeing the bitch part of this story."

"It's coming," Doreen answered with grim determination.

"She didn't have any friends, so Selesia, who was a few years older, took Rose under her wing," Vera continued. "She was always out there on the Reserve. As she got older, Selesia showed her how to look after herself:

3

makeup and stuff. And then she…umm…blossomed."

"Blossomed?" I laughed. "That sounds like something from a Victorian bodice-ripper romance."

"Well," Doreen bristled, "that's what happened. One day, she was a filthy little stick of a girl, and the next, she was a voluptuous…" she stumbled a little over the word, "woman."

"And she was stunning. I mean, beautiful," Vera added. "Just like she is now. Those big blue eyes and thick gold hair."

"Still not seeing the bitch part."

"Oh, you will. Suddenly, she was getting a lot of attention." Doreen paused to let that sink in for a moment. "From men."

"Older men," Vera added. "Married men."

"I'm beginning to see where this is going now."

"Rosalie realized that her beauty was a way to get attention, affection, and money. And so she took all three. From many men."

"Many?"

"Many," Vera repeated. "Between the ages of fifteen and nineteen, she ran through most of the available men on the island."

"And several of the unavailable," Doreen added. "It was as if her beauty was some magical potion that drew them in."

"I'm guessing the women on Wynter were immune?"

Vera glanced over at Doreen. "Well, there was that painter lady who spent one summer here…"

"It doesn't matter, Vera," Doreen continued. "The point is that she used whomever she could, man or woman, and didn't care about the consequences."

"She broke up more than one marriage …" Vera let that trail off.

Doreen clamped her lips together in a solid, unforgiving line. "She slept with my best friend's husband," she said in a brittle tone, "and he was stupid enough to believe they had a future together."

Vera nodded her head in agreement. "It was very sad. He left Alice, and she, well, she…"

"Killed herself." Doreen's chin trembled slightly. "Shot herself out in the woods near Wynter Mountain. It was days before we found her."

"Oh shit."

"Yeah, oh shit, is right."

"By that point, she had managed to alienate everyone on the island except for Selesia."

"What happened with Selesia?"

The General Store door tinkled as Dougie rushed in. He had his hood up on his waterproof jacket and held both hands over his head as if that might offer extra protection.

"Yes, b'y, is it raining outside or what! If it keeps pissin' like this, we won't have any summer at all!"

"Good morning to you, too, Dougie." Doreen pointed to a half dozen brown boxes sticking out of the back room entrance. "The Amazon parcels are over there."

"G'morning, Doreen, Vera. Hi Kate, how are you doing? I haven't seen you for a bit."

Dougie smiled his ever-present grin. It sliced across his red cheeks to expose bright white teeth, clenching a scotch mint in one corner. No matter what the problem, Dougie was a perpetual optimist, the stereotypical jolly ginger. I immediately smiled back at him.

"Yeah, I know. I took a bit of a break after..." I hesitated as everyone already knew the story.

How I had been suspected of murdering my ex-boyfriend, only to have the actual murderer attempt to drown Jupiter and me in an attempt to tie up all the loose ends.

Sometimes, in my dreams, I was back there again, sinking deeper and deeper below the surface, the dark, watery depths dragging me down. I would jolt awake and, in the inky blackness, reach out for the silky, sleeping form of Jupiter, relief flooding through me at the thump of his gently wagging tail against the bed.

Yes, it's just a dream. Everything is alright. We survived. We're home.

"I drove back East with Jupiter to visit my family."

Doreen hesitated before speaking to Dougie, her eyes watching me with wary concern. "Dougie, have you seen Greg at all?"

Dougie shook the rainwater off the arms of his jacket. "Yeah. He's doing okay. Worried about his mom." Dougie also glanced at my face with a flash of concern. "She pleaded guilty to Second-degree murder, so she has ten years to go before she has any chance of parole. She's in Maple Ridge, at the women's correctional center."

"And Greg's sentence? It's not as bad as hers, is it?"

Dougie shook his head no. "Because they both pleaded guilty and accepted a plea deal, he's got five years before he can request parole."

The three of them watched me. I glanced away to study the candy rack, fingering a Coffee Crisp while trying not to remember that day. The day I had watched as the two of them, shackled at their hands and feet, stood in court to accept their punishment. When the judge struck his gavel and adjourned the courtroom, my anger dissipated like a fine mist. All that was left was loss. Loss for Daniel, loss for me, loss for everyone.

"Umm, I've got to get going." I gestured with my hand for Jupiter to stand. "Can't talk all morning. I've got to get some work done!"

I assumed my smile looked as forced as it felt as I quickly hurried out the door and into the pouring rain.

Chapter Two

I couldn't believe the station was finally finished. At times, it had felt like an insurmountable Everest, what with the difficulties of construction on a small, isolated island. But the construction crew had worked miracles and completed it during my six-week recuperation break, transforming a single office space into a functioning TV station. The wall of windows overlooking the street now lit an open-plan office/meeting area of desks, tables, comfy chairs, and editing bays. The studio was hidden behind a dividing wall, with two access doors and a soundproofed control room attached. The odd whiff of new paint and freshly sawn wood still hung fleetingly in the air, but the space was usable. Jupiter, still suspicious that the noisy men would return, waited warily in his dog bed for their reappearance.

"It's nice to see everyone again."

I smiled at the looks of surprise from the volunteers, glancing around in wonder at the transformed space. Doreen quickly stuck her hand up like an eager child in a classroom.

"You don't have to put your hand up, Doreen. This is just our monthly volunteer meeting."

"Sorry, Kate. When we ask questions at the Garden Club, Bob makes me raise my hand first." She laughed, the dimples pushing up into her cheeks to dot both sides of her nose in quasi-punctuation marks.

Sitting next to Gwen on the folding chairs I had placed out, Vera rolled her eyes heavenward. "Of course he does," she muttered. "An anal-retentive if ever I saw one."

"We started a woman's group while you were on vacation," Doreen continued. "It's called Crafting with Cocktails."

"Which comes first," I asked with a grin, "the crafting or the cocktails?"

"Definitely the cocktails," Vera replied without hesitating.

Today, Vera had chosen to adorn herself in an unseasonably light sundress. It was her stiff middle finger to the rain blanketing the island. *So there! It's July. I'm wearing a sundress.*

Gwen continued. "Each week, we rotate houses and try a new cocktail." She added, almost as an afterthought, "And work on crafting projects. We're doing decoupage right now."

"Please tell me you're not driving yourselves home after this?"

Doreen shook her head. "No, Dougie drops us off and picks us up afterward. We're calling him 'Wynter Island's Uber driver.'"

"Where is Dougie, by the way? I thought for sure he'd be here today."

"He's over at the Zoloffs, I think," Shea answered. "They had a big pine tumble over last night, so he's got to clear that away. We've had so much rain the soil's saturated. Everything even close to the shoreline is unstable."

"Yeah, I saw that the Sydney Cliffs are closed again."

The Sydney Cliffs. One of the highest and most breathtaking viewpoints on the island. It was a place of both beauty and sadness for me: the place where my ex-boyfriend, Daniel, had fallen to his death.

Shea nodded her head. "That's part of the reason why Selesia isn't here today. They had a section of fence give way. She and Brad are trying to fix it to keep the horses in."

I glanced out the window at the drizzling rain outside. "In this? How terrible. Well, at least it's not pouring, I guess."

"That's the best we've been able to hope for all summer," Shea said. "Light rain rather than a torrential downpour. It's been God-awful for the businesses. Barely any tourists."

I sighed. The B&Bs and outdoor recreation companies on Wynter Island were barely holding on. A disastrous summer might just be enough to finish off a few more of them.

"How about Kurt and Harald?"

An uncomfortable silence met my question. Gwen finally broke it.

"Business-wise, I think they're okay. They've got the income from the Legion to keep them going, even if they aren't getting many bookings at the B&B. On a personal level ..." Her voice ebbed away into silence.

"Immigration Canada is investigating Harald," Vera continued for her. "Their marriage is valid, so that's one good thing, but he's been charged with falsifying immigration papers."

I remembered Kurt's face, overwhelmed with grief, an overgrown stubbly beard skirting the bottom half of his haggard face. It had been horrible for him to learn that Harald had been married previously and, even worse, was going to be arrested for the murder of Daniel.

Thankfully, the real killer was found, and Harald was released from jail. But that did not change the fact that his attempt to keep his first marriage secret by lying on his immigration paperwork had been uncovered. The police had no choice but to notify Immigration Canada.

"We're all trying to stay hopeful," Shea offered somewhat weakly.

Which hopeful? I wondered. Hopeful Harald manages to stay in Canada? Or, hopeful his marriage to Kurt survives?

"Fish Bingo is going great," Nate added. "We had two shows while you were away. We got a ton of live streams."

"A ton of what?" Vera asked.

Nate's thin, lantern-jawed face broke into a smile. He was almost eighteen, the dusky shadow of a bad shave cloaking the lower half of his face. "Live streams, Vera. You know, YouTube. The internet. The fancy, new-fangled computer stuff. Like radio, except better."

Vera turned to fix him with a steely glare. "Don't you get cheeky with me, Nate Rossino."

"Did Phil cause any problems?" I redirected the conversation back to safer ground.

Fisherman Phil was a lifer, born and raised on this island set in the Salish Sea between Vancouver and Vancouver Island. He was a small commercial fisherman known for his cantankerous nature and miserly need to hold on to every nickel he had ever earned.

"He tried to get me to overpay for the salmon by saying it was better than A1 quality. I don't think there is such a thing. I handled it. I'm hoping the viewing numbers will switch from our YouTube channel to the TV station when we move from online to over the airwaves."

"Great! So, of course, the big news is that we're going on-air for the first time with our live call-in talk show, Vox Pop."

"Yes, Michael is going to be the first guest," Shea said.

I glanced out the glass door at the blue Subaru Forester parked in front of the Island's Trust office across from us. I tried to push down the complicated emotions rising in my throat. Michael. Michael Rossino. He was like a potato chip; impossible not to want more. This was complicated by the fact that there was someone else there, too: his wife, Anna. Although, to be fair, the only one who knew anything about our relationship was me—probably because it existed only in my imagination. Michael was utterly oblivious to my feelings for him, which I suppose was for the best. But things were changing in the Rossino household. I had heard stormy waters were brewing on the marriage front. Details about Anna's extramarital assignations had come to light during the investigation into Daniel's death.

I hadn't seen Michael since returning to Wynter Island. I hadn't seen Ben either, the handsome veterinarian who had been sniffing at my heels since I arrived on Wynter. It was almost like I was trying to avoid all possible romantic entanglements. Or feelings. Feelings brought me back to Daniel, and that wasn't a space I was comfortable in yet.

"Sounds good. And Shea, Selesia is going to be the host?"

Shea nodded, her thin blonde hair straggling forward to brush against her face.

"Does she know about Rose yet?" Vera asked, drawing out the end of her question.

"Yeah, she knows."

Before I could ask anything, Nate spoke up. "She's moved into the old Wintford place."

"The Wintford place? Where's that?" I asked.

"Oh, it's one of the big waterfront mansions just down from Coho Bay,"

Doreen replied. "The islanders call it the Glass House because it has so many windows."

"Has anyone seen her yet?" Gwen asked. "They arrived a few weeks ago. Big black Cadillac Escalade with California plates."

"I'm surprised she didn't fly in on a private helicopter," Vera said. "Isn't that what celebrities do?"

The acidity of her tone left no doubt of Vera's opinion of such Hollywood accouterments.

"Apparently," Nate added, ignoring Vera's comment, "there's three of them. Rosalie, her manager, and a personal assistant."

"Why on God's green earth would she need a personal assistant on Wynter Island?" Vera sniffed. "To tear off individual pieces of toilet paper for her when she's sitting on the john?"

"I wish I had an assistant to help me get the new fruit shed up," Gwen sighed.

"How's that going, Gwen?" I asked.

My mind wandered back to the day I spotted what looked like a carton of eggs on Gwen's front porch. It was still hard to believe that I had stumbled over an IED on tiny Wynter Island, British Columbia. Gwen and I were lucky to have survived the explosion. Unfortunately, Gwen's old fruit shed had not.

Gwen exhaled with a hiss of impatience. "With all this rain, I'm going to have to get the lane from the road properly graded so it's safe for cars and equipment to get up there. Right now, it feels like I'm taking my life in my hands every time I drive up or down."

"I know," Vera added. "When I dropped your eggs off yesterday, I thought I was going to start a landslide. Chunks of the gravel driveway kept slipping away. Scared me to death."

"Okay, so no filming at Gwen's house for the foreseeable future," I said, laughing. "The last thing I need is to end up sliding down her mountainside in the station truck!"

As I waited for a polite titter of laughter, there was nothing but silence. Vera, instead, leaned out of her seat, her neck stretching like an elongated stork, to get a better view out the front window. If she stretched any further, she would end up sitting in Gwen's lap.

"What are you looking at, Vera?" I asked as the entry bell on the front door jingled happily. "You're acting like it's the Second Coming or something."

I turned to see a stunning, golden-haired woman flanked by two men standing by the door.

"Returning home is kind of a Second Coming," she replied, a smile spread across her oval, cream-skinned face, "but I think it's a bit much to put Biblical implications behind it. I'm Rosalie. Rosalie Morgann. Although most islanders remember me as just plain old Rose Morgan."

She was as stunning as they had said. Her oval face perfect, her big blue eyes and bee-stung Bardot lips like something from a French impressionist film, Brigitte Bardot, with a touch of 21st Century Hollywood. Her hair hung in long, loose waves of gold on either side of her face. I'm sure it would have shimmered in the sunlight if there had been any sunlight to shimmer in. She was a present-day Pre-Raphaelite goddess. The Lady of Shallot, in real life.

She walked over to me, her hand extended. I grasped it, noticing that one finger was weighed down with a diamond-studded platinum ring.

"I'm Kate Thomas. CWYN station manager," I said.

Rosalie gestured to the two men beside her, both in their mid-thirties. "This is my manager, Jason Bálachet, and my personal assistant, Scott Quillimento."

The first man, Jason, could have been a model if not for the slight crookedness of his nose. His black hair was clipped short, his mono-lid eyes hinting at some Asian ancestry. At 6'1", his taut body gave him the appearance of someone who drank kefir for breakfast and worked out daily on his *Peloton*.

The other man was a bit shorter in stature and carried a few more pounds on his frame. He wore a starched oxford shirt tucked into a pair of neatly pressed khakis, his belt matching his tan loafers. His dark brown hair was parted on the side, bangs brushing loosely over the left-hand side of his olive-skinned, round face. His eyes, which appeared to be quietly assessing me, were partially hidden behind tortoiseshell glasses. The lower part of his face was encased in an artfully trimmed five o'clock shadow.

He certainly cares about his appearance. Must do since maintaining a facial grooming style that holds you perennially at 4:30 pm must be difficult.

I nodded my hellos. "What can I help you with?"

"I was wondering if we could speak privately?" Rosalie asked.

I glanced around the open-plan office. It was many things, but private was not one of them.

"Of course. Everybody," I gestured to the volunteers to stand, "why don't we call it a day. I'll see you on Friday for the show. Crew call is 9 am."

"What? You want us to go? Now?" Nate asked, his lanky face shifting from amazement to dismay.

"Yes, of course, she wants us to go," Vera snapped. "They need to speak in private. And you need to stop drooling."

"Dougie will be so pissed that he wasn't here."

"C'mon everyone, let's do what Kate asked. Everybody out." Gwen walked over to open the front door, gesturing everyone outside. "And no, you can't all stand here on the sidewalk and stare in the window at them like they're animals in a zoo!"

Doreen, the last to leave, dramatically slowed her steps as she came level with us. She clearly wanted Rosalie to notice that she was there. Their eyes connected, the anger in Doreen's so sharp and brittle that I wondered how Rosalie could hold her gaze. But she did. The breadth of her shoulders stayed rigid and firm until Doreen had passed.

Well, she knew she would get hate for returning to the island. Doreen is just the start of it.

I led my guests to the now empty folding chairs, Jupiter trailing suspiciously behind me. "Please, have a seat."

We sat down in a small semi-circle, Rosalie casually draping one honey-colored leg over the other beneath her short cotton dress. Her calves were shapely perfection, like something from a magazine advertisement for ladies' razors.

I can never show my legs again.

13

Scott reached over to pet Jupiter, but he gave him a look that very clearly said, *I don't think so, buddy.* Scott quickly withdrew his hand. That was odd. Jupiter had gotten so much better at tolerating strangers. Why had he taken against Scott?

"I'm sorry you had to shoo away all your volunteers," Rosalie said.

I waved away her concerns. "It's perfectly fine. We were pretty much done for today anyway. But I'm curious about what you need to discuss with me."

Jason spoke up. "It's nice to meet you, Kate. I'm Jason, Rosalie's manager and boyfriend." His mouth split open in a cheesy, theatrical way.

Hmmm, a huckster.

"She gets two for the price of one with me."

I chuckled politely. "Bálachet. Êtes-vous Français?"

"Sort of. Half Korean, half Quebeçois. I grew up in Manchester, New Hampshire."

"And I'm Scott Quillimento," the other young man offered. "From San Diego originally."

I glanced over at him, the smile across his full moon face feeling more honest than Jason's if no less theatrical.

"Nice to meet you both. But I still have no idea why you're here."

"I would like to be a guest," Rosalie answered, "on your upcoming television show, Vox Pop."

"You? You want to be on one of our shows?"

Rosalie nodded.

"You do realize that this is public access television, right? Made by volunteers with a lot of heart but not necessarily much talent. Our audience is comprised of a few hundred retirees and one particularly grumpy fisherman."

"Is that Phil? Of course, it is. Who else would be the grumpy fisherman on Wynter Island?" Rosalie laughed.

"You know Phil?" I mentally checked myself. "Of course you do. You grew up here."

"Yes," Rosalie glanced out the front window at the volunteers, now gossiping in front of the Tru Value. "I have a lot of memories from Wynter

Island."

Good memories? I wondered. Or bad?

A silver dollar-sized mother-of-pearl disc moved on her bracelet as she shifted in her seat, its spoke-like engraved ship's wheel design catching the light. "Is that the Wheel of Dharma?"

"Yes, it is. You know something about Buddhism?"

I shrugged my shoulders. "A bit."

"I started practicing a few years ago. I needed something to help me deal with the stress of working in Hollywood. The meditation helped a lot. And then I began to learn more about the religion."

"More?"

"Yes. Do you know what the wheel represents?"

"Not really."

"It represents Samsara, the process of life, death, and rebirth we must all go through to achieve Nirvana."

I examined the beautiful young woman sitting in front of me. In the eyes of many, Rosalie had already achieved Nirvana. She had everything she could possibly want: great beauty, wealth beyond her wildest dreams, and worldwide fame. What else could she need?

"So you've returned here because you're looking for Nirvana? I don't know if Wynter Island qualifies as that."

The three of them laughed, Jason leaning forward, his well-manicured hands opening towards me in a car salesman-like way. "We realize that CWYN is a small community television station."

"Well then, why," I started, but he cut me off.

"It's imperative that Rosalie appear on your channel."

"But it has to be Vox Pop," Rosalie insisted. "Selesia Sixto is the host, right? It airs live for the first time this Friday?"

"Yes, that's right," I answered slowly, drawing my words out as I tried to figure out where this was going. "But we already have a guest for our first show."

"A guest better than Rosalie?" Scott asked, drawing his head back in surprise, a smirk of doubt lifting his rosy lips.

"Well, I don't know if I would say better, but ..."

"I'm sure they wouldn't mind if Rosalie took their place," Jason stated, putting a decisive end to the conversation. "After all, who better than Rosalie Morgann to be your first on-air guest? The local girl who became a Hollywood star?"

Chapter Three

The drizzling rain, which seemed to be our permanent state of weather these days, leached all color out of our normally lush, green island, turning it into a black-and-white, soulless world.

For Christ's sake, I know we live in a temperate rainforest, but this is just ridiculous!

I turned out of the station parking lot and headed the truck north toward the Reserve.

Jupiter sat shotgun—like usual—his nose pressed against the passenger window while his rosy tongue tried to catch the trickles of water sliding by.

"Jupe, you're never going to get one. They're on the other side of the window."

Jupiter turned at the sound of his name, tilted his head questioningly, and then returned to his task.

The Reserve sign appeared on the road up ahead of us. Selesia's house was the third on the right as you drive in, a blue split level straight from the Sixties. I pulled into the gravel driveway, the absence of any cars hinting that there was no one home.

"Okay, Jupe. Where next?" I said after an unsuccessful attempt to rouse anybody at the house.

Jupiter looked at me, his body stiffening with excitement, his ears lifting hopefully.

"No, I didn't say W.A.L.K. It's too wet. I'm sorry, no walks today."

With a slump, Jupiter returned to the passenger window.

"Let's see if Sam is around. Maybe he knows where I can find Selesia."

Sam's ranch-style house sat at the end of the main road in the Reserve, a stunning piece of waterfront property overlooking the Salish Sea.

"C'mon, Jupe. We know you're welcome here," I waved Jupiter out the driver's side door, and we dashed through the rain to the front door.

A quick knock brought the sound of scrabbling paws on the opposite side of the door.

"See, Jupe? Jojo is excited to see you again!"

Jupiter gave me a healthy dose of side-eye. The front door opened, and a small black lab exploded onto the front step, sniffing and jumping all over him.

"Hi, Kate," Sam said, his burnished skin breaking into a broad smile. "I wasn't expecting to see you here today."

Comfortable as always in his faded jeans and a white t-shirt, he leaned against the open door frame. His long, silver-grey hair was held back in a ponytail, pulling his fissured skin tighter around his eyes.

"Hi, Sam. Well, actually, I'm looking for Selesia."

Sam opened the door wider and gestured for me to come inside. "Well, you came to the right place. She's right in here."

Sam's home may have had a million-dollar view, but its interior was much more modest. More 1980s rec-room than Architectural Digest, with its well-worn La-Z-Boy chairs and lacquered wood-paneled walls. I turned the corner into the kitchen to see Selesia seated at the table.

"Hey, Kate. How're you doing?"

I had met Selesia a few times before, either out and about on the island or when we had crossed paths at Shea's farmhouse. She was in her early forties. Her body, strong and lean, had been carved into shape by the marathon running she did in the free time she had outside of her job as a Social Worker who specialized in First Nation's cases. Her straight brown-black hair hung in thick sheets around her face, a face that was a rectangle of unsoftened lines and angles. This gave her a somewhat cold and forbidding appearance. But when she smiled, her brown eyes shone, lifting her features to make her appear far less intimidating.

"Hi, Selesia. Glad I found you here."

Selesia reached down to pet Jupiter. He tolerated her pats as he had something more important to focus on: finding a safe space away from Jojo. With a last push, he squeezed up against the wall beneath the table, glaring at Jojo as he did so. "Yeah, just needed a change of scenery, so I came down here to bother my brother."

"Coffee, Kate?" Sam asked as he pulled a spare mug out of the cupboard.

"Yes, please. Two sugars and a little milk. How's everything? Have you heard anything from Will?"

Will, a recent high school graduate, and Selesia's eldest son was away from home for the first time, working at a First Nations summer camp in Williams Lake.

Selesia rolled her eyes. "Will's great. He loves it up there. No mom to tell him what to do. It doesn't hurt that his girlfriend, Tessa, also works there. It's Brad I'm worried about."

Brad, her other son, was a year younger than his brother and as different from him as night was from day. Will, a star academic who had earned a full scholarship to the University of British Columbia for the coming fall, was pleasant and outgoing. He was also well-liked throughout the island. That was no small victory, as he was rubbing up against the deeply ingrained racism toward First Nations Peoples that had only begun to dissipate in the past decade or two.

Brad was quieter and less social. A loner. I saw far less of him roaming around the island than I did his big brother.

"Why?"

She sighed. "This is a tough time for him. It's his last summer as a 'kid'. He's got a lot of important life decisions to make in the coming year. It's weighing on him, I think."

Sam fussed around fixing the coffee before placing a mug in front of me and sitting down himself. "So, what's up, Kate?"

I took a sip, quickly placing the mug back down as the scalding coffee burnt the tip of my tongue. "Whoa, that's hot, Sam." I took a moment to collect myself before starting again. "I was placed in a rather difficult situation this morning."

"What happened?" Selesia asked.

"I was forced into changing the guest for Vox Pop on Friday."

"Forced?" Sam laughed. "That sounds menacing."

"Well, it was more that they wouldn't take no for an answer."

The smile slipped from Selesia's face, leaving only the unforgiving bone structure beneath it.

"They?" she asked, the word slipping slowly off her tongue.

"Yes, they."

I glanced back and forth between Selesia and Sam as the emotional temperature of the room skidded rapidly downwards.

Oh shit, this is worse than I thought.

"Who are *they*, Kate?" Selesia repeated, her voice gaining strength but not warmth.

"Rosalie Morgann, her manager, Jason, and her personal assistant, Scott."

Selesia's mug collided loudly with the tabletop, causing a splash of coffee to wash over the rim and onto the table.

"No! I won't have that bitch on my television show!"

"Selesia, at least hear her out," Sam pleaded.

"No! How can you say that, Sam? You know what she did to me! To the kids!"

"I know. I know." Sam leaned across and grasped her hand, pinning it against the table. "But smashing your coffee mug isn't going to change anything. So just calm down."

Selesia leaned back in her seat, her chest heaving with the sudden adrenalin of rage. "Okay," she said once she had calmed herself down. "I don't want that bitch anywhere near my kids or me. Alright? Is that calm enough?"

"If you insist, I will tell her she can't come on the show," I said.

Selesia breathed out another exhalation of anger and then glanced over at me. "You really don't know what she did?"

"Well, not all of it. I mean, I've heard that she 'slept around' with a lot of men."

"Yeah, ruined a lot of marriages, including mine."

"You see, Kate," Sam started out, "Rose was a very troubled girl."

"Troubled," Selesia sniffed, "more like trouble than troubled."

Sam glanced over at Selesia, his hazel eyes a mixture of sadness and exasperation. "Rose lost her mom and, to all intents and purposes, her dad as a young child. She ended up basically raising herself. The island kids were quite mean. Selesia tried to help her."

"What a mistake that was!" Selesia retorted, taking an aggressive swig of her coffee.

Sam continued on as if she had said nothing. "Selesia became like a big sister to her, and Rose spent a lot of time out here on the Reserve. Then she hit her teens, and it got complicated."

"Yeah, if complicated is what you call being a slut!"

"Selesia," Sam barked out. "Throwing names around doesn't help anything."

Selesia grumbled and retreated into silence.

"For the first time in her life, Rose had something other people wanted. And that gave her power and a weapon she could use against the women on the island."

"But why?" I asked. "What did she have against the women on the island?"

"I guess she had hoped that one of them would save her—from the poverty, from her home life—and they didn't. That sense of betrayal, especially when you're a child, doesn't necessarily have to make sense."

"So she hurt them by sleeping with their husbands."

"And sons. And then she would move on to the next person who would give her what she thought was love."

"Or money. Or expensive gifts," Selesia inserted. "She had a wealthy 'mystery lover' who would fly her all over the West Coast for shopping trips and little get-togethers. Quite the racket."

"But I still don't see how she hurt Selesia?" I asked.

Sam sighed. "She was very close to Selesia, almost too close. And when Selesia and Rick got engaged, Rose viewed it as another betrayal."

Selesia leaned forward across the table towards Kate, her eyes deadly serious. "She told me that she had slept with Rick. That the only reason he was marrying me was because I was pregnant with Will."

I, in mid-sip, clunked my now-cooling coffee back onto the table. "That's horrible. Was it true?"

"No, we don't believe it was," Sam shrugged, "but you never truly know. Rose had planted a seed of doubt. And once something like that takes root, it grows until it eventually strangled their marriage."

"We lasted five years. He remarried and moved with his new wife up to Prince George. That's why the boys don't see that much of him."

"What happened to Rose?"

Selesia laughed, a bitter, harsh sound that grated against the air in the small kitchen. "She ran away. Caught the first ferry out the next morning. No one had any idea what happened to her until someone spotted her on a TV soap. That's when we discovered she had moved to L.A. and become Rosalie Morgann, the actress."

"And then, out of nowhere, she decides to return to Wynter Island," I murmured. "After how many years?"

"Eighteen or so," Selesia said. "She better be careful, that's all I've got to say. There are a lot of people on this island who have axes to grind with her. Me included."

"Selesia," Sam scolded, "being dramatic is not going to help anything."

"Like I give a damn," Selesia spat out.

"Okay," I raised my hands and made a T out of them. "I think I've got the whole picture now."

"Good, so you can cancel the interview."

Selesia pushed her chair back with a long, low squeak and carried her mug to the sink.

"Yesssss," I said, drawing out the word into one long syllable, "but there will be some fallout."

"Fallout?" Selesia spun back around to face me. "You said you could cancel it!"

"And I can," I repeated, anxious to make things clear. "it's just that they've gone out of their way to make that difficult."

"Why? What have they done?" Sam asked.

"Well, over and above coming to the station and demanding that Rosalie be the guest this coming Friday—"

"Yes—"

"They told me that a press release listing Rosalie as the first guest on Vox Pop had already been emailed to all the major media outlets in Southwestern B.C."

"What?"

"Yes, like I said, they're trying to make it impossible for me to refuse to have Rosalie on the show."

"What does that mean?" Sam asked.

I sighed. "It means they know we can't afford any bad publicity for the station. And it would look pretty bad to get all this attention for CWYN because of Rosalie's participation and then, out of the blue, cancel her."

"I'm not doing it," Selesia said, leaning against the sink. Her lip had jutted out into a bowl-like rim protruding from her face.

"Selesia, listen to me," Sam started out.

"No, not doing it."

"Selesia. It's been a terrible summer for the island. You know that as well as I do."

"So?" Selesia's lower lip jutted out even more.

"Think about it. What does Wynter Island need more than anything else right now? Tourists. If this publicity brings people to the island, that could be lifesaving for our businesses, Selesia."

"Why do I have to fix that for them? It's not my problem."

"You know that's not true," Sam said as if repeating a well-known fact to a toddler. "Every living thing on this island is interconnected. Hurt one, you hurt them all."

Selesia walked over to the kitchen window. The room was silent, except for the dripping rain on the roof and the scratch of Jojo's toenails as she tried to squeeze underneath the table to be with Jupiter. Selesia's lean body seemed to be battling some kind of internal struggle as her hands balled up into fists and then released. Finally, she turned around to face us.

"Okay, I'll do it. But I don't want anything to do with her other than asking the questions on-air. No friendly greetings, no thank you for doing this, no goodbyes. Nada."

"Agreed," I said in relief. "Only the interview. I promise."

Chapter Four

"How do I look?" Shea asked as she sat in the host's chair and looked straight into Nate's camera.

Shea looked quite smart, having changed from her usual jeans and t-shirts to a more professional-looking pair of charcoal slacks and a light tan sweater. She was Librarian Shea today, rather than my normal BFF/Animal Rescuer cohort. I had been so lucky when she had taken me under her wing on my arrival on Wynter Island. She and Gwen Wynter, my boss at the station and the unelected Matriarch of the island, had been my solid supports during those first dreadful days after Daniel's death. And also in the weeks that followed as I battled to prove my innocence.

I gave her the thumbs up from behind the soundproofed window of the control room. She moved to the guest's chair and settled herself in that seat, adjusting her posture to make the best use of the lighting. Earlier that morning, I had set up a simple set: two thrift shop wing chairs facing each other against a lit backdrop.

"Dougie, tell her that the lighting looks great," I said into the microphone connected to Dougie and Nate's headphones and Selesia's earpiece. "She can head over to the control room now."

"Kate says everything looks fine," Dougie said. He looked over at Nate, who was on the opposite side of the set with Camera Two, with a smile of amazement. "Can you believe we're actually going live in half an hour, Nate?"

Nate spoke into his mic headphone. "I know. I just hope I can remember everything."

"Don't worry, Nate," I said from the control room, "you'll do fine. So will you, Dougie. Just remember, I'll tell you the shots when I need them. Got it?"

"Yeah, I think so," Nate said.

Selesia walked out onto the set in a cream linen skirt and blouse, her perilously high heels adding a few inches to her already tall frame. Her hair had been pulled back off her face in a simple chignon that Shea had done in the washroom. Her makeup was just strong enough to make it appear on camera as if she was effortlessly attractive.

"You look great, Selesia," I said into her earpiece.

"Thanks, Kate."

Her cell phone jingled from her purse. She pulled it out and placed it to her ear. With a nod to me, she pulled off her earpiece and walked off-set to talk in private.

"When she's done on the phone, Dougie, can you get her miced up, please?"

The front doorbell tinkled through the station.

"Here we go," I muttered and stepped out into the hallway, locking Jupiter in the control room behind me.

Rosalie and Jason were already in the open-plan office by the time I got there, placing their coats and bags down on one of the empty chairs.

Rosalie wore a pale pink sheath dress with a silver necklace and matching earrings. Her hair was loose again, the golden waves bouncing off her tanned shoulders.

"Good morning. How's everyone doing today?" I asked.

"Hi, Kate," Jason looked up from their bags as Rosalie continued to rummage in her purse. "We're ready to go. Rosalie did her hair and makeup before we left the house."

"Great."

"There it is." Rosalie pulled a metal tube out of her bag, swiveling it open. She swiped a fresh layer of lipstick on. "Just need a quick touchup with my Charlotte Tilbury."

"It's a lovely shade," I said.

"Very Victoria. My absolute favorite." She dropped the lipstick back into

26

her bag.

"I don't know how many copies of it she's got," Jason said, his eyes narrowing with worry as he looked at her.

I examined her more closely, spotting what Jason had already seen. There was a faint sheen, almost like dew, of sweat across her forehead. I would have thought it was fabricated, some makeup trick, if not for the fact that I could see the discomfort in her eyes.

"Yes, I've got one in every bag I carry. Always best to have your HG lippy with you." She smiled bravely and then wiped two fingers over her forehead. "I'm afraid I'm not feeling all that great this morning, Kate."

"Are you well enough to go on?" I said, suppressing any irritation that after all this trouble, we might not be able to go ahead with filming today after all.

"Yeah, I think so. It's just a bit of a fever. Probably a bug coming on. I took an ibuprofen in the car. Jason has some more if I need another."

"Are you sure?"

She nodded her head firmly. "Yes, I'm sure." She looked towards the closed studio door, the red filming light waiting to be lit. "I need to do this."

"Well, you don't have to ...," I started, but Jason shushed me.

"Yes, Kate. She has to do this."

They were reading from the same script, so I changed the subject.

"Where's Scott? Your assistant."

"Oh, it's his days off. He left a couple of days ago to go and have a break in Victoria," Jason answered.

"Alright," Rosalie breathed deeply a few times and then pointed towards the studio. "Let's get in there."

She headed briskly down the hallway, Jason and I scuttling to keep up with her. She pulled at the heavy, soundproof studio door, hesitating for a moment as if unable to find the strength to fully open it, before stepping through.

"Hey, Rosalie, wait for me," I said, but it was too late. She was headed directly across the studio floor towards an unknowing Selesia, like two cars skidding toward each other across an intersection.

"Hi, Selesia," Rosalie said as she stopped in front of her. "It's been a long time."

Selesia's head jerked up, momentarily surprised. As I watched, anger replaced the shock, the angles of her face slipping so rapidly into frigid disapproval that they might as well have had icicles hanging off them.

"Excuse me. I have something I need to do," she replied with a blunt tone that veered into rudeness before turning on her heel and walking off the set toward the washroom.

"Well, that could have gone better," Rosalie muttered to herself before turning back to me.

I marveled at the calm of her Madonna-like face. She had just been rudely shut down by Selesia and didn't seem offended at all. In fact, it felt as if she had been expecting it. Perhaps the expectation was understandable, but the calm with which she faced it was surprising.

"Rosalie, we need to get you miced up. Nate?"

Nate walked over. "Hi, Rosalie. It's nice to meet you. If you don't mind, I'm just going to attach this microphone to your dress."

He gestured her towards the guest's chair and then clipped a small lavalier microphone onto the neckline of her dress.

"Is there anything we can get for you?" I offered. "Water? Soda or coffee?"

"That's very nice of you, but I brought my own drink. Pro-energy. I think Jason left it with my bag out there." She pointed vaguely towards the office area.

"I'll go and get it," Dougie volunteered and dashed out the studio door. Within a couple of minutes, he returned holding the glass bottle. "Here you go, Rosalie. I mean, Miss Morgann. I mean, Rosalie Morgann," he stuttered to a stop and handed her the bottle.

"Thank you. Is your name Dougie?"

Dougie nodded like a spring-necked dog on a Cadillac dashboard.

"Well, thanks, Dougie. You can call me Rosalie."

"Dougie," I inserted, "you should get back to your camera. And remember, you're going to count Selesia in for me, right?"

Dougie nodded once more before turning and dashing back to his camera.

Selesia eventually returned from the washroom and seated herself in the host's seat. She did not look up at Rosalie. She did not speak. Nate quickly attached a mic to her blouse as she focused all of her attention on the piece of paper she was holding in her lap.

Well, this is going to be fun, isn't it?

I returned to the control room, hooking my mic and earpiece over my right ear.

"Okay, everyone. We're coming up on the hour. Is everyone ready?" I glanced up at the large clock in the control room. It read 9:59 am. Shea and Jason settled themselves down in seats on either side of me.

Thumbs up from everyone, including Selesia.

"Okay, count her in now, starting on five, Dougie."

Dougie stepped away from the camera, moving his fingers from five to two. On one, he pointed at Selesia to start reading the teleprompter.

I flipped the switch. We had done it! CWYN was now live on televisions throughout Southwestern British Columbia!

"Good morning, everyone. My name is Selesia Sixto, and I am your host for Vox Pop, Wynter Island's live call-in show. Welcome to the inaugural broadcast for our TV station, CWYN, the voice of Wynter Island. Today's guest," She glanced over as Rosalie took a quick drink while still off-camera, "is Hollywood actress and Wynter Island native, Rosalie Morgann."

"Camera two, close-up of Rosalie," I said from the control room. "And then Camera one, go to a two-shot."

"Thank you, Selesia, for having me here today. I do appreciate it. I have several things I need to discuss." Her voice cracked, and she reached down to grab the bottle and take another quick sip. "Sorry about that. What I was trying to say is," Rosalie hesitated, and a spasm swept over her face like a wave breaking and then retreating over a sandy beach.

"Camera two, close up of Rosalie."

Rosalie swallowed a few more times and then smiled determinedly at Selesia. "I'm sorry, I don't know what's up with me today. I must have a bug."

Rosalie's features spasmed again. Her hand suddenly reached out to grab

Selesia's. In horror, Selesia attempted to shake it off, but Rosalie would not let her go.

"Okay, Camera one, go to a wide shot. We may have to cut to a break if she's sick," I said as Jason leaned forward toward the glass separating the control room from the set.

"Selesia," Rosalie repeated, her words barely discernible. "Listen to me." She kept her hand on Selesia's, using its strength to pull herself closer. "Selesia—"

Before she could say another word, a gush of blood and vomit shot from her mouth, covering her and Selesia in a crimson-splattered mess.

"Rose!" Selesia screamed and leaned forward to grab Rosalie's body as it crumpled to the floor, foam oozing between her lips, her eyes sightless.

Chapter Five

"What happened, Kate?"

People pushed past me to join the volunteer EMTs working on the prone body on the floor. She wasn't Rosalie anymore. She was just a body.

A body.

"Kate, I asked you what happened?"

Stewart, his RCMP chief constable jacket hastily pulled on over his uniform shirt, was breathless from the dash over to the station from the detachment. His normally stoic face, bracketed by his short russet-colored hair and neatly trimmed beard, was red from lack of breath.

"I don't know."

Someone was screaming and sobbing. I turned to see Jason sitting on the floor, Shea and Nate kneeling beside him. Shea reached out a hand to rest comfortingly on the young man's heaving back as she murmured something in his ear.

"Shea tried," I said to Stewart and then paused to breathe. "She tried to resuscitate her."

The images flashed back into my memory. Selesia screaming, holding on to the bloodied, unconscious body of Rosalie as she slipped to the ground. Me, flipping the switch to stop all video transmission from the station and then racing out of the control room. Shea taking Rosalie from Selesia's arms and placing two fingers against her neck.

There was a pause as we waited. Any desperate hopes we still clung to were dashed as she began CPR on Rose's lifeless body. One and two and three and, Shea said as she pressed urgently on Rosalie's chest. Twenty-eight, twenty-nine, thirty. Two breaths into her tilted mouth, and then back to the compressions again.

"Shea tried, but she couldn't resuscitate her."

The EMTs had taken over as soon as they arrived, one doing chest compressions while another searched for any vital signs. I suddenly realized that it was Ben's delicate-fingered hand checking for a pulse, Ben's narrow, sensitive face leaning forward to listen to Rosalie's chest, and that gave me a measure of comfort. At least Ben was here.

"Did she give you any sign that something was wrong?" Stewart asked.

"Well, she said she wasn't feeling great when she arrived. And then..."

"Then what?"

"Once she got on the set and started the interview, she looked like she was in pain, or nauseous, or something."

"And how long did that last?"

"Not long, maybe five minutes. She tried to catch her breath and take a drink, but it didn't help. She reached forward, grabbed Selesia's hand, tried to say something, and then threw up this massive amount of blood and was...gone."

Stewart and I examined the inert body, her pale pink dress covered with congealing blood and vomit. Her golden hair spilled out onto the floor behind her head, looking in the stage lights like a glistening, metallic trail. Ben sat back on his heels, staring at the young woman's face, before glancing at his watch and then shaking his head. The other EMT stopped the compressions.

"No! No! Don't stop! You've got to save her!" Jason screamed and tried to get to his feet, but Nate and Shea held him down. "Don't let her die! Rosalie!"

Ben walked over to where Stewart and I were standing. "I'm afraid she's gone. There was no pulse when we got here, and we've had no signs of life since then. I called it at 10:55. We'll have to get Dr. Lee to check her and sign the paperwork." Ben turned his attention to me. "Kate, are you okay?"

I reached out a hand to grab onto his arm. "Ben," I whispered, "not another death."

"I know."

He reached over and wrapped his arms around me, his fluorescent emergency services jacket encasing me in a wet hug. I felt the ends of his waist-length russet hair brush against the back of my hands. His grasp was warm and lovely, like a strong cup of hot tea on a cold winter's night. I wanted nothing more than to stay in his arms, but knew I had to push myself away.

"What caused this, Ben?"

He shrugged his shoulders in confusion. "I don't know. Someone said the onset of symptoms was rapid?"

"Yes. When she arrived, she was feeling a bit off, feverish, but nothing more. And then, within twenty minutes, she was dead."

As I said the words aloud, I realized they seemed almost laughable. How does someone mysteriously pass from youthful vim and vigor to death in that short a period? In front of half a dozen witnesses? Live on television, damn it!

It's ridiculous!

"It looked like things suddenly got worse about five minutes before she collapsed. She looked like she was in pain and took another drink to try and calm her stomach ..."

"Drink?" Stewart asked. "What drink?"

"That energy drink over there. The bottle got knocked over and smashed when she fell out of her seat."

Stewart walked past the body to the pieces of glass on the floor. He reached into his pocket and pulled out a pair of latex gloves and a specimen bag. He gingerly picked up the shards of the empty bottle and held them up to his nose before placing them in the bag and sealing it shut.

"Ben, don't let anyone touch this," he gestured to the pool of liquid on the floor. "I'm going to dash out to the car to get a specimen swab and bottle."

"Okay."

Within a few minutes, Stewart was back, scooping up the remaining drips of liquid enmeshed with the drying vomit and blood.

"Do you think it was something in the drink?" I asked.

"Who knows," Stewart answered, "but I have to try and collect any evidence I can. Lesley is over in Sidney today at the Provincial courthouse. She won't be back until the late ferry."

"But if it was the drink," Ben said and then hesitated, "does that mean she was poisoned, Stewart? Intentionally poisoned?"

"Yes!" Jason dragged himself to his feet and staggered towards us, with Shea and Nate each holding one arm to keep him upright. "She was murdered!"

"Jason, you don't know what you're saying," Shea scolded gently.

"I'm aware enough to know a crime when I see it!" he screamed. His face was blotchy, a mottled mess of crimson and white, his eyes swollen from the tears. "She was feeling a little feverish when we got here, but that was it. And look at her now! She's dead! Oh, Rosalie!"

He staggered forward toward her body.

Stewart moved towards him, blocking his path. "I'm sorry for your loss." He hesitated and glanced over at me.

"Jason," I supplied for him.

"Jason. I'm very sorry for your loss, but I'm afraid I can't allow you to touch anything."

"Just let me say goodbye to her," he sobbed.

Stewart sighed. "You can't. We have no idea what caused her death, so I have to work under the assumption that a crime may have been committed. I need to protect a possible crime scene. When the coroner releases her body, you will get a chance to say your goodbyes then."

He swung around to face Stewart, drool dripping from his open mouth as he choked with sobs. "You're in on it, aren't you? All of you," he swung around wildly, Shea and Nate trying to keep him on his feet. "You all wanted her to die. Everyone did. And all she wanted to do was finally come home."

"Take him out of here and find him a seat out in the lobby." Stewart gestured towards the studio door.

Shea and Nate led him shakily off the set.

"Who else was here?" Stewart asked as Ben returned to assist the other EMTs with lifting Rosalie's body onto a stretcher. They would take her to the small morgue at the local emergency medical center where Dr. Lee, the island's resident doctor, could confirm her death.

"Other than the people you've already seen, I guess there's only Selesia and Dougie. Selesia was the host of the show. She caught Rosalie's body as she collapsed. Selesia's pretty upset, so I had Dougie take her into the control room to try and calm her down."

"Okay, let's go and have a chat with her."

The control room door was closed, securing Jupiter behind it. I turned the handle and pushed it open as Jupiter rocketed across the room to me.

"I'm back, Jupiter. It's okay." I knelt down and rubbed his black and white fur back and forth between my hands as he circled round and round in joy at my reappearance.

"Selesia," Stewart said as he stepped past me. "I'm sorry, but we have to talk."

Selesia was sitting in the director's high-backed chair, where I had been sitting only a short while ago. Dougie had pulled another seat next to her and was holding her hand while keeping the chair turned away from the grim scene through the control room window.

Her crying had slowed to ragged breathing, her breath occasionally catching on a soft sob. Selesia's chic chignon had tumbled down to hang in random chunks around her face; her stylish blouse and skirt covered in bits of drying vomit and blood. Her hand, gripping tightly to Dougie's, was stained with a rusty wash of blood, deepening to dark brown around her nail beds.

"She's dead, isn't she?" Selesia asked, her voice quivering with shock.

Stewart stared at her for a moment. "Yes, I'm afraid she is."

Her breath became more ragged as she slipped back towards hysteria. "Why? I don't understand why?"

"We don't know that yet, but it may not have been an accident."

Selesia's hazel eyes opened wide. "Are you saying someone murdered her?"

"Perhaps. I don't know yet, but we've got to be open to all possibilities. She appeared to be a healthy young woman. They don't usually just keel over and die. Jason seems to think she was murdered, perhaps by the drink she had."

"Her drink?" Dougie said. "The one I picked up in the lobby for her?"

"You got it for her, Dougie?'

"Well, yeah. But I didn't do anything to it!"

"It was her own drink, " I inserted quickly, "not something she was given here. She brought it into the station herself."

"Where was it?"

I pointed to the office/hangout space. "She left it by her bag out in the lobby. A green leather tote."

Stewart walked over to the door, opened it, and gazed over at the open seating area. "I can see it. Was that where you found it, Dougie?"

"Yup, but I didn't touch anything else," he replied, panicked. "'I promise."

Stewart closed the door and turned back to face us. "Nobody touches anything. I'm going to have to bag all of that stuff. Kate, is it possible that someone may have been able to get in here while the rest of you were busy on the set?"

"I suppose so," I said. "I mean, I didn't lock the door. But I didn't hear the door alarm go off. You know, that tinkling sound."

"Perhaps you were too busy to notice." Stewart hesitated before continuing. "What about people already here in the station? Did anyone have an opportunity to tamper with the bottle without being seen?"

I thought about this for a moment. "Well, I suppose it's possible. But after Rosalie arrived, everyone can be accounted for by someone else. Nobody left except Dougie and …."

"And who?" Stewart asked.

"Me," Selesia finished for me. "I stormed out when Rose arrived. By myself. I went to the bathroom and swore at the mirror for five minutes. No one saw me. No one can vouch for what I did during that time. No alibi."

Chapter Six

"We're here for a good time, not a long time."

My voice warbled along with the radio while I drove down the winding road to Coho Bay. I remembered my mother singing along to this old Seventies hit from the Canadian band *Trooper*. How old would I have been then? Six? Or seven? I couldn't have been much older, as Mom left two weeks before my eighth birthday.

I turned the volume up and focused on the song. "So have a good time; the sun can't shine every day."

Well, isn't that appropriate.

I pulled into a long driveway that ended at a tiny white cabin. It was a simple square box with a peaked cedar-shingled roof and an oak front door. The trim around the door and the windows had been painted a bright, clear sky blue, which, when matched with the white cotton curtains, gave the small home an old-fashioned charm.

"C'mon, Jupe. We're here."

I climbed out of the jeep and headed up to the front door, Jupiter right beside me. The honeyed scent from a bed of sweet peas wafted over to us.

A sharp bark from inside followed my knock, and Ben, dressed in a casual t-shirt and faded jeans, opened the door. A brown and white springer spaniel quivered excitedly beside him. The dog ran out the front door, skidding to a stop a few feet behind Jupiter. She paused, her coat shining from a recent brushing, and then sidled up beside Jupiter.

Jupiter stood stock still, eyeing her with wary suspicion. She casually stepped towards him, nose sniffing, working her way from tail to head. He endured her entreaty to become friends, only relaxing when she turned and trotted back into the house.

"Now that the dog introductions are over," Ben said, opening the door wider, "C'mon in."

The cottage itself was surprisingly rustic. I didn't know what I had expected, but it hadn't been this. For such an exclusive part of the island, there was nothing grand or expensive about Ben's cottage. The front door led straight into the main living space. On my right lay a small kitchen. Monastically simple, it held a fridge, hot plate, toaster oven, and microwave. There were only a few simple pine cupboards and a strip of butcher block countertop. The cups and dishes were stacked neatly on a thick timber shelf secured into the wall, its rough edge left unfinished.

A loveseat and club chair were set to my left, angled towards the wood stove. A bookcase stretched across the rest of that wall, holding a hodgepodge of everything from Veterinary texts to Bernard Cornwell novels. The kitchen's two-seater table sat beside the glass doors at the back of the room, a small vase of wildflowers brightening it up.

"I should have asked what you like to eat." Ben gestured me inside. "I hope you don't mind Asian."

I walked towards the large glass doors overlooking his back deck and the deep emerald Pacific beyond that. 'No, that's fine. I love Asian food. Where in Asia, specifically?"

"Thailand. Well, with a touch of Vietnam."

"That's fine with me." I gestured out the window. "This view is absolutely gorgeous!"

"Yes," Ben busied himself pouring two glasses of pinot grigio. "I lucked into this place."

"This isn't that far from Rosalie's house, is it?" I paused. "Well, I guess what used to be her house."

Ben handed me the long-stemmed glass. "About a mile or so. She's at the other end, close to the Provincial Park. The islanders call it 'Millionaire's Row'. I was lucky to get an old summer cabin that hadn't been renovated in years; that's the only way I was able to afford this address."

I sipped the flinty white wine. "Wynter is a beautiful island, isn't it?"

Ben moved to stand behind me, the hairs on my arms prickling as I felt the heat from his body reach mine. "Yes, but not always a beautiful place to live."

I turned around to face him. "Did you know Rose at all?"

"No." He stared down at my face, so close to his that I could watch his carotid artery hypnotically throbbing. "I moved here long after she left. But I heard the stories. I couldn't believe she had the balls to come back and face everyone."

"I know. That's the part I don't understand. Why return to a place that held nothing but bad memories? I mean, she was wealthy enough. She could have retired anywhere."

"Yeah, I love Wynter Island, but if my budget extended to Bali ...." He waved goodbye out the window. "It would be bye-bye, Wynter. In all senses of the word."

He gestured me towards the table. A Vietnamese salad roll had been placed on my plate. The pale pink shrimp rested in a curling line beside the green onions in the semi-transparent molded rice paper. A small bowl of mahogany peanut sauce sat on the table beside it.

"I don't know what I was expecting, but whatever it was, Rosalie wasn't it." I sat down and dipped my salad roll in the thick brown peanut sauce before placing it in my mouth. A dribble of cooked rice noodles escaped one corner of my mouth, and I slurped them back in.

"Why? What had you been expecting?"

"I don't know. A diva? A narcissist? Someone who just uses people and then throws them away. Basically, the bitch that everyone on the island described to me."

"I take it she wasn't that? How long did you actually get to talk to her, though? Not that long, I'm guessing. The people on this island had known her for years, and not one had a good word to say about her. Well, except for Phil."

"Phil? What did he say?"

Ben sighed. "He was waiting at the medical center this morning when we got there with the body. I got out of the ambulance and tried to talk to him, but he was hysterical."

"Phil?" I asked, my voice rising with surprise. "Fisherman Phil? The guy who would sell you a sardine for a salmon if he could get away with it? Hysterical?"

Ben nodded his head. "He said someone had told him there'd been an emergency at the station. That Rose was sick. He begged me to tell him what was going on, to let him see Rose."

"What did you do?"

"I tried to get him to calm down, but he wasn't having it." Ben ate his last mouthful of salad roll and chewed it meditatively for a few moments. "I finally had to put my hands on his shoulders and tell him she was gone." Ben glanced down at his empty plate before looking up into my eyes, his own pools of sadness. "He was just … broken."

Phil. Broken. It seemed incongruous to compare the sharp-tongued, bad-tempered fisherman I knew with something delicate enough to break. But I had once believed myself to be strong, and I had broken, too.

"I would never have guessed."

Ben cleaned away our plates and returned with two bowls of steaming Pad Thai. The sweet tanginess of the lemongrass and tomato sauce wafted up to me.

"Me either. But one of the other EMTs said that Phil had been close to Rosalie's dad. In fact, he's the one who looked after his funeral. Phil notified her, but Rosalie didn't come home."

"She didn't come home for her father's funeral, and yet she came back now. Why?"

"I don't know. I don't think anyone does, other than perhaps that boyfriend/manager of hers."

"Jason."

"Yeah, him. How's your dinner?"

I dragged my thoughts back to the meal in front of me. "Lovely. This is all so delicious, Ben. Thank you for inviting me."

Ben smiled sheepishly. "Easy enough to cook for two as one."

I glanced to my side to see Jupiter staring at Ben with what could only be described as malevolent intensity. "I think Jupiter would prefer it to be three or," I glanced over at Lucy stretched out on the sofa with her brown and white feathered forelocks spread over the pillows, "four."

"Jupiter, may I bribe my way into your affections?" Ben laughed and held out a small chunk of chicken.

Absolutely not, said Jupiter with a silent glare. But he took the treat regardless. Lucy's long-snouted head popped up over the sofa arm as she watched Jupiter, the interloper, get a treat.

"Come here, Luce. I've got a piece for you, too."

Lucy scrambled off the sofa, her nails clicking frantically over the wood floor as she rushed to the table.

"I thought vets say you shouldn't spoil your dog."

"Yes, well, do as I say, not as I do." Ben stood up and collected our dirty plates and cutlery. "Not too much, but I do. They're like family, aren't they?"

I reached over to ruffle my hand over Jupiter's silver-topped head. He leaned closer against my chair, his eyes tipping adoringly upwards.

Yes, they were family. In some ways, more than family. You can't pick your family, but you can choose your dog. Or rather, I thought to myself and smiled, they choose you.

"Do you like games?"

"Excuse me?"

After placing the dishes in the sink, Ben pulled a four-foot-tall box from the bookshelf.

"Games? You know, board games? Checkers, Parcheesi." He gestured dramatically towards the box as he lifted it off to reveal a wooden block tower. "Mega-sized Jenga."

I laughed and walked over to where the wooden tower wobbled slightly in the middle of the living room floor. "That thing is huge! The Jenga I remember was small enough to put on your kitchen table."

"Why go small when you can go unnecessarily big?" His smile pushed out the boundaries of his face, brightening it with an almost childlike glow of happiness. "Do you want to play? I'm afraid I'm a bit of a game nerd."

"Game nerd? Like competitive chess game nerd or Dungeons and Dragons game nerd?"

"I feel I will look more attractive to you if I say the former rather than the latter."

"Yes," I nodded as I roamed around the tower's perimeter, "you will. But I might not believe you."

"How about we leave it at equal opportunity game nerd. You go first."

Jupiter had skittered behind me, his lip raising at the living room's unexpected structure.

"It's okay, Jupe. It's just a game. It's not going to hurt me."

Jupiter gave me some doubtful side-eye before sitting down to keep watch.

"Okay, let's try this one." I gingerly plucked a thin block of wood from the structure and pulled it out cleanly. "Okay, one down."

Ben stepped up and nonchalantly pulled a brick out.

"Show off."

I pulled another brick, but this time the structure trembled. "Okay, maybe not that one. Let's try this." I grabbed another piece further down the structure and began to inch it tentatively out.

Jupiter growled as the piece got stuck in the tower. I walked around to the opposite side and tried to push it through.

"It's fine, Jupe. I can do this."

With another slight shove of my finger, the brick pushed out, hovering dramatically in mid-air before slipping out and dropping loudly to the floor. Jupiter barked suspiciously. Lucy joined him, the two oddly in-sync voices barking together.

"C'mon, guys," I said. "It's okay."

But as I spoke, the edge of my sleeve brushed against the tower, and it began to sway like a hotel in a bad Seventies disaster film.

"No! No!"

I tried to steady it, but it swayed back in my direction again. That was all Jupiter needed. He leaped up and bit at one of the blocks, grabbing it in mid-air and throwing it viciously to the floor. Strong arms pulled me to the left, clearing a path for the wooden structure to cascade onto the wood floor beside me.

"Oh," I exhaled loudly, only realizing a moment later that Ben's hands were still gripping my shoulders.

He turned me around to face him, his skin's warmth seeping into mine. His head dipped down, and his lips, tasting faintly of coconut and lemongrass, touched mine.

I pulled back sharply, so much so that I almost over-balanced the other way, tipping Ben and myself back onto the tumbled Jenga blocks.

"I'm sorry," Ben said awkwardly, letting go of me and stepping back. "I thought ..."

I stepped further away, searching frantically for my bag, "No, that's fine. I mean, not exactly fine, but still nice. No, that's not what I mean. I mean, where the hell is my bag?" I spotted it and grabbed it to my chest, my blathering stumbling to a stop. "I think I should go home, Ben." I paused at the surprised and somewhat wounded expression on his face. "I'm sorry. It's not you. It's me. Really, it's me. God, I feel like such an idiot." I covered my eyes with one hand, desperate to not embarrass myself by slipping into tears.

His bare feet squeaked towards me over the wood floor, one tanned hand reaching up to pull my hand away from my face. "It's okay. I'm sorry if that was too soon."

"It's not that it was too soon; it's just...that it was...maybe too soon." I stopped jabbering and tried to catch my breath. "I mean, Rosalie dying this morning. And then there's Daniel. He's only been gone a few months." I sighed and pushed the image of Michael from my mind. Would I have pulled away from his embrace? I didn't know and didn't want to think about that. "Ben, this is a bit embarrassing, but I haven't been with anyone since Daniel," I murmured. "Although it makes me sound like an overwrought teenager, I don't think I'm ready yet."

He smiled with such sweetness and compassion that I suddenly regretted pulling out of his arms. "It's okay. It is. If you don't mind, I think I'll wait. My guess is you're probably worth waiting for."

Chapter Seven

"*It's like rain on your wedding day.*"

I rummaged blindly on the side table for my cell phone, trying to turn off the chorus from Alanis Morisette's *Ironic*. "I've gotta change that ringtone. It's just not funny anymore." I held the phone up to my ear. "Hello?"

"Hello? Kate?" Gwen's voice rattled through the line, sounding weak and shaky.

"Yes, it's me. What's up, Gwen?"

"We have a situation."

"What kind of situation? I'll need coffee before I can focus on anything this morning." I sighed and glanced over at where Jupiter had rolled spreadeagled on top of the blankets; his legs stretched out like a canine centerfold.

"It's Rosalie."

"What about Rosalie?" I sat up straighter in bed.

Shit, how could I forget about what happened to Rosalie!

"Jason released a statement to the media last night."

"He said he was going to wait! We were going to write one together and include the station's perspective!"

"Yeah, well, he didn't wait. And we have bigger problems than him cutting us out of the statement."

A slither of dread began to snake its way down my spine. "What did he say?"

"A lot, but the main gist of it was that Rosalie was murdered, most likely by those evil, small-minded islanders who rejected her sincere efforts to make peace. In other words, she's dead, and we killed her."

"That's slander, Gwen."

Gwen sighed. I imagined her sitting by the old black rotary phone in her smoke-hued farmhouse kitchen. "Slander or not, that's what he said. The volunteer fire chief just called me from the ferry. He's on the first boat out of Tsawwassen this morning, and he's far from the only one on it."

"Media?"

"Yeah, thick with them. He says they're roaming around trying to identify islanders so they can question them about Rosalie." She paused as if reading from a newspaper. "They're apparently saying that 'Actress's dramatic pleas for peace and quiet in retirement end in public bloodshed and death.'"

"That's a good lead," I muttered to myself.

"What?"

"No, sorry, it's just that headline will catch people's attention. Editors will be all over this."

"It's not just the press. T.V. and digital media are coming as well. Scott said they were talking about heading straight up the mountain to my place. I guess my name and address are linked with the station."

"Lock the doors and shut the curtains, Gwen. I'm on my way."

* * *

The steep winding road to Gwen's homestead on the top of Wynter mountain was not an easy drive at the best of times. This summer was definitely not the best of times. The months of constant grey drizzle had weakened the friable soil, creating small landslides at the slightest pressure.

"Gwen's gotta get this graded and secured somehow," I said to Jupiter, who, as usual, was riding shotgun. "It's much worse than the last time I was up here." I swung the station truck through the farm gate and ground to a sliding stop. "And they aren't helping things."

In front of me, Gwen's front lawn and parking area was crammed with a mishmash of cars and trucks stuck in an oozing sea of mud and muck. Station logos were emblazoned across the sides of vehicles: CKOG—the voice of the Okanagan; CKNV—Vancouver TV. Camera operators busily propped satellites up on van roofs to beam the latest news from Wynter Island back to their stations.

I turned off the ignition and pocketed the truck keys. "Head down and keep moving forward, Jupe. That's the only way to deal with a press scrum like this one." I shoved the jeep door open and stepped out with Jupiter behind me.

Jupiter stopped in his tracks, torn between his need to stay close to me and his innate desire to avoid this noisy pack of humans.

"It's okay, Jupe. Come here." I patted my stomach encouragingly, and Jupiter jumped into my arms. I adjusted his body to carry his weight over one shoulder and began pushing through the crowd.

"Coming through. Coming through. Out of the way, please. Thank you. Thank you. Don't want the dog to bite anyone."

The pack grudgingly parted, pelting me with questions. Eyes focused straight ahead. I barreled through them and up the front steps of Gwen's house.

"Who are you? Do you know Gwen Wynter? Do you have anything to do with CWYN? Were you there yesterday when Rosalie Morgann died?"

Jupiter lifted his upper lip at them and growled menacingly.

"You show them, Jupiter. Show them what a fierce pup you are," I whispered.

I had just raised my fist to knock on the side door when a hand reached out and pulled me into the kitchen.

"Thank God you're here."

Even though it was mid-July, Gwen wore a thick sweater hanging loosely over a pair of grey corduroys. In the dim light of the shuttered kitchen, her grey hair pillowed away from her face in a mass of messy waves. I put Jupiter down on the yellowing linoleum floor and unshouldered my bag.

"It's going to be okay, Gwen. Don't worry. But we do have to make some kind of statement."

Gwen gestured towards the front lawn. "You mean, out there?"

I nodded my head. "Yes, out there. We don't have to say much. Just state the station's viewpoint on what happened yesterday. I don't know what Jason was thinking, or if he was thinking at all, but we can't allow him to control this narrative."

"In plain language, that means what?"

"That means we can't allow Jason's perspective to become 'the truth' or 'the story'. And if we don't provide them with another viewpoint, that's exactly what will happen. I'm sure Jason feels that his press release is accurate, but he had just watched his girlfriend die. That's enough to skew anyone's perspective."

Gwen walked to the kitchen table and sat down with a thump in a chair. "What do we say?"

I pulled my laptop out of my bag and sat down beside Gwen. "Luckily, you have a journalist on your payroll."

Gwen glanced out the window. The figures on the front lawn, shapeless grey blobs when seen through the protective screen of her white floral curtains, moved around like amoebas on a glass slide.

"Alright, then. Let's do this."

* * *

"Good morning."

Reporters jostled in front of Gwen's house, jockeying to get the closest to the front porch where Gwen, Jupiter, and I stood. DSLR bursts snapped with a rapid series of clicks that made Jupiter's hackles rise.

"It's okay, Jupe," I murmured and gave him a comforting pat. "Everything's okay." I straightened up and breathed deeply before starting again. "Good morning, everyone. My name is Kate Zoë Thomas. I am the station manager of CWYN. This is Gwen Wynter standing beside me, the station's owner."

"Do you believe Rosalie Morgann was murdered?" a woman shouted from the back of the crowd.

"Before we answer any questions," I continued as if no one had spoken, "I have a statement that I would like to read." I glanced down at the hurriedly printed document in my hand. "On behalf of the station, its staff, and volunteers, we would like to offer our sincere condolences to the family, friends, and fans of the late Rosalie Morgann. She was a beautiful young woman who should have had many years of life ahead of her. We are saddened not only by her passing but also by the fact that this tragic event occurred while she was a guest at CWYN. What we had hoped would be an historic first live broadcast for CWYN has become a nightmare for us all. We have no information regarding the cause or circumstances behind Miss Morgann's death. We request that you address any such questions to the RCMP. Thank you."

"Who do you think did it?" Another voice bubbled up from the scrum.

"Did it?" I repeated.

"Yeah," a male voice chimed in, "who killed her?"

I sighed. "I think I made it quite clear that we have no idea who or what caused Miss Morgann's death. As far as we are aware, neither do the police. I'm sure they are still in the early stages of figuring that out."

"Her manager, Jason Bálachet, believes she was murdered," the male voice continued, "by someone on this island."

I hesitated for a moment. "I realize that is what Mr. Bálachet said in his statement, but I'm sure we can all agree that he must be going through a challenging time right now."

"Are you saying he's lying?" A young woman with a camera and a raised microphone asked from the front of the crowd.

"We are not accusing anyone of anything. Like Jason, we are struggling to understand what happened yesterday."

"So when he said," the young woman continued, reading from her phone, "*Many islanders were jealous of Rosalie's success. They attempted to thwart her desire to recapture the peace and joy of her childhood by trying to scare us off from moving back here. This saddened us, but we hoped that with time, things might change. Perhaps these hard feelings would pass once we lived on Wynter Island for a while. We never imagined this deep-seated hatred might lead to Rosalie's murder.*"

"What piffle," Gwen murmured under her breath.

"As I said, Jason is going through a difficult time. He has just lost a woman who meant a great deal to him. That can affect anyone's perspective on a situation. Perhaps it would be best if he took some time to grieve and leave any suppositions to the police."

"What, like you did, Kate?"

I glanced up sharply, scanning the crowd to try and pinpoint the male questioner. Whomever it was, he had ducked back into the thick of the group.

"I'm afraid that's it for us," I said abruptly, scooping Jupiter into my arms and waving Gwen back to the kitchen door. "Thank you for your time."

"But wait," the young news reporter closest to the porch moved up onto the first step. Jupiter growled and snapped his jaws with a loud click in the direction of her microphone. She staggered back, pulling the microphone into her chest.

"Jupiter, no," I said loud enough for the crowd to hear, and then bent my head to his ear and whispered, "but thanks for the help, boy."

"Wait, we're not done. We've got more questions...." The hubbub of voices built to a roar behind me as I gestured Gwen back into the house.

I paused and turned back to the crowd. There was someone out there. Someone who knew me but wasn't willing to be seen. Someone who knew what had happened on Wynter Island in the past six months and wasn't afraid to throw it back in my face.

I shivered with a sudden chill and followed Gwen into the house.

Chapter Eight

"I forgot that she bought the old Wintford Place," Gwen said as we drove down the narrow seaside road toward the area known as 'Millionaires Row.'

Although unhappy about our destination, Gwen had jumped at the chance to get away from her home and the scrum of media, still stuck in the mud pit of her front lawn. "They named it Wynterhaven, but everyone just calls it the Glass House. You'll see why. It's very modern in style and has huge windows."

After a quick stop to drop Jupiter back at the cottage, we headed north toward W'en'e'win Provincial Park. Was part of the allure of this area that the road dead-ended at an unmarked entry to the large provincial park? No through traffic to bother them and their own private entry to the hiking trails scattered along the shoreline.

I turned in the second from the last driveway and headed toward a two-story modernist-style cement block. The cement had been painted white, giving it a clean, crisp feel. And then there was the glass. Acres and acres of it, not a speck concealed by conventional curtains.

I could see where the nickname came from. It was definitely a house of glass. The best house, I suppose, for an exhibitionist, or perhaps, an actress....

"I don't know why we had to come here today, Kate. After that press release last night, it's not like we can expect a warm welcome."

I braked the truck to a stop on the driveway behind a moss-green Range Rover. "We're not here for a warm welcome. We're here to see how Jason is doing."

"You mean the man who just labeled us all spiteful murderers?"

"Yep, that's who I mean."

"I didn't take you for the Mother Theresa type."

I pointed to the top of my unadorned head. "You've never noticed my halo?"

With a snort of derision, Gwen jumped out of the truck and followed me down the long cement path across the golf course-like lawn. A checkerboard pattern had been mowed into its damp surface, reminding me of Fenway before a Red Sox game. Who on earth was doing that? I couldn't see either Jason or Scott riding around the sizable lawn on a John Deere lawnmower.

Dougie. It must be Dougie. But then, how come he never told us he was working for them?

My mind flashed back to Dougie's flustered meeting with Rosalie in the studio. I could have sworn they were strangers. How odd.

"It also won't hurt if we can find out why he said what he did. And see if it's possible to get him to tone it down a bit," I added.

"Good luck with that."

We arrived at a pair of massive front doors, the top of their frames towering ten feet above ground level. Who needed doors that big, other than the Jolly Green Giant?

"Well," I raised my hand to knock on the dark, smooth wood, "here goes nothing."

The knock echoed back at us, bouncing off the glass windows and thick cement walls. "Should I knock again?"

"No." Gwen grabbed my elbow. "Listen. I think I hear someone coming."

Yes, Gwen was right. Steps were slowly shuffling across a tile floor. Their path seemed labored, almost as if the owner had lost their way. The door finally opened, and we found ourselves face to face with Jason Bálachet, an older, sadder version of the man I had seen yesterday morning. His face was unshaven, his eyes swollen, big violet-black circles dragging his pallid face downward.

"What do you want?" he spat out, his jaw clenching in a spasm of irritation.

51

"Hi Jason," I said, striving for pleasant but instead sounding fake with my overly bright, chipper tone. "We wanted to see how you're doing. You know, after yesterday."

His eyes shifted from me to Gwen before his mouth erupted in a harsh, unfunny rasp. "How do you think I'm doing? Fucking awful."

"That's what we assumed," Gwen replied with an edge to her voice sharp enough to cut through glass. "We thought it might be good to check in on you."

"Fine," Jason stepped back and made an overly dramatic sweep of his arm, gesturing us inside. "Come in if you want to. I don't care. I need another drink."

He turned, leaving the door wide open, and headed back down the wide hallway.

"C'mon," I hustled inside, "let's follow him."

We scuttled in after him. The corridor, glassed on both sides, connected two separate wings of the house. Through the glass, I could see the backyard stretching down to a rocky beach and then the ocean. We followed Jason as the hallway opened up into a massive kitchen/great room. The interior was clean, spare, and starkly chilling, an immense white cube. The ceilings, easily fifteen feet high, stretched back to panoramic windows, which showcased the waterfront in a single, unbroken image.

The furniture was sparse, like a composed gallery installation. Here, a minimalist sofa and chair are angled toward the water view. There, a huge statement piece of a dining table separates the great room from the high-end European kitchen. It was an ode to minimalism: black, white, and a thousand muted shades of grey.

For Christ's sake, couldn't they find a single piece of art with some color in it?

Jason stopped at the immense marble island, his hand reaching toward a half-empty bottle of Jack Daniels. He poured a hefty shot of bourbon into a glass and lifted the cut crystal to his lips. He gestured vaguely towards the bottle. "Help yourselves if you want to."

Gwen glanced at her wristwatch and snorted her disapproval. "It's barely past noon."

"Jason," I stepped toward him, "how are you doing?"

His eyes, red and swollen, momentarily met mine. Yes, there was grief there, but also fury. A red-hot rage arced across the narrow space between us like an electrical spark.

"My initial answer still stands. Fucking awful."

"I'm sorry, we're both so sorry," I glanced back at Gwen, whose stiff facial muscles belied her agreement, "about what happened yesterday. It was a tragedy for everyone."

"For everyone? Huh." He coughed out his disbelief. "Not for the islanders, that's for sure."

"Yes, we got that impression from your statement to the press last night." Gwen paused as brackets of irritation settled deeper into the skin around her mouth. "For some crazy reason, you seem to feel that Wynter Island is to blame for Rosalie's death."

"Yes, I do." He didn't attempt to hide his defiance, his eyes blazing. "It took me a while to process everything yesterday, but I figured out who was at fault."

"Who?" I asked, already knowing the answer.

"All of you!" His finger stabbed in the direction of Gwen and me.

"So all 2,492 residents of Wynter Island got together and conspired to kill your girlfriend?" Gwen responded dryly. "That's a surprising amount of cohesion. Especially when you consider we can't even get everyone to agree on the days the library should be open."

"Gwen," I muttered, "this is not helping."

"Neither is throwing around blame for an unfortunate accident, Kate! Especially saying something as stupid as it was 'all islanders'." Her pupils had opened up, dark and dilated, against her light green irises.

"Okay, just try to calm down, Gwen. Deep breaths." I turned my attention back to Jason. "Why did you write your own press release? We agreed yesterday that we would release a joint statement this morning."

"Because I realized who had killed Rosalie, and I wanted the world to know about it. I wasn't going to wait around to be muzzled by you two."

Gwen snorted. "Muzzled. Huh, more like—"

"Gwen, that's enough. Why would the islanders want to kill Rosalie? C'mon, Jason, think about it. It doesn't make any sense."

I paused as Selesia's words resurfaced in my memory. What had she said? Rose had better watch out that there were a lot of islanders who had an axe to grind with her.

"How much time do you have?" he snorted. "This island has always had it in for Rosalie. If only we hadn't moved to this god-damned place, she might still be alive!"

"Oh, for God's sake, what a load of cow pies!" Gwen muttered.

He turned his rather wild, swollen eyes towards her. "Do you know how we've been treated? Like scum. Like a disgusting odor in a small room. One old bat stormed up and told us to go back to Hollywood, where we belonged."

"Which old bat?" I asked. After all, there were quite a few to choose from.

"The woman who runs the convenience store in the hotel."

"Doreen," both Gwen and I murmured together.

"Yes, her. Every time I go in that damn shop of hers, she looks like she's going to pull a rifle out from underneath the counter. And if that wasn't bad enough, we started getting crap left at the house." He marched over to the monolithic dining table. He rummaged around in numerous paper piles before brandishing a square of crumpled brown paper that appeared to have been cut out of a paper bag.

"Do the police know about this?" I asked.

"Yes, we complained about it, but there wasn't much they could do. We didn't even bother to take this one to the station. I'm guessing the RCMP will take it as evidence. A forensics team from Victoria is going through the house this afternoon."

I wondered for a moment if adding my fingerprints to the evidence was dangerous, but I took the brown paper anyway.

"Go home SLUT!" I read aloud, "We don't want you on Wynter Island! Leave or else!"

I turned the paper over in my hand, noticing the tiniest shred of red or perhaps orange ink on one ripped corner as I did.

54

"Or else what?" Gwen asked.

"Murder, that's what," Jason replied before collapsing into an armchair. "And that's not even including the box of rotting fish left on our doorstep. If we'd managed to get the security system up and running, we'd at least have some idea who did it. But there was no one on this damn island to install it for us! Still, Rosalie refused to leave."

"So someone killed her. An angry islander. Case closed," Gwen said.

His head tilted back, and I could see his Adam's apple bobbing as he swallowed another long slurp of bourbon. He nodded his agreement.

"Well, the RCMP are going to need more evidence than a few scrawled notes and a box full of rotting fish to arrest someone for murder," I said.

"If it is murder," Gwen interjected. "We won't know that answer until the Coroner's findings from the autopsy are released."

"Good afternoon." A voice spoke from behind us. I spun around to see Rosalie's assistant, Scott, standing there. His dark navy polo shirt and black jeans elongated his short torso, making him appear taller and more dignified. He wore them with an almost ceremonial sadness, like one of those Victorian mourners paid to follow caskets as they were carried through a town.

But who does that anymore? Not for the funeral, but alone at home? Dresses in full black, like they're sitting Shiva?

"I thought I heard someone talking down here." He walked over to me, his right hand extended. "Scott Quillimento. We met at the station."

I shook his hand. His fingers were long and delicate, almost malleable, as they rested in my grasp. His blood-stained eyes and mottled skin showed that he, too, had been crying. But he carried his grief with more...I don't know, perhaps acceptance? Jason appeared like an angry child. Scott was much more of a somber adult.

"Yes, Scott, I remember. I came—well, we came—to check in on Jason and offer our condolences. We're both very sorry for your loss."

His lower lip trembled as his hazel eyes misted over with tears. He quickly wiped a hand over his face before regaining control. "Thank you. Thank you both for coming. I'll never forgive myself for going to Victoria. If only I'd been here..."

55

"Scott," Jason said, "there's nothing you could have done. These people weren't going to stop until she was dead."

I studied Scott's face, interested to see his reaction. Did he believe Jason's theory that someone on Wynter had planned and executed Rosalie's death? That this was all part of some vast island conspiracy?

His lips tightened in irritation, like the zip closing on a snug dress, before quickly switching back to his easygoing smile. "We don't know who did it, Jason. It could be ..." His hesitation was momentary, but I still caught it, "anyone."

Why the hesitation? And why the sudden flash of irritation? Did he, too, realize that Jason's rantings were more fantasy than reality? And would not help the investigation into Rosalie's death?

"If you don't mind me asking, Scott, how did you meet Rosalie?" I asked.

Jason's head snapped up, his eyes and Scott's connecting across the vast room. "I don't think that's any of your business..."

Scott raised one hand in the air. "It's okay, Jason. She just asked a simple question." He gave Jason a silent nod that said very clearly, 'Calm down and back off', before turning his attention back to me. "Jason is feeling suspicious of everyone right now."

"Do tell," Gwen murmured.

Scott's lips lifted in a half smile. "But I'll answer your question. Jason and I met each other when we worked in Vegas."

"Vegas?" Gwen repeated. "What were you doing in Vegas?"

"Working as magicians."

"Magicians?" I blurted out in surprise.

"Well, not Penn and Teller, but it was a good living. We would cross paths occasionally. That is until Jason pulled Rosalie from the audience at one of his shows and managed to bewitch her. In all senses of the term."

A tremulous smile spread across Jason's face.

"They fell madly in love, and he followed her back to L.A. One day, when I was in town, I called him. He invited me over to the house. That's when I met Rosalie for the first time. It was fate."

"Fate?"

"Yes, fate. We were destined to meet. Rosalie said it's called Niyati in Buddhism. We became instant best friends. I'd never felt that kind of connection with anyone else before." His voice cracked with emotion. "She asked me if I would consider working as her assistant. Before I knew it, I had moved to L.A. and was living in their guest cottage."

"And then we ended up here," Jason said morosely.

A wave of sadness spread over Scott's face. "Yes. I guess, perhaps, this, too, was fate. Niyati."

Chapter Nine

"Staff Sergeant Singh? What a surprise!"

The tall figure in an RCMP windbreaker swiveled away from the counter of the Lind General Store toward me. "Kate." A broad smile spread across his narrow face. "It's nice to see you."

"Nice to see you, too, Staff Sergeant Singh."

He picked up his change from Doreen and gestured for Jupiter and me to follow him outside. "I think we know each other well enough now that you can call me Ian."

As we stepped out the door, a whoosh of cold, damp air rushed off the ocean, slamming into our faces. We both stopped in our tracks, momentarily gasping to catch our breath.

"Well, at least it isn't raining," I laughed. "That's about the best we can hope for this summer. What brings you to Wynter Island, Ian?"

"Do you have a few minutes? Maybe we could sit down and have a chat?"

He pointed to one of the dark green benches on the Lind hotel's back patio. In better weather, they would have been packed with tourists awaiting the arrival of the next ferry. Not this summer.

I zipped my jacket closed and pulled the collar up around my neck. "Sure. I don't have to be back at the station for another half an hour."

"Great. Follow me."

Jupiter and I dropped into step beside him. His 6' 2" frame, spare but athletic in appearance, suited his RCMP uniform. His molasses-colored skin stretched from one cut cheekbone to the other, making his Sikh ancestry apparent even without the traditional dress turban. He hadn't changed much since he had investigated my ex-boyfriend Daniel's death a few months ago. What had brought him back to Wynter Island?

Duh.

"You're here about Rosalie, aren't you?" I asked as we settled ourselves down onto a bench.

He nodded, his eyes examining the rows of empty sailboats bobbing forlornly in the marina. "Yes, I am."

"But why? Weren't you a part of the RCMP Forensic Explosives Team?" I patted Jupiter absently. He disappeared underneath the bench to use my clamped-together legs as a windbreaker. Even furry creatures were finding it nippy these days. "There weren't any explosives involved in Rosalie's death."

"I transferred from the RCMP E division to take a position with VIIMCU."

"VIIMCU? What's that? It sounds like a vacuum cleaner manufacturer."

His lips raised in a smile, exposing his bright white teeth. "No, we're not a vacuum cleaner manufacturer. Although we are trying to clean up crime." A small chuckle.

"That is a terrible Dad joke, Ian."

His smile stretched even wider. "Yes, I know, but I couldn't resist it. VIIMCU stands for Vancouver Island Integrated Major Crimes Unit. We focus on homicides, suspicious deaths, and missing person cases where foul play is suspected."

"Now I'm beginning to see the connection."

"Yes, the murder of Rosalie Morgann. I took the case mainly because of my previous experience here on Wynter Island."

"Mainly? Was there another reason?"

His hazel eyes settled on my face. "Yes, a personal one. I've been thinking of buying a weekend place here since I relocated to Victoria."

"Really? I wouldn't think investigating Daniel's death would create a 'that's where I want to live' vibe. It's usually the exact opposite. Murder keeps home buyers away."

I felt a sudden jolt of pain in my gut as my memory traveled back to the image of Daniel's body floating in the ocean.

No! No! No! Don't think about it!

He smiled. "It felt like a community to me when I was here, a place where people cared about their neighbors. I thought, in my spare time, I'd look at some real estate."

He sighed, an ineffable exhalation of sadness. Was there another reason he wanted to move to Wynter Island?

"Part-time detective, part-time real estate hunter, then."

He smiled again. "Yes, but mainly the detective. I'm staying at the Lind for the duration of the investigation."

"Does the coroner have a cause of death yet?"

He dropped his chin decisively, once. "Poisoned. They're not sure with what, but they're sure that's the cause."

Poisoned. I let the word settle into my consciousness. Poisoned meant intent and planning. Poisoned meant murder. Another murder here on Wynter Island!

"Poisoning. Wow, that isn't something done in a sudden moment of passion or anger, is it?"

He nodded his head in agreement. "No, it isn't. We assume it was in her energy drink, but we won't know for sure until we get the full toxicology report back. Unfortunately, the bottle shattered when she dropped it, so the remaining liquid intermingled with her vomit and bodily fluids."

Vomit and bodily fluids. My body shivered reflexively.

"We, Stewart, Lesley, and I, are trying to follow the path that bottle took in the days leading up to her murder."

"Where did she buy it?"

"She didn't. Jason, her manager, did. From the General Store, just before they were due to leave for CWYN. Rosalie stayed back at the house to finish getting ready while Jason dashed out to buy one for her. She usually has a bottle midday as a pick-me-up, but there were none left in their fridge."

"That's suspiciously convenient, isn't it?"

He shrugged his shoulders. "That's the difficult thing about coincidences, Kate. It's hard to tell whether the sound of hoofbeats means horses or zebras."

"Excuse me?"

He laughed. "Haven't you heard that old saying before? When you hear the sound of hoofbeats, think horses, not zebras. In other words, the most commonplace answer is usually correct."

"So, the most commonplace answer would be that they just ran out of the energy drink. Not that it was planned."

"Yes. Apparently, that happened quite a lot. Scott said it was on his shopping list for his trip to Victoria. He was over there for a couple of days off."

"Yes, I know."

"You've met him?"

"Gwen and I stopped by the house the day after Rosalie's death to check in on Jason."

"And how did you find him?"

"Scott or Jason?"

"Both."

I thought about that for a minute. "Jason was distraught, Scott less so. I mean, there's no point in beating around the bush. Jason believes that an islander killed Rosalie."

"Yes, he was quite vocal about that with me, too."

"Scott struck me as not so hysterical. And—"

"And what?"

"I don't know. It's just something I felt."

"What was it?"

How could I explain the strange, tenuous vibe I had gotten off the two of them? Like there was something that Jason did not want Scott to speak about. How else to explain his sudden panicked look at Scott when I asked about their history together? And from Scott, there had been that subtle thread of irritation toward Jason. Not obvious, more of a distant melody running beneath the main score.

"He seemed as if he was irritated with Jason for some reason."

"Because he didn't agree with Jason's theory that an islander had killed Rosalie?"

"I guess. I'm not sure. Did you get the note that was left at the house?"

"Yes, along with anything that could have been poisoned: food, drinks, meds, makeup, lotions."

"Lotions? You mean, like hand cream?"

He nodded. "Yes, poison can also be absorbed through the skin. No sign so far that anything at the house was tampered with."

"Which leads us right back to the energy drink."

"Yes, which brings its own complications."

"Well, you'll be happy to know, Ian, that I am not going to butt into this investigation. My days of sleuthing are over. You may not realize this, but I'm not actually an RCMP constable."

He laughed outright. "Really, Kate? You gave a pretty good imitation of one the last time I was here."

"That was different. I had to investigate that murder. I needed to find Daniel's killer to save myself and put Shelley behind bars. But there's no reason for me to get involved with this case." I shivered at the memory of Rosalie's golden hair trailing behind her dead body on the studio floor. "I'd be happy to have nothing more to do with it."

"I doubt that. She died in your studio, under your supervision," he replied, his expression tipping towards somber reflection. "Once again, you and murder on Wynter Island are inextricably entangled."

Chapter Ten

The new open-plan work area of the station bubbled with the voices of volunteers. Most had found a place on the folding chairs I had hurriedly placed out, but a few stood near the front door chatting.

"Alright, can everyone grab a seat? We need to get this meeting started."

"This emergency meeting, you mean," Vera clarified as she settled herself in a metal chair. "This secret *emergency* meeting."

"It's not a secret, Vera."

"Well, do you know what it's about?"

I glanced over at Gwen, standing beside me. Her eyes met mine, her brows furrowed with concern. Something was definitely up, but I had no idea what it was.

"No, I don't. Gwen is the one who called this meeting."

Shea raised her hand to get my attention. "Well, before we get to all that, can I introduce Betty Wu?" She gestured to a silver-haired Asian woman sitting next to her. "She came into the library the other day to introduce herself. She and her husband Gordon bought that new home near Coho Bay."

"Millionaire's Row," Vera said, not quietly enough.

"Well, we call it Salish Rd," Betty corrected her, "but I guess it's known as Millionaire's Row to all of you. It makes it sound very fancy." Her laugh tinkled in the air.

"It's right next to the Glass House, isn't it?" Dougie asked.

"The Glass House?" Betty paused. "Oh, you mean the place where that poor girl used to live? The one who died on TV? Yes, we're right next door."

"They sold their home in Vancouver and decided to retire here," Shea continued.

"My husband was a dentist in Kerrisdale for thirty years. When I finally convinced him to retire, I had to ensure he was far enough from his old practice that he couldn't bother the new dentist!"

Her smile expanded the round doughiness of her face. It lit up her kind eyes, which were settled among the lines on her face. I liked her. Fun, but still full of common sense. The kind of practical mom who just throws another plate on the table when her children bring home an unexpected guest.

"I mentioned that we were looking for new volunteers at the station," Shea continued, "and asked if she might like to come to our next meeting. I didn't," she hesitated, "think it was going to be quite so soon."

"None of us did," Vera muttered.

"Well, it's nice to meet you, Betty," I said. "And it's great to have a new volunteer for CWYN. Any idea of what you might be interested in working on?"

Betty smiled at the other volunteers, the arched parentheses around her mouth deepening into shadow. "I have been brainstorming with my husband, and, well, the thing I enjoy the most is cooking. Chinese cooking."

"A cooking show! That would be fantastic," Dougie said. "Kate, the crew gets to eat the food afterward, right?"

"With everything going on right now, Dougie, that's what you're focusing on? Free food?"

He sat a little straighter in his chair. "A man has to have his priorities."

I sighed. "Yes, the crew eats the food after a shoot."

"I was thinking we could call it Wokking with Betty," she offered.

"I like it. You'll need a producer and a crew. There'll be a lot of preparation work to get done. I hope you're up for that."

"That's fine," she said. "I've got a lot of time on my hands now."

"Great." Gwen tugged sharply on my elbow. "But I need to hand this over to Gwen. Gwen, you're up."

Gwen paused for a moment and looked out over the faces of the volunteers.

Her normally healthy complexion was pallid. "I'm afraid I have some bad news, everyone. I received an upsetting telephone call last night from the gentleman who supports CWYN. Financially supports it."

"Who's that?" Dougie asked.

"He wants to remain anonymous."

"He's gotta be rich. Lumber business? Gotta be lumber," Dougie said, glancing around the volunteers to see if anyone might have anything to offer. "Maybe mining?"

"Don't bother trying to figure out who he is, Dougie," Gwen commanded. "What's important is that he's worried. Worried about CWYN."

"Why?" I asked. "Because of Rosalie's death? I mean, it's unfortunate that it happened here at the station, but we had no involvement with it."

"He doesn't care about the facts. He cares about the optics."

"Optics?" Vera asked. "Like glasses?"

"No, not that kind of optics, Vera. The optics of how this situation looks, for both him and us."

"In other words, he doesn't want any negative publicity," I said.

"He doesn't want any publicity, period. That's why he won't let me release his name."

"But if we don't know who he is, how would the press find him?" Shea asked.

Gwen sighed. "A journalist with some time on their hands could probably figure it out. And then he would have to deal with the media asking a lot of uncomfortable questions."

"So our benefactor is feeling a bit antsy because Rosalie was murdered at CWYN," I said. "I get it. What do we have to do to reassure him that everything will be okay?"

Gwen's eyes met mine, the seriousness in their depths making my palms tingle.

How bad is this going to be?

"He's not looking for reassurances, Kate. He wants the whole thing to go away."

"So do I, but I can't just snap my fingers and make a murder investigation vanish."

"Well, that's what he wants. Murder solved, criminal captured, and the story off the front pages and out of his hair."

"Or what?" I asked.

She hesitated momentarily. "Or he pulls his funding from the station. That's why I called this meeting. If this murder investigation drags on for too long, we may lose our funding."

A sudden hubbub of angry voices filled the room.

"How in hell's bells can he get away with that!" Vera shouted, her German accent shrilly canceling out the other voices.

"Because," Gwen stated, "there is a clause in our paperwork."

Shit! A morals clause!

"It's a morals clause that allows him to terminate our agreement if the station or its representatives engage in misconduct that may negatively affect his company's reputation."

"Say that again in English," Dougie asked.

"It means," I said, "that a murder, perhaps involving one of us, will make him—and therefore his company—look bad."

"Well, boo hoo," Doreen answered sharply. "He's just going to have to get over it. There's no proof that any of us were involved in the murder or even considered suspects by the police ..."

Her voice trailed away as all eyes turned to Selesia.

Selesia's chiseled features stiffened. "Yeah, I know. It's not rocket science, people. I know I'm a suspect," she said, her voice flat and featureless.

"Well, you're not the only one, Selesia," I said.

Every head swiveled back to me, including Gwen's.

"Kate, what are you talking about? What do you know?" Gwen asked.

"Not much, really." I hesitated. "I crossed paths with Staff Sergeant Singh this morning."

"Wasn't he the police officer who came over to investigate Daniel's murder?"

"He's staying with us at the Lind," Doreen added. "Lovely man."

"He's leading the investigation into Rosalie's death," I continued, "along with Stewart and Lesley. He told me they now have a definite cause of death. Poisoning."

A gasp from everyone.

"Is that why Stewart wanted to know who brought her energy drink in from the lobby?! Oh my God, am I a suspect?!" Dougie's voice rose so high that his testicles must have reinserted themselves into his body.

"I think everyone is a suspect right now, Dougie. At least everyone at the station who came in contact with her drink."

Vera counted them off on her fingers. "Well, as far as the drink is concerned, that would be Dougie; whoever bought her the drink, probably her boyfriend; and then, of course, whoever sold it to him..."

Silence seeped across the room as a new realization spread through the volunteers. It was apparent from the stunned look on Doreen and Bob's faces that the RCMP had not informed them yet that Rosalie had been poisoned.

Why can't I remember to keep my stupid mouth shut?!

Doreen's face blanched as she held one hand gripped to her chest. Whether it was shock or an imminent heart attack, I couldn't tell.

Bob's gravelly bass voice boomed out from the back of the room. "Doreen didn't have anything to do with that woman's death. Neither did I. And anyone who says anything different will have to deal with me!" His meaty hands balled up into fists as if preparing for battle.

Oh God, this is going from bad to worse.

"Nobody is accusing her or you, Bob," I said. "I was just repeating what Ian,"

"Ian?" Gwen repeated.

"Yes, Ian. He asked me to call him that."

"Hmm, first names now," Vera said with a suggestive lilt to her voice.

"Don't be ridiculous, Vera. He said that anyone with access to that bottle would be considered a suspect."

"Her boyfriend bought it first thing on Friday morning," Doreen murmured. "I remember because, you know, I wasn't thrilled to see him."

"You hated his guts," Dougie clarified.

"No, well, ah—"

"You didn't hate his guts? Okay then, you hated her guts," Dougie continued on.

The color began to seep back into Doreen's cheeks as her emotions shifted from shock to anger. "Yes, I did," Doreen said, her eyes emitting sparks of fury. "I hated her. I didn't wish her dead, but I'm not sorry she's gone. She got what she deserved."

There was an audible gasp in the room. Vera turned around in her seat, her waggling eyebrows signaling Doreen to shut up.

"Alright," I said, "that means that Dougie, Selesia, Jason, Doreen, and whoever had access to the bottle at the store—"

"What about you?" Dougie asked.

"Me?" I stuttered out. "Why would I be a suspect?"

"I don't know why, but some guy from the press is wandering around asking questions about you."

My mind harkened back to that male voice at the press conference. Was that who Dougie was talking about?

"Who is it?"

"I don't know his name." Dougie swiveled around to look at the other members. "Does anybody know who it is?"

The volunteers shook their heads no.

"But you know who I'm talking about, right?"

Several nodded their agreement.

"See, I told you. He's been asking about you all over the island."

"What does he look like?"

"Thirties. City type: soft hands with clean fingernails; no tan to his skin. Dark hair with those Ray-Ban sunglasses. Wears a black leather jacket."

"Doesn't ring any bells for me."

At least not visually. Internally, I was sure he was the anonymous voice from the press conference.

"What was he asking about, Dougie?"

Dougie hesitated. "He wanted to know about your life on Wynter Island. Particularly," he swallowed before continuing, "about Daniel's death."

I squeezed my eyes tightly shut. Would this never end? I had been so excited to start my new job on Wynter Island, so pleased at the thought of having a fresh start after my time in Afghanistan. Until I found the body of my ex-boyfriend floating in the Salish Sea.

Daniel. My lovely Daniel.

A smack reverberated from the front door as Fisherman Phil pushed it open with a thrust of one hand and stumbled into the lobby. His entrance was immediately followed by the pungent aroma of rum.

"I heard there was an emergency meeting today," he slurred. "I got here as fast as I could."

"Please tell me you didn't drive, Phil!" Gwen asked.

Phil shook his head, causing the laces at the top of his rain jacket to flap back and forth across his chest. "No, got a lift."

A beat-up Chevy pulled out of the parking lot with a young man behind the wheel. Was it Brad Sixto?

"Well, thank God for small mercies," Vera muttered. "You've missed most of the important bits, Phil, but I'll give you a quick recap. The person funding the station is getting antsy with all the publicity around Rose's death. He's threatening to shut us down."

Phil's milky eyes welled up, turning his features from the grumpy, caustic fisherman I knew into a sad, lost soul.

"Rose." He sat down heavily in a seat.

I walked over to him and reached out a hand, pausing before placing it lightly on his shoulder. God only knew what forms of microscopic sea life might be living on that jacket.

I had never seen him like this before. Just the mention of her name had moved him to tears. I remembered Ben's description of him sobbing over Rosalie's body at the island hospital. Yes, he was definitely a broken man.

"Phil, are you okay? How much have you had to drink?"

His eyes swam towards me. "Not enough." He paused. "It's never going to be enough. She's dead, you know."

"I know, Phil. We all know. It seems like you had a special connection with her."

He nodded. "Such a beautiful girl."

I gestured to Nate. "How about you let Nate take you home, okay? Maybe have a rest and let some of the alcohol wear off. We can talk about your new show, 'Fishing with Phil', another day."

He nodded and allowed Nate to help him to his feet before following him out the door.

"What a horrible way to end a horrible meeting," Vera said as she stood up. "He loved Rose like a daughter, you know. God knows why."

I watched as Nate reversed out of his spot with Phil slumped in the passenger seat.

Yes, that's true. Only God knows why.

Chapter Eleven

"I like Gene Kelly, but I've gotta say, I'm not a huge fan of singin', dancin', or even walkin' in the rain," I said, huddling under the broad branches of my pop-up umbrella.

"My mom says that it builds character," Shea replied, forging across the Enchanted Forest Park in her purple patterned rubber boots.

"Causes illness, more likely," I muttered, following her in my new blue Bogs: waterproof and warm, just what my tootsies needed.

Jupiter had refused to leave the truck and sat balefully watching us through the front window. His white and grey arched brows spoke volumes: Kate stupid. Me smart.

"Why are we doing this, Shea? We could talk anywhere, Annie's bakery, my house, your house..."

She shook her head. "Not my house. Lesley is home this morning."

"Okay, so we need to talk about Lesley?"

Shea stopped suddenly in her tracks, her purple boots kicking up an errant splash of mud. "This has been a tough summer for me, Kate."

I moved closer. "More than just the weather?"

She looked grimly towards the edge of the park, whose uncut grasses obscured the drop to the sea. "Way more than just the weather."

"Is this about Rosalie? I didn't realize you knew her."

She started to walk once again. "No, I never knew her. She left before I arrived on the island. It's about Selesia," she paused as her voice cracked, "and a lot of other things."

"Let's start with Selesia."

"Well, first off, she's a suspect in Rosalie's death." Shea gazed down to watch the toe of one boot tunnel into the mucky soil. "Not just one of the suspects, but THE suspect."

"That might be jumping the gun a bit. Right now, my money is on Jason, the boyfriend."

"Well, Selesia stated that she would like to see Rosalie dead. Not just once but several times, and in public, to boot. And then she vanishes while Rosalie's drink is left unattended in the lobby? No one saw her during the ten minutes she said she was in the washroom. Everyone else was on set or in the control room. She could have been anywhere in the station."

"True, or she could have been right where she says she was: in the bathroom. It takes a lot of chutzpah to poison someone with only a closed door between you and everyone else."

"Chutzpah is something Selesia has in spades."

"I can't disagree with you there, but do you really think she's capable of killing someone?"

There was a long silence before Shea finally spoke. "I don't know."

"That doesn't sound like an I don't know. That sounds like a yes."

Shea turned and started to stride towards the hill's edge. "I need your help, Kate. I've got to clear her."

I struggled to keep up in the soggy soil. "Why me in particular? I mean, have you talked to Lesley about this? She's trained in this kind of thing."

"I can't talk to Lesley about this. We try to keep at least a little separation between her work and our relationship."

"Alright, but you can still talk to her about how concerned you are for Selesia."

"So that she gets more validation for her theory that Selesia did it? I don't think so. We need to do more than that. She could lose custody of Brad to Rick, her ex, who lives 20 hours away in Prince George." Shea paused to look out over the roiling waters of the Pacific, the raindrops landing like silver bullets. "I don't think she could survive that."

I turned to watch the mist of rain descending into the ocean below. "What does Sam think?"

"He agrees with me. And that's just the start of it. I don't want to think about what she would face as an Indigenous woman in the Canadian penal system. We like to kid ourselves that justice is blind, but you and I both know it isn't."

"Let me get this straight. You think Selesia poisoned Rosalie Morgann."

"I didn't say that."

"Okay, I am inferring that is what you meant. And you need my help to try and prove she didn't?"

"Basically."

"I can see why you didn't want Lesley to overhear us."

"Lesley is another issue entirely."

"You don't think she's the murderer!" I laughed, trying to lighten the mood.

Shea's glower didn't budge. "No, I don't think she's the murderer. At least of Rosalie Morgann."

"Of someone else?" I replied, shocked.

"There are different kinds of death," Shea replied. "There's also the incremental death of a relationship, like a frog in a tepid pot of water coming to a boil. You think everything is fine for the longest time—until it isn't. We've been together for four years. Four happy years, or at least that's what I thought."

"Lesley doesn't agree?" I hesitated. "You don't think she's cheating on you?"

"Yes. I do."

We had arrived at the edge of the park, the unobstructed wind whipping rain steadily onto our faces. The force made it painful, like tiny pinpricks over my cheeks.

"Ahhh," I said, spitting out the bits of rain that splashed into my mouth, "what a lovely day for a walk."

I turned to see Shea silently sobbing, the only visible sign being the upward hiccupping of her shoulders.

"Shea!" I wrapped my arms around her, trying and failing to keep our umbrellas untangled. I finally just gave up and dropped mine to the ground.

"Are you sure?"

Indecipherable sounds emerged from where she had burrowed her head into my shoulder. She raised her head so that she could speak clearly. "Yes. She's having an affair."

I tilted her chin with one finger to look directly into her blue eyes. "I find that hard to believe. Lesley loves you."

"Loved."

"No, not loved. Loves. What proof do you have?"

"She's been acting strange for quite a while. There was all the craziness with Daniel's death and Gwen's house being bombed, so I assumed she was preoccupied with that. But everything calmed down. You went back East to visit your father and sister. Everyone began to get ready for the summer season...."

"And then it started to rain," I added.

"Yes, so no tourists. No crime. The island ground to a stop. And yet she kept on disappearing at the oddest of times."

A chill slithered down my spine. "Like when?"

"There was no rhyme or reason to it. She started going to that crazy "Crafting with Cocktails" get-together— as if Lesley ever crafted a day in her life! I'd stop at the station to talk to her, and she'd be out 'on a job.' But Stewart wouldn't tell me what the job was or where she had gone."

"Shea! Come on! Do you think Stewart would allow Lesley to go off and have some romantic assignation in the middle of the work day? And then lie to you to cover for her?"

Shea shrugged. "Who knows? I don't know who to believe anymore. But that's not it, Kate. There's more."

"Go on."

"I went through her cell phone."

"Illegal but understandable."

"There were calls to and from a number I didn't recognize. And a few text messages from it, too."

"What did the messages say?"

"Not much. Need to see you. Got your message, will call later to discuss it. Let me know when you can come by."

"Sounds pretty tame to me."

"How about: I'll be home tonight. Does seven work for you? You like chardonnay, right?"

I hesitated, scrambling to find a positive slant. "A work meeting?"

"A work meeting? At night? With an RCMP constable? Where you offer them chardonnay? I don't think so."

A sigh escaped my mouth, a low, drawn-out exhalation. "Do you know who it is?"

"Yes. I called the number, pretending to be a survey taker."

I watched as her face froze into an impenetrable block of stone. "And? Who is it?"

"Gretchen Steubbs. That artist who has a cabin not far from Michael and Anna. That newly single artist."

"Single?" My voice wavered. "I thought she was in a long-term relationship with that pop star, Tonya something or other?"

"She was. Tonya dumped her for a high fashion model a few months ago. Gretchen must have been," She ground the last few words out through her teeth, "lonely."

"But Shea, we still don't know if that's true. There may be a reasonable explanation for all of this."

"There is no reasonable explanation for any of this." She stared out into the grey mist. "I don't know which hurts more: clinging to the desperate hope that I'm wrong or the thought of living the rest of my life without her."

"Oh, Shea." I wrapped my arms around her, hugging her tightly in a futile attempt to ward off her pain.

"You've got to help me, Kate. Help me save something, someone. If I can't save my relationship with Lesley, at least help me prove that Selesia is innocent. I can't bear to lose her as well."

I remembered Ian's words on the bench beside the harbor. Was it true? That I was somehow intrinsically entangled in murder on Wynter Island? It certainly felt like it.

I gripped her tighter and whispered, against my better judgment, "Yes,

Shea. I'll help you."

Chapter Twelve

I shook my umbrella several times, making sure not to splatter Jupiter, before leaning it against the outside wall of the Lind General Store. I stomped my boots in a futile effort to return circulation to my feet and blew on my icy, chapped hands. I had no idea a place without snow and ice could feel colder than Boston in mid-January. But that's what a combination of rain and wind blowing in off the ocean does for you.

"C'mon, Jupe. Let's go in." Jupiter, who had suddenly found the energy to leave the comfort of the truck, stood waiting expectantly beside me. "You're not fooling me. I know why you're willing to brave the rain now but weren't willing to go on a walk with Shea and me. You're hoping Doreen has a treat for you, aren't you?"

His ears pricked up excitedly at the sound of the magic word.

"Yeah, that's what I thought."

The ferry had just arrived. A few vehicles, mainly locals but with a few hardy tourists sprinkled amongst them, motored off the ferry and started up the hill. A sparkling new white pickup was in the lineup. I squinted and recognized Dougie's ginger hair as he drove past me.

Hmm, Dougie's bought himself a new pickup. That must have cost him a pretty penny.

I stepped inside the steaming warmth of the store, happy to get a warm cup of coffee and a liter of milk to take home.

"What the hell?"

Standing beside the long counter that stretched across the front of the store, Ian and Lesley were deep in conversation with Doreen and Bob. From the fevered crimson flush spread across Bob's face, it was not good news.

"We didn't have anything to do with this!" Bob growled, his fists clenching reflexively beside him. "How can you even be sure it happened here? That bottle could have been poisoned anywhere along the supply chain!"

Ian's lips clenched together as he visibly struggled to maintain his calm demeanor. Ian was usually pretty even-tempered, which meant Bob was being particularly difficult this morning.

"Yes, it may have been tampered with before arriving on Wynter Island, but that's highly unlikely, Mr. Corker. If we are working under the assumption that this was a targeted crime, then the poison could only be administered once there was a good chance the bottle would get to Rosalie."

"But how could the killer know which bottle would be picked from the cold case?" Doreen asked.

"Jason bought the same brand and flavor frequently," Lesley explained. "The murderer might have known that and used it to their advantage."

"But how did the bottle get into the store?"

Lesley and Ian, exchanging a brief glance, said nothing.

Doreen continued. "And what would have happened if someone else had gotten to that bottle first?"

"Then we would have a random poisoning on our hands rather than the murder of a Hollywood star," Ian said. He spotted me at the door, his lips clenching even tighter in irritation.

My presence here was making a bad situation even worse. I smiled in my most obliging way, and he nodded back in a brisk up-and-down greeting.

"Remember, this is a woman with enemies. Several people publicly stated that they wanted her dead." He hesitated as we all watched a flush crawl up the surface of Doreen's neck. "It's possible that Rosalie got the bottle accidentally, but not likely."

"But you're still not sure it happened here," Bob countered, his bluster starting to lose steam. "That the bottle was tampered with in our store?"

"That's correct. It's just one avenue we have to investigate. All the other bottles that Constable Akiyama removed from your cooler tested negative for poison."

"So it was only in the one bottle?"

"As best we can figure out right now."

"And what about once the drink left here? Someone could have poisoned it after it left the store," Bob said.

"That's true. It did pass through several hands."

"Was it at the studio long enough for someone to poison it there?" Doreen asked.

Lesley nodded. "Yes."

"So that's most likely how they did it."

"We can't say for sure," Stewart said as he walked out the open door of the back storage room, his fist closed loosely around something. "Hey, Kate. I didn't realize you were here. And Jupiter, too."

All eyes turned to look at me. "I just came in to get a cup of coffee and warm up. After a walk."

"A walk? In this weather?" Doreen asked.

"Yes. If you want to go for a walk, there aren't many other options these days. What's going on?"

"That's none of your business," Bob barked in brittle irritation.

"Who has access to the back room, Doreen?" Stewart asked, drawing all eyes back to him.

Doreen hesitated, the pupils in her eyes bobbing manically back and forth. "Well, Bob and I, of course."

"And Dougie," Bob added.

"That's where we store all the Amazon packages. Either people come and get them for themselves, or Dougie picks them up when he's got some free time and delivers them for tip money."

"So anyone can go in there and rummage through the boxes?" Stewart asked.

Doreen nodded.

"That's not a very secure operation, is it?" Ian asked.

Doreen turned back to him, a little spark of color returning to her cheeks. "They won't fit in the P.O. Boxes, so we have to store them somewhere, Staff Sergeant."

"Yes, but—"

"But nothing. I've never had a complaint that a box was stolen. If it ain't broke, don't fix it, I say."

"So anyone can access your back room?" Stewart repeated.

"Yes, that's right."

He nodded for a few moments before glancing up at the CCTV camera facing the cash register. "Do you pay much attention to your security system?"

Doreen followed his gaze to the camera, confused. "No. Why?"

"Did you set it up yourself?"

"Yes," Bob answered. "A few years ago. We haven't needed to access the video on it, so it just copies over when it runs out of space."

"Our candy counter is right at the front of the store." Doreen gestured to the display of Aero chocolate bars and Smarties boxes nestled directly beneath the counter. "The only theft we have is the occasional gobstopper, and I can usually grab the kid's arm before he runs out the door."

Stewart tilted his chin toward one of the ceiling cameras. "Do you notice anything now?"

"What in the Sam Hill are you talking about, Stewart?" Bob bellowed. "Just tell us what you found!"

"If you look up at the camera, Bob, you'll see there's no light. "

All eyes turned to the ceiling.

"You're right, Stewart," I said. "It looks like the system is dead."

"It is dead."

"What do you mean?" Bob asked, his eyes widening in confusion.

"Exactly what I said. Someone—or something—severed the power to your CCTV security system." Stewart opened his fist to show a few large brown pellets resting in the palm of his hand.

"Rats?" I asked in surprise.

He nodded. "It looks like it. There is not only rat poop, but several traps set around the back room. You obviously knew there was a problem back there, Bob."

"Yes, I did. So what? This building is almost a hundred years old and sits right next to the ocean. You know as well as I do that there's a rat problem on all of the islands."

"Don't you dare make it sound like we don't keep our place clean, Stewart," Doreen piped up angrily. "We're cleaning all the time. It's just part of living so close to the water."

Stewart walked over to a garbage can and dumped the pellets into it before wiping his hands on his trousers. "I know, but it adds an extra layer of difficulty to this investigation."

"Why?" I asked.

Stewart looked directly at me, his hazel eyes serious. "Because it's impossible to tell whether the wires were damaged by rats or humans."

"They were gnawed at?"

"And pulled. But I can't tell by whom."

"So that means we don't know if this power outage was purely coincidental or if it was something the killer did on purpose."

"Are you sure you can't tell by looking at the wiring?" Lesley asked.

"No," Stewart shook his head. "There are signs of chewing damage, so it's reasonable to assume it was rodents. But the timing of it is highly suspicious, to say the least. I can't believe it's purely coincidental that the security system was shut down at that exact moment."

"But why would someone need to shut down our security system?" Doreen asked in confusion.

"I would think the answer to that would be obvious," Ian stated. "To stop the camera from recording any attempt to poison a bottle or place an already poisoned bottle into your cooler."

"Which means," Lesley offered. "we have no way of knowing whether the bottle was poisoned before it arrived at the store, while it was in the store, or sometime after Jason purchased it."

"Were you able to look at the video that was shot just before the power cut out?" Ian asked.

"Yup, just Doreen puttering around behind the front counter. It's angled to cover the cash register rather than the door, so it's possible someone walked in and just wasn't filmed."

"I have a question, Stewart," I asked.

Bob scowled in my direction. "Are you still here, Kate? Shouldn't you and your dog be doing something other than butting into our business?"

From the corner of my eye, I saw Lesley's lips tilt in a half-smile. "That's never stopped her before, Bob."

"Well, I came in here for a cup of coffee," I reached over to grab a paper cup and filled it with hazelnut coffee before walking towards the cold case, "and some milk. How was I supposed to know an investigation was going on?" I innocently grabbed a container of milk, walked to the cash register, and placed several toonies on the counter. I grabbed a treat from Doreen's dog bowl and gave it to Jupiter.

"What's the question, Kate?" Stewart asked.

I pointed to the cooler's juices, iced teas, and energy drinks. "Those are all glass bottles with metal caps. How on earth did someone tamper with that? Nothing's going to pierce through that lid."

Stewart walked over and took out one of the juice bottles. With a twist of one hand, he removed the lid. "This type of bottle doesn't have a tamper-evident band like sodas do." He screwed the top back on and held it out to me. I leaned closer to look. "It's almost impossible to tell if your drink has been opened. The seal is released, and a small hump appears on the lid, but it's easy to miss."

"Talk about lucky for the killer," Ian muttered. "Any other type of bottle, and they couldn't have gotten away with it."

"There is no such thing as luck," I murmured, mainly to myself.

"What was that, Kate?"

"It's a quote. From Patton, I think. 'There is no such thing as luck. Merely opportunity meeting preparedness.'" I pointed to the coins on the counter. "That's for the coffee and milk, Doreen. Keep the change."

And with my mind still mulling over these new details, I led Jupiter out of the store.

Chapter Thirteen

The grey mistiness of another rainy day blanketed the island, the tops of the fir trees pointing up like distant arrowheads through the mist. Jupiter had settled on a woolen blanket I had set out at the station, cozily toasting himself beside the portable electric heater I had brought in. Although the station was heated, the icy dampness in the air called for something a little toastier. Not that I got much access to it.

Nate's small blue Kia pulled into a parking spot in front of the station. The door alarm tinkled as he dashed inside.

"Sorry I'm late, Kate. There's a tree down on Rte. 97."

"Oh no, a car accident?"

He shook his head. "No, too much erosion in the soil from all the rain. Luckily, it didn't hit anyone on its way down. Although it came pretty close to Dougie's new truck. He must have been sweating!"

"I saw him driving it off the ferry the other day. A white Ford 150. They don't come cheap."

Nate nodded. "Yeah, he came into some money unexpectedly."

"That's a lot of money to come into. How'd he do that?"

"I don't know, an inheritance or something."

Or perhaps payment for a big job? Like poisoning Rosalie's drink?

Even though I knew it was ridiculous, my mind still ran through the details. Dougie had easy access to the back room at the Lind General Store. In fact, no one would have noticed if he had spent any time alone in there. They would just assume he was picking up Amazon packages to deliver. He had also been the last person to touch the bottle before Rosalie drank from it.

He could have easily tampered with it out in the lobby before returning to the set. And he had volunteered to go and get it for her. I hadn't asked him to do it.

He volunteered. And then pretended he didn't know Rosalie. Even though it's pretty obvious he's been doing some landscaping work at her house.

But...no, this was craziness! It couldn't be Dougie. Dougie wouldn't hurt a fly, let alone another human being. I pushed this theory to the back of my mind.

"Stewart had to get out there with his chainsaw to clear a path for traffic to get through," Nate continued.

I smiled. "Calling it traffic might be a bit much for Wynter Island."

"Okay, well, cars then."

Nate stripped off his soaking rain jacket and pulled out a chair. "So, what do we need to go over today?"

"I thought we should touch base to see how Fish Bingo went while I was away."

Fish Bingo, our first program on CWYN, had turned into an unexpected hit. Not only did all of the islanders watch, but a small piece in the Victoria Citizen newspaper alerted Vancouver Island to the wonders of our small TV station streaming on YouTube. They couldn't play bingo without a copy of the Wynter Island Times but were happy to watch the inevitable fights between Fisherman Phil and me over Phil's desperate need to win back the salmon he had just sold to us.

Only on Wynter Island.

"Fine. We're shooting it at the Community Centre since Doreen won't let us use the hotel restaurant during tourist season."

"Did Phil call in to complain?"

"Of course."

"I think that's why most people watch it! To hear Phil rabbit on about his rights as enshrined in the Canadian Constitution. Hopefully, he'll stop fussing about that now that he has his own show to focus on."

"I can't believe he came up with 'Fishing with Phil.' And that Brad Sixto is crazy enough to want to work on it with him."

"A little birdie told me he is hoping that the publicity from the show might lead to some lucrative fishing charters."

"Fishing charters? In the Wet Witch? That old thing is held together with chewing gum and prayer."

"I know, I know. But Phil's got it into his head that this is his path to a lucrative retirement."

"Old Age Pension is going to be the only path he's going to have to retirement," Nate said with a grin.

I smiled as well. "Probably, but we can keep our fingers crossed that Fishing with Phil will be as successful as Fish Bingo."

Nate's mouth tipped over into a doubtful frown. "I don't know about that, Kate."

"Don't know about what?"

"Whether Phil is in decent enough shape to do either."

I remembered the drunken husk of a man who had stumbled into our last meeting. It was as if Rosalie's death had sapped away whatever minimal joy he had in his life.

"Is he still drinking?"

"Yup. He only leaves the cottage to go to the liquor store. Luckily, Brad drives him, so he doesn't kill anyone on the way over."

"Fishing at all?"

Nate shook his head. "Not that I've seen. That's the problem. If he isn't fishing, I don't know if we'll have a prize for next week's Fish Bingo."

"Which means I have to go and see him," I said flatly.

Shit. The only thing more uncomfortable than a social visit with Phil would be one where he was drinking and sobbing simultaneously.

"I'm sorry, Kate."

I shrugged it off. "It's okay. Responsibility brings with it the crappy jobs that no one else wants to do. You'll soon learn that when you venture out into the big, bad world. You're starting twelfth grade this fall, aren't you?"

"Yes, it's hard to believe I'll be graduating in less than a year from now."

"Brad Sixto graduates this year as well, doesn't he?"

Nate nodded. "Yeah, from the tribal high school over in Saanich."

"Do you know him well?"

Nate turned toward me, his eyebrows lifting in surprise. "Not really."

"Because he's First Nations?"

He considered that for a moment, his face scrunched into a perplexed frown. "No, I don't think so. I'm not racist. I mean, I hang out with Will occasionally. But Brad has always been a loner kid. Kind of, " he paused to think of the term, "troubled. He mostly hangs out with his brother."

"So, not a lot of friends on Wynter."

"No. I think he made some friends at his school, but they live on the Reserve in Saanich. Why? What's up with Brad?"

"Oh, nothing. I've just been hearing that he's having a tough summer. I'm glad he's got Phil's show to focus on."

"Yeah, God knows how that pairing came together."

I smiled. "Yes, God is probably the only one who knows the answer to that, Nate." I smiled and changed the subject. "Enough about Brad. Do you know what you want to do when you graduate? Where you'd like to go?"

"Not sure yet. A toss-up between SFU and Capilano University. I like both of their film programs, but I haven't had a chance to go over and tour the campuses with my parents."

His lean face shifted toward sorrow.

"Are things getting any…" I hesitated, "better at home?"

The island had been gossiping all summer about the affair Anna, Michaels' wife and Nate's mother, had with a Green Party coworker. It didn't help that Michael's position as the sole lawyer on the island and its representative on several municipal boards drew a lot of attention to their family. Anna had brought her own notoriety. There had been whisperings that when our present provincial representative retired, Anna would run in her place. I hadn't heard anyone mention it recently, so perhaps the scandal had scuppered Anna's hopes for a political career.

He shrugged. "It's hard to say. Mom says it's all over with that guy. I think she's telling the truth. I don't know whether Dad believes her, though. They're still sleeping in separate bedrooms."

My heart fluttered. An image flickered in my mind and was just as quickly pushed away. It was of Anna packing up and leaving their island home, Michael standing on the front doorstep watching her go. His face was riven with sadness but there was a brief moment of hope. A hope that there might be something else, someone else, out there waiting for him.

Someone like me.

"Kate?"

"I'm sorry, Nate. You were saying?"

"It's all my mom's fault."

I sighed. "It's never as simple as that, Nate."

He harumphed. "Yeah, in this case, it is. We had a great family, and she ruined it."

"Try not to judge your mother too harshly." I smiled inwardly at the irony of my defending Anna, the woman married to the man I wanted. "There may be other issues in their marriage that you don't know anything about. Problems don't usually occur in a vacuum."

Yes, that was true. Problems didn't usually occur in a vacuum. Although the reasoning may seem obvious on the surface, so much more lay beneath. Rosalie was an excellent example of this. A woman utterly reviled by the islanders as a heartless home breaker and yet adored by both Jason and Scott as well as her many devoted fans around the world.

How could she be such a contradiction?

It was like a tapestry. From the underside, it was nothing but a mass of jumbled, colored yarn. But once you flipped it over, the true picture was suddenly revealed. The underside was the path. The top was the final destination.

What was your destination, Rosalie? And why did it bring you back to Wynter Island?

Chapter Fourteen

hil's cottage lay on a small lane in Harrow Village, just off the central green that ran down to the left-hand side of the ferry dock. The other houses surrounding it, neat and painted bright whites and pastels, looked picture-postcard perfect. Phil's did not.

Tumbledown. That was an excellent word to describe Phil's home. I stopped the truck on the narrow tarmac and climbed out. It looked like a hoarder's house. When you opened the door, if you could manage to open it, you would be greeted with tottering piles of paper and other detritus. Dead cats and such. Yuck. I tentatively knocked on the front door.

"Brad, it's open," a shaky male voice called from the interior.

I turned the doorknob and pushed the door open a few inches. "Um, it's not Brad, Phil. It's Kate. Kate from CWYN."

"Kate?" His voice rasped with annoyance. "What do you want?"

I pushed the door open a few more inches to see chipped stains on the original wood floors and a thick layer of dust on the elderly pieces of furniture. The cottage was small, a straight shot from the front door into the living room and right through to the kitchen at the back of the house. The bathroom and bedrooms, I guessed, were beside the kitchen. It didn't appear like a fisherman's cottage, more like the abandoned home of an elderly aunt.

Duh! I mentally smacked myself in the head. Phil must have lived here with his parents until they passed away. That would explain the dirt-encrusted china figurines on the mantel and the embroidered samplers on the wall.

"I've just come to check on you, Phil. That's all."

I entered the room, spotting Phil in an old wicker rocking chair. An end table sat beside him. A bottle of Captain Morgan spiced rum, along with a small glass, rested on top.

"I don't need no one checking up on me," he muttered, still sober enough to be irritated by my presence. I took a quick glance at my watch: ten am.

Oh, Phil! Drunk already?

"Well," I realized I was speaking louder than usual and lowered my voice, "You didn't look that great when you came to the station a few days ago."

He myopically reached for the bottle of rum and poured some into the water glass. "That ain't any of your business."

"Well, actually, it is." I weighed up the choice between standing or sitting on a delicate living room chair that looked like it might crumble beneath me. I pulled the chair back and sat down facing Phil. "What's going on, Phil?"

Belligerence wavered on his cratered, wrinkled face before he slipped back into melancholy. His eyes teared, and he took a quick drink of rum.

"Rose is gone. Dead. They killed her."

"Who are *they*, Phil?"

He gestured wildly towards the front window, almost knocking over his glass. "Them. All those prissy busybodies who had it in for Rose."

"You mean, the islanders?"

"Yeah, all those women who gossiped about her when she was young. They hated that she'd come back home. Jealous is what they are, all of them. Jealous of her beauty." He petted the back of his grizzled grey head. "Her hair was like gold. Did you ever see it?"

I nodded my head. "Yes, I did, a couple of times. She was one of the most beautiful women I've ever seen, Phil."

Phil's lips stretched into a weak smile. "Yes, she was. My Rosie is what I used to call her."

I settled back in my chair, hearing an ominous creak as I did so. "How did you know her?"

Another glug from his glass of rum. "I was best buddies with her dad, Frank. And her mom, Nancy. That's where Rosie got her looks, you know. I courted Nancy, but she ended up choosing Frank."

A sadness crossed his face. Was this perhaps part of the reason for his breakdown? That he had lost her mother to another man and then lost Rose as well?

"Nancy died in a car accident on the Pat Bay highway. Frank never recovered, so Rosie was left to look after herself." A spark of anger flickered in his eyes. "They could have helped—all those bossy women who gossiped about her. But no, they were too busy with their own perfect lives. Nosy bitches, the lot of them."

It appeared Phil had been drinking from the same Kool-Aid that Jason had been imbibing.

"Did you see her much? Once she returned to Wynter Island?"

His eyes narrowed. "Why are you asking? Who've you been talking to?"

"No one, Phil. I just wondered if you'd had a chance to see her before she, ahh, passed."

His face relaxed, and he nodded his head once. "Yeah, she came to visit a few times."

"Was it just a social visit or...?"

His face closed shut again. "Why are you asking all these questions?"

Before I could answer, footsteps clomped up Phil's gravel front walk. Brad Sixto sauntered into the house, stopping as he spotted me sitting in a chair.

"Oh, hi, Kate. Didn't think I'd see you here today."

"Ditto, Brad."

Brad was a younger, softer version of his older brother, Will. They shared the same pale chestnut skin tone, not yet hardened into the walnut-like seams on Sam's face. They both had the same lanky height and shoulder-length, stick-straight black hair. He was dressed in faded jeans and a leather jacket, owing to the chilliness of the weather. During the week, Brad attended a tribal school in Saanich, only returning home on the weekends. But it was now summer vacation, and Brad was at loose ends. Will had taken a job as a camp counselor at a summer camp. For the first time, Brad didn't have his big brother around for companionship.

I had heard the whispers about Brad Sixto. That he was running wild without the sensible counsel of his older brother. That maybe he was drinking or doing drugs. I didn't know whether they were true or just the fevered fears of a predominantly non-native population.

But what I couldn't get over was that, in his loneliness, Brad had turned to Phil. Why, of all people, Phil? Desperation?

"Phil, how you doing, man?"

He walked over and gave Phil a quick handshake. Phil smiled in return, a natural reflexive reaction to Brad's wide grin.

"Middlin', I'd say. But I've got company, as you can see."

I returned Brad's smile. "I heard you're going to be in twelfth grade this fall."

He nodded his head. "Yes, I am."

"Any idea what you might want to do? Any colleges look interesting?"

As soon as the words left my lips, I knew I had made a mistake. The room temperature plummeted as Brad's smile slipped from his face.

"Why does everyone think you've gotta go to college?" Phil shouted before Brad could speak. "I never went to college and look what I made of myself." He waved his hand around the small, filthy room.

Not the best example, Phil.

"You're right. Not everyone has to go to college. There are excellent trade schools …"

"I don't want to go to any more school," Brad said, his shoulders squaring with fierce determination. "I just want to get my high school diploma and get out of there."

"Leave the boy alone!" Phil barked, his voice getting quite agitated.

"I'm sorry. I was just asking a question. I didn't mean to upset everyone."

"It's okay, Kate. Phil, calm down, or you're going to have a heart attack."

Phil gave me one final glare. "These folks and their interfering ways," he muttered.

"I wasn't trying to interfere, Phil."

"It's alright, Kate. I'm dyslexic, so school has always been tough for me. Will is the star academic of the family, not me. He's going to UBC for Computer Science this fall. Full ride scholarship."

His self-effacing grin couldn't hide what I suspected was the hurt he felt at always being second best.

91

"No, I didn't know, Brad. You're right. There are many different ways for young people to make their way in the world."

Brad's eyes met Phil's, but they both remained silent.

"Not if you're my mom. She has all these plans for what she wants me to do, where she wants me to go."

"Well, she's your mom. That's understandable."

"She thinks if I'm not in a special college for the learning disabled or a government-sponsored work training program, I will end up like Greg."

Greg. The name sent a jolt through my system. He had been a drug dealer on Wynter Island and involved in my ex-boyfriend's death.

"Just cause he's native, the islanders think he'll go off the rails and end up in prison or something," Phil said.

"So, to get away from her nagging, I come here to see Phil."

Once again, they glanced over at each other.

Did I see that correctly? Did Phil just wink at Brad?

"Well, I stopped by to make sure Phil can provide our salmon for next week's Fish Bingo. And that he's, um, 'well' enough to start work on 'Fishing with Phil.'"

Defiantly, Phil took a gulp of his rum. "I'll get you your bloody fish. And I'll also make it to the station to talk about the show. Or at least Brad will, 'cause he's gonna be my producer."

I must have looked doubtful, for Brad chuckled. "I'll make sure he gets it done, Kate. Or I'll get the fish for you myself."

Brad has changed, I realized as I headed back to my truck. A lot. This was not the sullen teenager I remembered. Something had given him a new sense of accomplishment, of power. A belief in himself and what he could accomplish. It was lovely to see but also surprising.

What happened?

Chapter Fifteen

The toxicology report was released the next day. Well, released makes it sound like everybody knew. It was more like the police were notified of the results, and Ian informed me. I jokingly asked him if that meant I was now on the RCMP payroll. He told me not to push my luck.

I didn't kid him about it again.

The next day was…rainy. People were beginning to whisper about the stability of the cliffside homes on Wynter and the other Gulf islands. With more rain and no sun to dry up the soil, there was the potential for severe landslides all along the coast. Million-dollar homes might slip right off their foundations and plummet into the Pacific.

Since my morning was free, I piled Jupiter into the truck and headed to Vera's farmhouse. Her house reminded me of a bit of butter-colored Victorian fancy plunked down in the middle of the Pacific Northwest rainforest. One of the original homeowners on the island must have had a soft spot for finials, pilasters, and various forms of molding, for they curved and sprouted all around Vera's front porch.

I couldn't see Vera anywhere in her yard. I parked the truck and dashed with Jupiter to the front door. A few knocks drew an exasperated shout from inside.

"I'm coming! I'm coming!" The door opened, and Vera owlishly looked out at us. Her outfit this morning was grey sweatpants and a very loud pink and purple striped top. "Oh, it's you, Kate. C'mon in. Jupiter too. Shake yourself off in the front hall and join me in the kitchen."

She turned on her heel and headed towards the back of the house. We did as we were told: Jupiter, literally, me not so much, and followed her into the kitchen.

I had never been inside Vera's cottage before. I don't know what I had been expecting. Perhaps an interior design that matched its fussy Victorian exterior? But there was a clean Scandinavian aesthetic throughout. A small IKEA couch and a comfy chair were the only pieces of furniture in the living room. No TV. No stereo. But there was music. I followed it back to the kitchen, where a song that sounded like Enya giving birth streamed out of an old beatbox on the kitchen table.

Vera was seated at a small pine table, sorting through a bowl of dried flowers. She was portioning them into small, mesh bags. "It's chamomile tea. I've run out, and since there's little hope of a crop this year, I've resorted to making my own from bought flowers." She shook her head in disgust. "Would you like a cup?"

"Well," I hesitated. How could I tell her that floral tea tasted to me like warm eau de toilette? "Umm."

"Coffee then?"

"Yes, please."

She scooped ground coffee into an Italian espresso pot and placed it on one of the glowing elements of her 1960s white stove.

"So what has brought you here today, Kate?" Her husky, robust voice dipped in and out of its Germanic consonants. "It's obviously not my chamomile tea."

"I'm sorry, Vera. Flower tea is just not my thing."

Her serious face split into a wide grin as one work-roughened hand reached over to pat mine. "That's fine. I'm just teasing you."

"Good," I sighed. "I'm here for your herbal expertise."

Her hand paused as she raised it from mine. "Herbal expertise? Is there something wrong? Are you sick?" She leaned down to look at where Jupiter had positioned himself under the table. "Is Jupiter alright?"

"No, we're fine. It's more general herbal expertise."

"Oh, okay. What is it?"

I hesitated. This was going to be tricky. How do you casually ask someone if they have any poison lying around the house? The same poison that has just killed a young woman?

"Lily of the valley. You know it, don't you?"

"Oh, of course. Convallaria Majalis. Beautiful flower, lovely fragrance, but it can be deadly."

"Yes, I know. The coroner is pretty sure that is what killed Rose."

"She was poisoned? By Convallaria Majalis?" Vera's stunned reaction slipped towards meditative thought. "Well, it's a good choice, I suppose. Its toxin, convallotoxin, is quite similar to digitalis, found in foxglove. Has a similar effect. You know, Cardiac arrhythmia. It's the cardiac glycosides."

"The what?"

"It affects the heart, Kate, either in a good or bad way, depending on how it's used."

"Have you used it?"

Vera considered this for a moment. "Not in quite a while. I don't even think I have any tincture anymore. It can help deal with irregular heartbeats in small doses, just as digitalis can. Also UTIs."

"But you don't have any?" I pushed.

"Well, not in my herbal apothecary. But I have lily of the valley growing in my garden."

"Why do you have it growing in your garden if it's poisonous?"

"For the same reason, I have foxglove and belladonna growing in my garden: they're also poisonous. Yews, those shaped evergreen hedges you see in Stanley Park and around older homes in Vancouver? They are the deadliest tree known to man. Almost instantaneous death."

"Really?"

"Yes, because a little of something can be good for your health, while a lot of it can kill you. It's the nature of pharmacology, either herbal or prescription."

"Okay, I've got to ask you this, Vera. What was your relationship like with Rosalie?"

Vera leaned back in her chair and laughed so loud and long that she began to cough, her hacking shaking her thin frame. "Oh, Kate. I don't know which is funnier: that you think I'm the murderer or that you think I might answer that question honestly if I was!"

The espresso pot burbled on the stove, and Vera stood up to take it off the element and pour me a small cup of espresso.

"Sugar?"

I nodded, and she dumped a heaping teaspoon in before handing me the cup.

"No, I was one of the few women on the island who didn't have a personal issue with Rose."

"Why was that?" I sipped at the boiling hot liquid.

"Because I was a child of the sixties. Drugs, free love, nudity, etc. That's how I came to live on Wynter Island."

"I wondered how you'd ended up here."

"My then-husband and I left Germany in '67 to travel across Canada in a VW van. We heard about a groovy commune starting up on this idyllic West Coast island, so we decided to try it."

"What happened?"

"Well, my marriage ended, and then the commune broke up. I decided to remain on Wynter Island and open the pharmacy."

"I see. Most everyone else left, though."

Vera nodded her head. "Yes, leaving me surrounded by a bunch of fishermen and farmers who didn't know what to make of a flower child. Over time, they warmed up to me."

"But not to Rose."

"No. They couldn't see that sex for Rose was merely another form of attention and affection. The women were scandalized because she didn't bring the moral weight to it that they did. Scandalized with both her and their husbands."

"But not you."

"No, I didn't care whom she slept with. But I wouldn't say I liked how she used sex to hurt people. I didn't like that at all. Even then, I could see that she was getting her revenge."

"Revenge for what?"

"Revenge for the fact that she was invisible to all of them until she grew into a beauty."

"I see."

"So I had no motive to murder Rose," she chuckled. "Unlike other women on this island."

"Like Doreen?"

"Unh huh."

"Did Doreen have access to your garden?"

Vera snorted. "Is that your not-so-subtle way of asking if I gave her some lily of the valley so that she could make Rose pay for the suicide of her friend?"

I nodded.

"No, Kate, I didn't. Have you ever heard the saying: A friend will help you. A good friend will help you hide a body."

"Yes."

"Well, as lovely as Doreen is—and we are quite good friends—I would not help her hide a body."

"But what about Gwen?"

"That's different. Gwen is like a sister to me. I would definitely help her hide a body." She hesitated. "You're not seriously thinking that Gwen had anything to do with Rose's death?"

"No, not really. Just thinking out loud."

"Gwen wouldn't have any motive to hurt Rose. She and Sam left for UBC in the early seventies."

"Gwen never met her? At all?"

Vera shook her head. "No. She and Sam left before Rose was born. They were madly in love back then. Did you know that?"

"Sam told me. Something happened, and they broke up."

"Yes, Gwen started dating someone else in their third year of university. Broke Sam's heart. And then, out of nowhere, she packed up and moved to Toronto to finish her degree. She never returned until about 15 years ago."

"Yes, I remember. After her father died."

"Yes. Rose was about 19 or so when she ran away. The late nineties. Long before Gwen came back to Wynter Island."

"Outside Gwen then, most islanders would have known Rosalie. Definitely, the old-timers would."

"What are you getting at, Kate?"

"You heard what Gwen said at the emergency meeting." I took another sip of my espresso. There was no reason to tell Vera what I had promised Shea. "We've got to find the killer. CWYN can't lose its funding. If it does, we're done."

"My money is on her fancy man."

Jupiter came out from beneath the table, looking for a treat. Vera leaned back to take a cracker out of a tin and handed it to him. "It's not dog food, Jupiter. It's human food, so you'd better be extra good."

Jupiter licked his lips and returned to his spot under the table.

"You mean her 'mystery lover'? The wealthy guy who was funding their little liaisons?"

"Yes."

"Did he really exist, Vera? It sounds like something a teenage girl would make up to try and impress people."

"I don't think so. Rose frequently caught the float plane out of town for the weekend, and there was no way she could have afforded that on her own. And think about it, Kate: Rose's murder was public and dramatic, almost theatrical. That leads me to think of the heart, not the head. An emotionless murderer would have their victim die in their sleep, not live on air. Perhaps she broke his heart when she ran away to Hollywood?"

"So the question then becomes: who is the mystery lover?"

Vera shrugged. "Your guess is as good as mine."

Chapter Sixteen

On the day of Rosalie's funeral, Stewart erected a barrier blocking off Millionaire's Row to everyone except mourners. He stood there gesturing us through, while on the other side, a small group of reporters, mainly photographers, stood huddled beneath their umbrellas. One of them caught my eye. He was dressed in a black leather jacket similar to the one Dougie had described, thin with dark hair, probably around thirty. His easy smile slipped into a sneer as I slowly drove past.

The line of cars parked in front of the Glass House was small, with no California or rental car plates that I could see. They had positioned their vehicles along the narrow road to have the most direct path through the rain to the massive front door. After all, nothing ruins a funeral like wet clothes.

I pulled my keys out of the ignition, tossed them into a small purse, and stepped out of the truck into the gently spitting rain. Gwen was right behind me. She was dressed in a simple black linen shirt dress, the rubber boots on her feet taking away from her funereal appearance. Luckily, I had found one piece of appropriate black clothing in my closet: a knit dress I had bought at the winter sales in Paris several years ago. I glanced down at my feet. At least my leather flats looked better than the Wellington boots I had considered.

"Let's do this, Gwen," I said.

"Do we have to?" she asked grudgingly.

It had taken quite a bit of coaxing to get her to accompany me this morning.

"Yes, we have to."

"I didn't realize until yesterday that the coroner had released her body, and she had already been cremated."

"Well, they did. Jason wanted to move forward with a memorial service as soon as possible."

We hurried through the rain to the open front doors. A young woman dressed in typical caterer's gear, a white dress shirt, and black trousers pointed us toward the vast family room. Her face was unfamiliar. Jason must have brought in a catering firm from Victoria.

As soon as we entered the hallway, the warm, patchouli fragrance of incense enveloped us.

"It smells like Vera's house," Gwen muttered.

We followed the fragrance into the family room. Someone had moved all of the furniture out to make room for the folding chairs that were now arrayed there. Two cedar tables had been placed directly in front of the massive glass windows.

On the first table, an intricately filigreed blue and white ceramic jar sat alongside a framed photograph of a radiantly beautiful Rosalie. The second table was identical, except that it held a framed image of the Buddha. Red tapered candles were placed on either side of the pictures, along with platters of fruit and rice. Crystal vases held gently smoldering incense sticks surrounded by lush floral arrangements.

"Look at all those flowers," Gwen whispered as we slipped into a seat. "If Jason had those done on the island, Nan must have made a fortune."

Nan was our island florist. She worked out of her garage doing everything from weddings to funerals.

"I don't think we should be discussing profits at someone's funeral," I whispered.

"I don't know why not," Gwen answered. "It's the only good news to be had out of all of this."

I glanced at the chairs around me. In the front row sat Jason and Scott. A few seats down from them were Phil, with Brad Sixto sitting next to him.

Brad? Why was he here? And sitting in the front row? Wasn't that kept for family and close friends? Had he known her? Or was he merely there to help support Phil?

Scattered amongst the mourners, I spotted Lesley and Ian sitting together, both in uniform. Anna, Michael, and Nate were seated with a woman I didn't recognize.

"Who's that?" I nudged Gwen and pointed toward them.

"That's June Greenwood. She's our provincial MLA."

Amongst those remaining were the Anglican vicar and his wife, Dougie, Shea, Vera, and what looked like Betty Wu and an older man, most likely her husband.

Silence settled over us as three bald monks walked up to the tables and knelt facing them. They were dressed in identical robes, each dyed a saffron-gold color and draped with toga-like coverings of rich red fabric. One held a small tambourine-shaped drum. Another had brass cymbals that he began to clash together in a chiming rhythm. The monk holding the drum began twisting its long handle back and forth between his palms, causing the leather strings attached to it to beat against the taut surface. The three of them began to chant as if on cue, the sound echoing through the room's cavernous space.

The chanting continued, with ululal peaks and valleys, for approximately twenty minutes. When the last crashing note hovered on the suddenly still air, two of the monks moved to one side while the older one stood and turned to face the audience.

The grey stubble on his newly shorn scalp brushed against the pockmarks of long-ago acne that was pitted across his cheeks. Settled in his narrow, some might say gaunt, face, two bright eyes surveyed us all. He smiled as our eyes connected, giving me a quick up-and-down inspection.

Oh, he doesn't miss much.

"Good afternoon. My name is He Kyabje Khenzur Rinpoche Kachen."

His voice was not loud, but in his distinctive Nepalese accent, his directness reached across the room.

"Sadly, I never got the chance to meet Rosalie Morgann. She sounds like a lovely person, much loved by her friends and fans." He walked soundlessly in bare feet, pausing now and then to gather his thoughts. "Many in the West come to our faith looking for peace. They first find this peace in meditation. I have been told this is how Rosalie started her journey toward Buddhism.

They then begin to ask questions to learn about our belief system. About who Buddha was, what he believed." He chuckled to himself. "Don't worry, I am not here to—what is it you call it?—proselytize. The purpose of a Buddhist memorial service is for the monks to pray for Rosalie's soul. Not for us to try and get converts. We pray that the actions, or karma, Rosalie created in this life will return to help her as she goes through samsara, the cycle of birth, death, and reincarnation that leads to enlightenment."

"She better hope her karma didn't return to help her," Gwen whispered out of the side of her mouth.

"Gwen!" I shushed her, "That's a horrible thing to say!"

"I will translate one of our prayers so that you can understand some of what we said here today. This prayer is from The Tibetan Book of the Dead:

> *May I know myself forgiven for all the harm that I have thought and done.*
>
> *May I accomplish this profound practice of phowa, and die a good and peaceful death.*
>
> *And through the triumph of my death, may I be able to benefit all other beings, living or dead."*

The room was silent, only broken by sobbing from the front row. Jason consoled a distraught Scott while Brad attempted to stop a furious Phil from getting to his feet.

"She don't need to be forgiven for anything!" he shouted as he finally wrenched himself free from Brad's grasp and turned to face us. "Not anything! No matter what all you busybodies think! She was better than all of you."

He turned and stormed out of the room, Brad racing to catch up with him.

As we all watched Phil storm across the front lawn with Brad in pursuit, Jason stood and moved toward the monk. "I'm so sorry for that outburst, Khenzur Rinpoche. He knew Rosalie when she was young and is distraught over her passing." The monk bowed his head in understanding. "Thank you for coming today. I'm so glad you could do this on such short notice. Having a Buddhist ceremony would have meant a great deal to Rosalie." He stopped to brush away a tear and gestured us all to our feet. "Everyone, please enjoy the refreshments that will be circulating in a moment as we share happy memories of Rosalie."

On cue, a team of neatly attired waitstaff spread amongst us, carrying trays of glasses and canapés.

Gwen and I took a fluted glass of pale pink liquid. Gwen took a quick sip and wrinkled her nose.

"Fruit spritzer. Not champagne."

I took a sip myself. "Of course. It's a Buddhist memorial service, Gwen. Buddhists don't drink."

"Whatever." She turned to walk over to where Shea and Vera were standing with Betty and her husband. I trailed after her.

"Hi, Gwen. You've met Betty before, haven't you?" Shea asked.

Gwen nodded. "Yes, at the emergency volunteer meeting."

"Well, this is her husband, Gordon." The older man smiled, exposing a set of perfect white teeth. "They've retired here. They bought the house next door."

"Yes, we didn't know Rosalie, but we've met Jason and Scott a few times," Betty replied. "We thought it would be nice to come and pay our respects as neighbors."

Out of the corner of my eye, I saw the leather jacket-clad man striding across the front lawn toward Phil. He must have somehow gotten past Stewart. I gulped down the rest of my drink and thrust the empty flute at Gwen. "Gwen, hold this for me. I need to talk to someone."

I managed to reach them just as they met in the middle of the lawn.

The young man grabbed at Phil's shoulder, either unaware or uncaring of his emotional state.

"Did you know Rosalie Morgann? Can you give me some details about her funeral?"

"Leave him alone," I skidded to a stop on the wet grass and yanked his hand off Phil's shoulder. "He's grieving, for God's sake. Have some common decency." I nodded for Brad to take Phil past us. "You get him out of here,

Brad."

The young man swiveled toward me, a sneer once again spreading across his face. "Well, look who it is. Kate Thomas."

"Do I know you?"

"Perhaps you should answer that for yourself," he asked, gesturing toward his face.

There was definitely something familiar about him, even though his face was partially covered by designer sunglasses—the last thing one needed with the weather these days. His skin was pale, and his black hair was left artistically long so that its moussed tendrils brushed his shoulders. Besides the black leather jacket, he wore a loose T-shirt over tight, straight-legged jeans. Doc Martens boots were on his feet, and he was enveloped in an aura of *Dior Sauvage.*

Ugh, a Johnny Depp wannabe.

"Don't you recognize me, Kate?"

His voice was thick with menace. It made the hair on my arms stand up.

I decided to try another tack. "How do you know who I am? Have we met before?"

He lowered his sunglasses to expose a pair of icy blue eyes filled with malevolent satisfaction. "Oh yes, Kate. We've met before."

Chapter Seventeen

W e have?"

He removed his sunglasses and stared directly at me. "Yes, we most definitely have."

"I'm sorry. I don't remember you." Something clicked in the back of my memory, making my palms tingle, but I just couldn't place him. "Can't you just tell me who you are?"

He replaced the sunglasses on his face. "I don't know about you, but I'd prefer to chat out of the rain. Perhaps we can move somewhere inside? Annie's Bakery? Twenty minutes?"

"Okay," I replied cautiously. I was curious to find out who he was, even though the thought of having coffee with him made my skin crawl. There was something so sinister in his manner.

"I'll see you there." He turned on his heel and dashed toward the cars.

* * *

I explained the situation to Gwen and figured out a way for someone else to give her a ride home before dashing back to the truck. I pointed it down Route 97 toward Harrow Village.

Harrow Village held the ferry dock, the Lind Hotel, and Annie's Bakery. Gwen had once told me their cinnamon buns were world-famous. I don't know if that was true, but they tasted pretty damn good.

Eighteen minutes later, I pushed open the door to the bakery. I instantly spotted him at a table near the windows. It wasn't difficult; there were only a few people seated inside. That was the problem with a single-source economy: if the tourists didn't come, no one got paid. There was definitely no trickle in this trickle-down economy. I grabbed a mug of coffee and a cinnamon roll from the counter and walked over to pull out a chair opposite him.

The more I looked at his face, the more certain I was that I did know him. The problem was that I had no idea of his name or how I had come to know him. He wasn't unattractive, with his slender frame and shoulder-length black hair, but the set of his mouth and the anger in his eyes was off-putting. He was around my age, early thirties, but the effect of the tousled hair and subtle black eyeliner felt like he was trying too hard. My palms began to tingle again.

"Okay, I'm here. Now, will you tell me who you are?" I said as I took a bite out of my cinnamon roll.

He was silent for a moment. "Jack Donahue."

Jack Donahue. I let the name cycle through my memory but still came up with nothing.

"Sorry, I've still got nothing."

He sighed, his lips puckering in anger. "I used to go by John Donahue."

"Yes!" My hand smacked down on the tabletop as the pieces fell into place. "That's who you are! John Donahue from Ryerson! You were in the same year as me, weren't you? In the journalism program?"

So that's who he was!

"Yes, that's right." He took a long sip from his cup of coffee.

"It's been a long time, John."

"Jack."

"Okay, Jack. What have you been up to?"

"I'm based in Vancouver now. I work for CGN."

"CGN? That online celebrity news site? So you're here covering Rosalie's death?"

He nodded his head. "Not quite up to your level of journalism, I'm afraid." He glanced out the window at the rain. "Not that you haven't come down a bit in the world."

I didn't reply, feeling a momentary sting at his words. He wanted me to snap back at his intentional rudeness, that was obvious, but I wasn't going to give him the pleasure. I just let his comment settle in the quiet air of the bakery and rest there for a few moments.

"What is this about, Jack?" I asked after waiting long enough to see him begin to fidget with his coffee cup.

"Oh, you know. Payback. Karma is a beautiful thing, isn't it?"

"Payback? Payback for what?"

He took another long sip of coffee before looking straight at me. "Don't pretend like you don't remember, Kate."

"I honestly don't remember, Jack. What are you talking about?"

He snickered. "You know, that shouldn't surprise me, but it does. Our final year at Ryerson. Everyone was getting resumés and portfolios ready, scrambling to head out into the working world and get a job."

"Yes, I remember."

"You were the editor of *The Eyeopener.*"

My mind flashed back to the crowded, messy classroom where we had put together Ryerson University's school newspaper.

I nodded.

"It wasn't that surprising you got the job. You got most of the top prizes that year, didn't you?"

"Well, I don't know about that..." I started.

"You did. You got everything you wanted. Lots of friends, great grades. I suppose it didn't hurt that your dad was the film critic for the Toronto Star. All the professors loved you—their golden girl journalist." The sneering in his voice was toxic and angry. "That meant you got the special coups, didn't it? All those little extra boosts that helped you get to the top."

"I don't know what you're talking about, Jack."

He leaned over the small table, a flinch of fear reflexively moving me an equal distance away. "Like the story that made your career. Remember that story, Kate?"

"The city hall story? The one about the mayor funneling funds to his secretary to keep her quiet about their affair?"

He nodded his head in satisfaction. "Yeah, that story. The one that was picked up by all the major newspapers. You got to be interviewed on CBC, didn't you? I guess it's not surprising they offered you a job after graduation." He paused, his voice deepening into fury. "The story that made you, Kate."

"Yes, of course, I remember that story. What I don't remember is what any of this has to do with you!" My patience was slipping, anger seeping through the cracks to sharpen my voice.

"Don't pretend like you don't know," he laughed.

"If you say that one more time, I swear, I'm going to walk out that door and never look back!"

"Who brought in that story, Kate?"

"It was ten-plus years ago. I've no idea."

"I brought it in, Kate. Me. I'm the one who put in all that research. I took it to Professor King so that I could have my moment. But he said it was too big a story for me, too important. I wasn't skilled enough to do it justice. They needed to have the best on top of it, so they gave it to you."

"I had no idea."

"A huge story just drops into your lap, and you don't ask any questions? You never tried to find out who discovered the story in the first place?"

"I-I don't know. I don't think so. All I remember is getting handed it by Professor King."

"Memory can be tricky like that, can't it? Easy to forget unimportant people."

"That is unfair!"

"Unfair! You're talking to me about unfairness! That's rich."

I took a deep breath and tried to calm down. "It's unfair to expect me to remember something that happened more than a decade ago."

"Yeah, well, I remember. Just like I remembered when I read that you'd been taken hostage in Afghanistan."

"I don't want to talk about that."

He continued unabated. "Just your luck; you got rescued. And then you took a job out here on the West Coast, only to find your ex dead in the ocean. Now, I thought, she'll get her due. Kate Thomas is going to find her ass in prison. But, no, you wriggled your way out of that one, too."

I shoved my chair away from the table and stood up.

"But you can't wriggle out of this one, Kate."

I said nothing, standing still as stone, anger bubbling from every pore.

"Your career, your home, your whole world is resting on this little chunk of land in the Pacific, isn't it? Wynter Island, British Columbia. CWYN. If this station goes under, you're done."

"What do you know about what's going on at CWYN!" I shouted, uncaring that the few patrons in the bakery had turned to stare.

"Everything, Kate. Who do you think convinced your philanthropist to reconsider funding a station that would only bring him and his business bad press?'

My hand slammed the table so hard my empty coffee mug smashed over on its side, tiny chunks of cream porcelain flaking my fingers.

"You bastard!"

He stood and brushed a few broken fragments off the table. "Yes, I am. I take great pleasure in it. I only wish I'd dared to be one twelve years ago."

He turned and left the bakery, leaving me standing beside the shattered crockery, torn between tears and fury.

Chapter Eighteen

Michael's Subaru Forester crunched down the gravel road toward the cottage. There was no point in going outside to greet him. Even though the rain had stopped, the threatening cement-grey clouds looked like they might open up again.

It had been a difficult twenty-four hours. I had returned home from the bakery so overwhelmed with fury that I needed to grip the wheel tightly to ensure I didn't accidentally smash the truck into a tree. And what made it worse, I couldn't talk about it. How could I tell Gwen or Shea that CWYN's downfall might be linked to a feckless decision I'd made when I was twenty-two?

Was what Jack had said true? Had I thoughtlessly taken someone else's story?

That didn't feel like me. I wasn't perfect, but I prided myself on being kind to others. But that final year of university had been so crazy. Our professor had told me about the story and asked me to write it up, and...I had. Jack was right. I hadn't stopped to ask any difficult questions. I had just pushed forward because...I wanted to succeed. I wanted to be a star.

Star. The word settled in the pit of my stomach like a piece of lead. And what had that success brought me? A kidnapping in Afghanistan, a murdered ex-boyfriend, and my present job on Wynter Island. He was right. Going from a well-respected television network to a small community TV station in the middle of nowhere was a step down career-wise—a big step down.

Michael jumped out of his SUV and grabbed his toolbox before heading to the house.

"Lovely weather again, Kate," he said as he stood in my small foyer, taking off his jacket and hanging it on a hook beside the door. His wet hair, tinged with grey, glistened in the glow of my hall light. "At least it's not raining."

"For the moment." I waved him into the living room and pointed through to the kitchen. "But now we've got other water problems to deal with."

"I was thinking of making an 'if it rains, it pours joke,' but it's too painful." He placed the toolbox on the linoleum floor and bent down to open the cupboard underneath the sink. "So you woke up this morning—"

"And came out to find a puddle of water on the floor."

"Which you checked to make sure wasn't dog pee, and then mopped up and called me."

"Yes, my handy-dandy property manager."

He looked back at me, grinning. " I don't know about that, but I'll see if it's an easy fix. If it's too complicated, I'll have to call in a plumber."

"Dougie?"

He laughed. "No, plumbing's a specialized trade. That and electrical work are the two things that Dougie can't do. Can you get me a towel or blanket that I can lie down on?"

I walked into the bathroom and returned with an oversized beach towel.

"Great. That'll do." He spread it out on the floor before laying down on his back and reaching his hands inside the cupboard. "It's been a while since we've had a chance to chat. How are things going?"

I grimaced. "Do you mean outside of Rosalie Morgann's death during our first live TV broadcast?"

He glanced up at me sitting on the countertop. "I suppose that's the most obvious place to start. That and this Noah's flood we're dealing with. Any idea yet what happened to Rose?"

I sighed. "The coroner says it's poisoning. Remember Staff Sergeant Singh?"

"Yes, the officer who came to help with Daniel's case."

My heart twisted painfully at the sound of Daniel's name. "Yes, that's him. He's leading the murder investigation into Rosalie's death."

"Oh, good. He seemed like a nice guy."

"Yeah, he is. But it means we're looking at another murder case."

"Holy Christ, that's two in one year! We're going to become the murder capital of British Columbia!"

I smiled. "I don't think we're quite there yet."

"Still. Who do you think did it?"

I paused to run over the scenarios. "Jason? The boyfriend-manager? If he's the beneficiary of her will, I'm guessing he could return to LA with a nice chunk of change."

"Anyone else?"

"The islanders who threatened to murder her, with Selesia and Doreen topping the list. But that's not our only problem."

"Something worse than murder?"

"Not worse, just not great. Our mysterious benefactor, the guy anonymously funding CWYN, has let Gwen know that he is considering pulling his money."

"Why? Who is it?"

I raised my hands in confusion. "No idea. You wouldn't happen to know, would you?"

He considered this for a moment. "I'm guessing it would have to be someone with some connection to the island. If not, why would they bother to fund CWYN? There are only a handful of millionaires with those kinds of ties."

"Like who?"

"Well, there's Robin Clatterey. He owns that sandwich shop chain that's gone international. And the Botowskis. Made a fortune in property development. Also, Frederick Stern, the pulp and paper billionaire."

I squirreled those names away into my memory for later examination.

"But why would he pull the funding?"

"Because he doesn't want the blowback of negative publicity if the station gets any more entangled in this."

"But how can he blame the station for this?" he asked as he thumped on a plastic pipe.

"You can if it was staff or a volunteer behind it. Or at least the media can."

Michael tapped on another pipe and peered up at it with his flashlight. "If it's not one thing, it's another."

I hesitated before asking, "How are you and Anna doing?"

He stopped tapping and stared up at the underside of the sink for a moment. "There's no way to keep something like that quiet on a small island, is there?"

"Not really, no. Perhaps I shouldn't have asked."

He sighed and moved the flashlight to examine another location under the sink. "It's okay. We're," he paused to mull over the right word, "co-existing."

"That doesn't sound great."

"It isn't. We go to Victoria once a week to see a therapist, talk things out, and then go and have dinner."

"Dinner in Victoria sounds nice."

"Yes, nothing like a cheeky bottle of chardonnay after your heart's been ripped out of your chest for 55 minutes." He put the flashlight down and peered out from under the sink to where I was sitting. "It's not just her. I'm at fault, too."

"Well, I don't know if you should blame yourself..." I started, but he cut me off.

"Yes, I should blame myself. She may have cheated, but I set the stage for it."

"What on earth does that mean?"

He slid out from underneath the sink and leaned against one of the cabinets. "I loved Wynter Island from the first moment I saw it. Anna didn't. She thought it was beautiful but never wanted to leave Vancouver. That was all my doing. Moving here was all about what I wanted. And I knew it."

"Nothing is ever 50/50 in any relationship, Michael."

"That's true, but I pushed aside her concerns. I said she wouldn't be lonely and isolated. And to start, she wasn't. Nate was a baby, and everyone was busy. But as Nate got older and more independent, time began to weigh on her. I encouraged her to volunteer for the Green Party so she wouldn't have an excuse to leave the island."

"That hardly makes you a horrible husband."

He paused. "I was fine with her spending nights and weekends at events in Victoria. I thought she was having fun."

"That's not the same as condoning an affair."

He said nothing, just stared off into the living room.

"Is it over? With the guy?" I tentatively asked.

He nodded his head. "She says it is. I believe her. I don't see why she would lie about it. If she wasn't serious about saving our marriage, why would she bother to stay with me and go to all this trouble?"

"See, that's a start."

"Either way, it may be a moot point. I think there's a good chance we may end up leaving Wynter Island anyway. Returning to the city may be the only way to save our marriage." He looked down at his sneakers. "And what's tying us to Wynter Island anymore anyway? Nate graduates next year. He'll attend university on the mainland. If anything, it makes logistical sense for us to move closer to where he'll be."

My heart plummeted directly into my stomach with the speed of a freight elevator headed for the basement. Michael leaving Wynter? He couldn't! I had no tie to him, but his occasional presence gave my unrequited love something to feed on.

No. No. No! He can't go.

He slid back underneath the sink again. "Can you hand me a wrench, Kate? I need to try and get this drain trap off."

I jumped off the counter and grabbed a wrench out of the toolbox. I crawled forward and held it towards his outstretched hand. As his fingers grasped blindly for it, they missed and connected with mine. I almost dropped the wrench as the heat of his skin rolled over the top of my fingers.

"Oh!" I said involuntarily.

He looked up from underneath the sink. "Oops, sorry about that. Missed the wrench and got your hand instead." He released my hand and took the wrench. "I think I might just be able to fix this myself. It looks like the trap needed to be cleaned and fresh plumbers putty put in."

His voice droned on about plumbing, but I couldn't move. His scent, that seawater and cedar cologne he wore, filled my nostrils. He hadn't even realized I was still on the floor beside him. It would be so easy to reach my hand out and rest it on his chest, letting my fingers stroke down over his stomach. To pull his shocked face over to mine and kiss him, taste him, disappear into him. What if I moved my hand underneath his shirt, trailing my nails ever so lightly over his chest? Would he arch in pleasure? Reach back and pull his shirt over his head. And then what? Push me back onto the damp floor as we wriggled out of our clothing, and he entered me, riding, riding, towards ecstasy.

"Kate?"

I shook my head. No, that wasn't possible. He was trying to save his marriage to Anna. I had no right to get into the middle of that. But....

"Kate? Are you okay?"

I stood up and stepped shakily back towards the entry to the kitchen. "Yeah, of course. I'm fine. How's the leak?"

He wiped his hands on a piece of paper towel. "I got the new putty in, so it should hold for now."

He placed his tools back into the box and got to his feet. "Thanks for listening to me. It was nice to have someone to talk it out with. Sometimes, it feels like my thoughts circle inside my head, like bats trying to find their way out of a cave."

I laughed hollowly and moved into the foyer. "That's me, your friendly neighborhood bat catcher."

His somber face split into a smile. "And a friend, too. Let me know if there are more problems with the sink, okay?"

I nodded my head, unable to speak. I raised my hand to wave goodbye and then shut the door against the rain that had started again before sliding down against it to sit on the floor.

Jupiter joined me there, licking the salty wetness off my cheeks.

Chapter Nineteen

"Betty, are you sure you want Vera to produce your new cooking show?"

It wasn't the subtlest way of putting it, and from the look of irritation Vera shot me, I could tell she hadn't missed my rather clumsy hint. But how else to frame it? Did Betty really want a strong-willed senior citizen with no experience telling her what to do?

I sure as hell wouldn't. But then again, Vera was as sharp as a block of cheddar, so she might surprise us all.

"Could you sound a little less doubtful, Kate?" Vera said, her German accent even more robust this morning as she battled a hoarse cough. She must have a cold. She took another sip from her travel cup of herbal tea before speaking again, her voice softened. "Betty and I have figured everything out."

Whatever was in that mug had undoubtedly helped.

Do I want to know what is in that mug? Probably not.

"Yes, we have," Betty chimed in. "We talked about it last night during Crafting with Cocktails."

"So they've roped you into that as well. You're becoming quite the social gadfly, Betty."

She smiled and nodded happily.

"Was alcohol involved?" I continued.

"Oh yes, it was Lesley's turn to bring a new cocktail last night. What was it, Vera? A Lonely Island Lost In...something, something."

"The Middle of a Foggy Sea. The stupidest name I've ever heard of for a cocktail," Vera replied, "but tasty."

Betty nodded. "Yes, lots of rum and pineapple and—"

I cut her off. "I don't need the recipe, Betty." I turned to where Vera was seated. "Are you sure about this? It's a lot of work producing a show, Vera. Scheduling shooting locations and volunteers, editing, picking music, yadda, yadda, yadda. Those are a lot of skills for you to learn."

"I did build a business from the ground up, Kate. I may not be young, but I'm not quite senile yet," she said.

Before I could reply, my phone vibrated with my new ringtone: *Hello, Goodbye* by the Beatles.

"You changed your ringtone," Vera stated.

"I couldn't take Alanis Morisette's *Ironic* anymore." I touched the screen and put the phone to my ear. "Hello?"

Lesley's voice boomed down the line. "Kate, we're trying to locate Vera Schmidt. Is she with you at the station? Last night at Crafting with Cocktails, she mentioned stopping by the station."

"Yes, she's here with Betty Wu."

"Great. Can you send her down to the Lind? We need to talk to her."

"We? As in the official 'we'?"

"Uhmm hmm," she said before disconnecting.

I placed my cell phone down on the table.

What on earth is that about? Something to do with Rosalie?

"Vera, Lesley wants to talk to you. She needs you to head down to the Lind."

"Hmm, I wonder what's going on?" Vera stood and grabbed her huge purse and travel mug off the table. "I hope nothing bad's happened."

I stood as well, an idea suddenly percolating in my brain. "Would you mind if I came along? My guess is that this has something to do with Rosalie's murder."

"I can come, too." Betty supplied.

Vera looked at both of us as if we had lost our minds. "Sure, why don't we invite everyone? Jupiter," she looked over to where he was nestled in his dog bed, "would you like to come, too? Apparently, this is some kind of social

117

occasion."

Jupiter's ears pricked up at the thought of a car trip, but I quickly dashed his hopes. "You stay here, Jupe. I won't be that long."

* * *

Stewart, Lesley, and Ian were waiting with Doreen and Bob for our arrival. Lesley ushered us into the General Store, which had the closed sign on the door even though it was almost lunchtime. Bob would not be happy about that.

"What's up?" I asked.

"Why are you here, Kate?" Lesley asked. "We just needed Vera, not a whole committee."

"Moral support. Good morning, Stewart and Ian. Hi Doreen, Bob."

"Are you butting into other people's business again, Kate?" Bob's voice rumbled up from where he leaned against the front counter.

"Yes, Bob. I consider that my second job after managing the TV station."

"Okay, enough small talk," Ian cut in. "I don't know why you're here, Kate and Mrs. Wu, but please stay out of the way. Vera, we need to ask you some questions."

"I didn't think I was coming down here to dance the samba, Staff Sergeant. What's up?"

"We believe Rosalie Morgann was poisoned by the drink that Jason bought for her here at the Lind General Store."

"Yes, I'd heard that." Vera's voice had slipped back into the gravelly roughness I had heard earlier this morning. She took a long glug from her travel mug. "Still don't understand what this has to do with me."

"We want to talk to you about Doreen."

"Are you accusing Doreen of poisoning Rosalie?" I asked in some surprise. "Is that why we're here?"

"Well, actually, Kate," he retorted angrily, "you two," He pointed at Betty and me, "were never supposed to be here in the first place." I started to say something, but he quickly shushed me. "Don't give me that moral support nonsense. You're here because of your amateur sleuthing."

"Or because she's nothing but a nosy parker," Bob threw in.

"So keep quiet, or you're out of here," Ian finished and turned his attention back to Vera.

"So you think Doreen is the killer?" Vera repeated my words as if she couldn't quite believe them herself.

"It's a possibility," Stewart answered. "She's certainly been very vocal about her anger toward Rosalie. And one of the threatening notes left at Rosalie's house was written on a Lind General Store paper bag."

Yes, of course! The faint orange stripe on the edge of the note Jason had shown me! It was the same color as the design on the Lind General Store's paper bags!

All eyes turned to Doreen, including Bob's, his eyes widening in surprise. She jutted out her lower lip stubbornly.

"So what if I wrote a note? That doesn't prove anything."

"Oh, sweetheart, why did you do that?" Bob murmured, his eyes, for the first time, betraying actual concern.

"You've got to admit, Doreen," Vera sighed, "it doesn't look great."

"I was angry. I wanted them to leave. That doesn't make me a killer."

"So you're admitting you wrote one of the threatening notes?" Ian repeated.

She nodded, the stubborn tilt of her lower lip beginning to tremble a bit. "One note. That's all. I didn't write any of the others. It was a mistake. I'm sorry."

"Let's take the note out of this for now, Staff Sergeant," Vera said quickly. "That's not why you brought me down here, is it?"

"No. We have a more fundamental question for you, Vera. If Doreen is the killer, where did she get the poison?"

Vera nodded, a sage smile spreading across her face. "Now we're getting to where I come into this."

"Yes," Stewart said, taking over for Ian. "It's possible to purchase lily of the valley tincture, but not easy. You would need to know someone with connections in the herbal or naturopathic movement to convince a seller to

119

let you buy some."

"But then it would be fairly easy to trace from the dispensary to me and then Doreen," Vera replied.

Stewart nodded. "That's true, which is why we think there's a good possibility it might have been homemade. Vera, you're the only person on this island with a lily of the valley plant growing in your garden and the know-how to distill it into a poison."

Vera chuckled. "Well, not exactly. Other people on this island use herbs for medicinal purposes, such as the Tsawout. But that's not what you're asking me, is it? You want to know if I gave Doreen the poison that killed Rose?"

"Yes," Lesley answered.

"If I did, do you think I would be stupid enough to tell you without a lawyer present?"

"A yes or no is preferable to a hypothetical question, Vera," she continued.

Vera's laughter veered towards anger. "Okay, here's your answer. No, I did not. I have no Convallaria Majalis tincture in my home, nor have I made any in quite some time."

"Did Doreen question you about distilling herbs or flowers?" Stewart asked.

Vera held up her hand to stop Bob before he exploded into a million little pieces. "No, she did not. And you are missing a couple of critical points."

"What points?" Ian asked.

"Doreen can't cook. She can't bake a decent pie, roast a chicken, or even dress a salad. How on earth could she distill a tincture and figure out the dosing?"

Doreen nodded, agreeing. "I am a horrible cook."

"So you don't think..." Lesley started.

Vera interrupted her. "No, I don't think. I *know* she doesn't have the ability to make a tincture." Vera put up her hand to stop all conversation. "Just listen to me without interrupting, okay?"

The three officers looked at each other for a moment and then nodded their agreement.

"Doreen, come over here, please." Doreen hesitated before walking over to where Vera was standing. "Can you take off that sweater?"

"My sweater?" Doreen asked in surprise.

"I am not asking you to do a strip tease, Doreen. Just take off your sweater." She pulled it over her head, revealing a white t-shirt underneath.

"Now, hold your arms and hands out to the police."

Doreen held her bare arms out toward the three of them.

"What are we supposed to be looking for, Vera?" Stewart asked.

"You'd know it if you saw it," she replied. "Her arms and hands look normal, don't they? No fading marks of any kind? No scabs or scratches?"

They nodded their agreement.

"Doreen, did anyone see you in the days before and directly after Rose's death? See your hands and arms?"

"Of course. Lots of people. Either here or in the hotel."

"Do you sell asparagus in your store?"

Doreen shuddered and pulled her sweater back on. "No, you know I don't, Vera. Can't take the risk."

Vera smiled, thoroughly enjoying her Perry Mason moment. "And what risk would that be?"

"A serious allergic reaction. I'm highly allergic to asparagus. Can't eat it, touch it, anything."

"Exactly." Vera folded her arms in satisfaction. One eyebrow arched with inquisitive glee. It was clear she knew what Ian would ask next, and she could hardly wait to tell him.

"So what does asparagus have to do with lily of the valley, Vera?" he finally asked, sighing.

Her smile grew wider. "Well, Lily of the Valley is a member of the Asparagaceae family. Asparagaceae: Asparagus. If Doreen had come within an inch of any part of a Lily of the Valley plant, she would have swollen up like an itchy, overripe plum."

Chapter Twenty

Jupiter heard the knocking before I did. I had fallen down the rabbit hole of a documentary on serial murderers on Netflix the night before and hadn't gone to bed until three. His body stiffened as he stirred from his spot curled up beside me, his tail ramrod straight behind him.

"What is it, boy? Did you hear something?"

A loud banging echoed from the front door down the hallway to my small bedroom at the back of the cottage.

"Okay! Okay! I'm getting up!" I shouted and pulled myself out of bed.

Whoever was doing the knocking must have heard my shouts because the thumping ceased. I pulled a fleecy robe over my PJs, not caring that it had a sizable Sleeping Beauty illustration, a gag gift from my sister after a trip to Disney World with my niece. I stumbled down the hallway and pulled open the door to find Shea standing, frantic, on the front doorstep.

"Thank God you're here, Kate," she said and stepped past me into the cottage, removing her damp coat and placing it on a hook.

"I don't know where else I would be first thing in the morning, Shea. Is everything okay? Did something happen?"

Shea made her way to the sofa and collapsed on it. Jupiter wandered over and sat in front of her, quizzically examining his previous owner. "Hey, Jupiter." She gave him a distracted pat. "Lesley's fine. She's at home right now. I couldn't talk about this on the phone. I had to see you in person."

I wandered into the kitchen and pushed the button to turn on the electric kettle. "I'm making tea. Is English Breakfast alright for you?"

"Sure."

"I don't have much to nibble on except for some leftover muffins from the bakery."

"I've already eaten. Tea is fine for me."

I poured the boiling water over tea bags in two mugs and carried one to Shea. I returned with my own and a plate carrying one of the leftover muffins.

"So, what's going on?" I asked as I settled into an overstuffed armchair.

Jupiter was seated dead center in front of me. He had forgotten Shea's existence now that he had my muffin to focus on.

"The Glass House was broken into last night."

"What?"

"Yeah, Lesley got woken up by the 911 operator in the middle of the night saying there'd been an emergency call."

"Holy shit! Was anything stolen?"

Shea shook her head no. "They're not sure, but I don't think so. It looks like the thief was looking for Rosalie's laptop."

"Doesn't the RCMP already have her laptop as evidence?"

Shea nodded her head. "Yes, but I'm assuming there were other computers in the house, as well as hard drives and flash drives."

"What on earth were they looking for?"

"They think it was a rough draft of Rosalie's autobiography. Apparently, she had been working on one for quite a while. That was part of the reason she returned to Wynter. She felt the quiet here would help her get it finished."

"I had no idea."

"Me either. Jason was in bed but heard something downstairs. He got up and went to investigate and came upon the thief going through Rosalie's office."

"Yikes. What happened? Did they catch him?"

Shea shook her head. "He had a metal club and hit Jason with it."

"Is he okay?"

"Lesley said it's just a bad concussion, but to be safe, the ambulance boat took him over to Sidney last night."

"So they didn't catch the thief?"

"No, Scott heard the shouting and ran downstairs to find Jason bleeding on the floor. He could just make out a dark figure in camo pulling away from the beach in a small zodiac."

"Without anything."

"Scott doesn't think anything is missing. Jason must have stumbled over him before he found what he was looking for."

"Rosalie's autobiography. I wonder what's in there that's worth a late-night robbery and assault?"

"Not just robbery and assault. Murder, as well."

"The police think this is connected to Rosalie's murder?"

"Yes. That whoever did the murder is behind this."

"Which means…what?"

"I'm not sure. Is there a clue in her autobiography? You would think there must be something particularly incendiary there if it's worth murdering Rosalie over and burgling her home to get rid of the evidence."

"But the RCMP have her laptop, which means they have her draft of the book. Whatever is in there is already known by the police."

"Yes, Lesley said they have read it, but she won't tell me anything."

"Well, it is police business, Shea."

"Whatever. But you're missing the bigger issue here, Kate."

After giving a piece to a waiting Jupiter, I took the last bite of my crumbly banana walnut muffin and washed it down with a slurp of tea. "It's first thing in the morning, Shea. I'm still in my pajamas. I'm missing a lot of things."

"We had three main suspects: Doreen, Jason, and Selesia."

"Okay."

"Doreen is off the list because Vera proved that she's highly allergic to the poison that killed Rosalie."

"That's right. I was there when Vera told Ian. It was brilliant courtroom technique."

"So then we move down to Jason. Now, he's off the list."

"Why is Jason off the list?"

"Because if the killer and the thief are one and the same, Jason could hardly split himself into two. Someone other than Jason smacked a metal tube over his head and was spotted by Scott escaping in a boat."

"Alright, I get your point."

"That just leaves Selesia."

I nodded my head. "And that's why you're here. Because you're desperate to prove Selesia's innocent, no matter what. And the only name remaining on that list is hers."

"Yes, there could be others we don't know about, but my guess is the investigation will focus on Selesia now."

I sighed. "I don't know what you want me to do, Shea. I can't fabricate evidence to help indict someone else. If Doreen and Jason are proven innocent, there's not much the police can do except focus on Selesia."

Shea's hand thumped the arm of the sofa, causing Jupiter to start. "She's hanging on by a thread right now, Kate. Rosalie literally died in her arms. Will's away from home, and she's worried sick about what Brad is getting up to."

"Well, I know what he's doing, at least part of the time. He's hanging out with Fisherman Phil."

"Fisherman Phil?"

"I know. An odd couple, isn't it? Phil's in a pretty bad way over Rosalie's death. Brad has been visiting and helping him buy groceries, do chores, etc."

Shea mulled this over for a minute. "I don't think Selesia knows anything about this. He just vanishes in his car at odd hours. And at home, he's a mess: an angry, moody, defensive teen."

"So, like all other teenagers then."

"Worse than average, I think. He's got a lot of extra stressors. Will is gone, and his mom is under suspicion of murder. He must know that if Selesia is taken into custody, he will have to leave Wynter Island. He's still a minor. Custody would go to Rick, his father, who lives in Prince George."

"Plus, when I ran into him at Phil's, I got the sense that his future is a touchy subject."

Shea nodded. "He's never been great at school: dyslexia, learning disabilities. Will was always the star in the family."

125

"It must be hard to try and not compete or compare himself with Will."

"Yes, and that's become increasingly apparent the closer he gets to graduation."

"He said he doesn't want to go to college."

"That's right. No schooling of any kind. Which is driving Selesia mad. She's been hunting up special training programs for the learning disabled, but he won't even look at them."

"Lots of people don't go on to post-secondary education, Shea. They get a nice job somewhere and carve out a career for themselves."

"Yes, but those aren't Indigenous teens. Especially not boys. However liberal and tolerant we think we've become, there's still that overarching societal perspective that an Indigenous kid will be irresponsible and untrustworthy. Nobody wants to say it, but it's true."

"I know," I sighed.

"If the choice is between a First Nations kid and anyone else for a low-level job, it will go to anyone else. Selesia is right. Some kind of education or specialty training is his path out of turning into the stereotypical unemployed guy on the Reserve, dipping into whatever substances he can find to pass the time."

An idea began to trickle into my mind, a not particularly positive one.

"You said a lot of anger, resentment, and frustration has been building up in Brad. That's not a great combination, Shea. Especially in a young man whose pre-frontal cortex is still developing."

"His what?"

"Pre-frontal cortex. The part of his brain that helps him make complex decisions and prevents him from doing stupid, impulsive things."

"You mean, growing up."

"Yes. That's why teenagers sometimes make incredibly dangerous choices: they don't have the skills to stop themselves. And then you throw into that mix that a woman his mother despises has just arrived in town, the same woman who broke up his parent's marriage…"

"You don't mean what I think you're saying, Kate!"

I nodded. "Yes, I do. If Selesia didn't do it, is it possible that Brad did?

And would that make things any better for Selesia if her son went to prison rather than herself?"

Chapter Twenty-One

"Could you bring in some extra power cords?" I shouted out the open front door of the Community Hall to Dougie, who was grabbing things from the station truck.

"Sure, Kate. I'll be in in a sec."

I continued setting up one of the long folding tables in the back storeroom. The Community Hall used them for the weekly farmer's market, one of the biggest tourist draws on the island. After pushing the legs open, I tipped it onto its feet and began dragging it towards the large meeting room.

As tourist season had arrived, or would have if the weather had been any better, we couldn't use the restaurant at the Lind Hotel for Fish Bingo. We could have started filming the show in the studio as planned, but no one had the heart yet to go in and film there after Rosalie's death. And there was something atmospheric about being out in the community doing a livestream. People had come to expect it, and I was not going to mess with success. After all, Fish Bingo was an undeniable hit for CWYN.

"Here, let me help you with that."

Ben's arm brushed against mine as he raced to pick up the opposite end of the table. A strong scent of Drakkar Noir, spicy and woody with a leather undertone, wafted over me.

"Thanks, Ben. This thing weighs a ton."

Drakkar Noir. It wasn't Michael's distinctive cologne. What was it that made Michael's cologne so enticing? The aroma of fresh seawater and pine trees? Or that it meant I was close enough to spot the veins bulging on the back of his olive-skinned hands and see the stubble of a fresh shave on his cheek?

No. Stop it! Stop fantasizing about the man you can never have, and focus on the single, handsome man in the room!

"How have things been, Ben?" I asked breathlessly as we settled the table in the center of the room.

The recently completed Community Hall had been a considerable investment of time and money for the islanders. It fit the bill for most island events: film nights, where students sold maple sugar popcorn to pay for after-school activities, weddings, wakes, and even the occasional dance.

"Great. I brought Lucy along. She's in the car." He nodded towards where Jupiter had curled up on an old blanket. "Do you think he'd mind if I brought her in?"

"Of course, you can bring her in. Jupiter is getting more..." I paused to consider my words, "tolerant."

Ben headed to the parking lot, returning with his brown and white springer spaniel. There was the usual dog greeting, sniff, sniff, with Jupiter prostrate like a martyr in a religious play while Lucy's bobbed tail vibrated with happiness.

"Hey, Ben," Dougie said as he walked in with a light stand. "Are you co-hosting with Kate tonight?"

"Yup, me and Lucy." He nodded towards the spaniel, who had left Jupiter to wander around the open room.

"I haven't seen Lucy for a bit." Dougie walked over to give her a few pats. "It's been a while since either of you did Fish Bingo."

I calculated the time in my head. There had been a six-week recuperation period after my near death in Steeltun Bay, most of which I had spent visiting family in Ontario. And then, of course, we had to cancel programming while the police investigation at the studio was underway.

"That's right, but I think we can manage. What do you think, Ben?"

A cheeky grin from Ben. When he smiled, I noticed a dimple on the left-hand side of his mouth, a small indent in his otherwise perfect face. I wondered what it would feel like, this slight depression underneath my fingertips.

"I think we'll do fine."

Ben went to retrieve two chairs while Dougie finished setting up the camera and lights.

"Here you go, Kate." Ben placed the seats behind the table, sitting in one while I sat in the other. "I haven't seen much of you around." he stated, lifting one eyebrow rakishly, "and I've been looking. I'm guessing you've been busy with the case?"

My surprise must have been apparent on my face. He laughed aloud.

"Don't worry," he whispered, "your secret is safe with me."

"I don't know what you're talking about, Ben," I replied before busying myself with setting up my laptop.

"The case. Remember? Rosalie's murder? I had to miss the emergency volunteer meeting because I was working, but I heard the news. Find the killer and put this story to bed, or the station might lose funding."

I sighed. "Unfortunately, that's true."

"So, that leads right back to my first question: Have you been busy? Sleuthing?"

"You make me sound like Sherlock Holmes."

Ben tilted his head flirtatiously to one side. "I could always be your Watson. You know, some people believe their relationship was more than just a friendship."

I stared down at my laptop keyboard. Ben as my Watson? But Shea had always been my partner in crime. But not any longer. She didn't know it yet, but I had begun to consider the unthinkable: that Selesia might be the killer. Or worse, her son Brad.

"We'd have to get you a bowler hat."

"And you a deerstalker?"

"Yes," I laughed.

"I think you'd look quite attractive in a deerstalker hat," he said. "Or anything else for that matter."

My eyes connected with his, and I felt a tingle of nervous anticipation in the pit of my stomach. What would I do if he reached over right now to kiss me? Startle and run away? Or lean into his warmth and enjoy the texture of his soft lips against mine?

"Well, Watson, we're down to one suspect."

"And who might that be?"

I hesitated. "We need to keep this between us. Some people," I paused, "are struggling with this theory."

He grinned. "My pleasure."

"It's Selesia."

I could not bring myself to mention Brad, even to Ben. The idea was too incredible, too incendiary. I felt like uttering it aloud would singe my tongue.

"Really? My money was on the boyfriend."

I nodded. "Yes. Jason was one of my first suspects, but he's no longer on the list."

"What about that other guy, the assistant?"

"Scott? He has an ironclad alibi. He caught the ferry to Victoria two days before Rosalie's death. And he had absolutely no motive for her murder. Ian told me that Jason is the main beneficiary of the will, with only a small bequest for Scott and Phil. Financially, her death was a terrible blow for Scott. In fact, it means he is out of a job and probably out on the street."

"So her death only makes things worse for him. But not for Jason, especially if he's the heir to her estate. I mean, that's a huge motive right there."

"I know. And it's not just her past revenue to consider. There's going to be future revenue as well."

"Future revenue? You mean syndication rights and that kind of thing?"

"Yes, but not just TV rights. Rosalie was working on her autobiography, which played a big part in her decision to return to Wynter Island. She wanted a quiet place to write."

"But if it wasn't finished...?"

"Jason will get a ghostwriter to finish it and tidy things up. The publicity from her murder will increase sales tenfold."

"Which brings us right back to Jason again."

"Yes, but he got an unexpected get-out-of-jail-free card this week. Did you hear about the break-in at the Glass House?"

"Yes. I assumed it was someone trying to get a piece of memorabilia."

"More like someone hunting for Rosalie's laptops and hard drives. Looking, we think, for a copy of her autobiography. And they would have gotten away with it, too, if they hadn't woken Jason."

"Is that how he got injured? I saw him in the village with a black eye."

"Yeah, he got whacked in the head by the thief. His shouting was loud enough to rouse Scott, who arrived downstairs in time to see the thief race away in a zodiac."

"The plot thickens."

"Which leaves us with only one suspect now: Selesia."

"Selesia." He paused to ruminate on this.

"She has publicly stated her hatred for Rose and her desire to get revenge. She, like all the other volunteers, had advance notice that Rose would be our guest. She also had access to the energy drink at the station when she went to the restroom. There are ten minutes where no one can confirm where she was. She could have poisoned the bottle and returned to the studio with none of us any the wiser. "

"Or she could have been in the restroom for ten minutes."

I nodded. "That's correct. But, like Vera, she also knows how to collect flowers and herbs and create tinctures. Apparently, several people on the Reserve do. It is a skill the Tsawout use in their medicinal treatments."

"So, anyone on the Reserve might have that ability."

"Yes."

"Like Sam or Brad. Those two would also have an axe to grind about the failure of Selesia's marriage."

I didn't say anything. I couldn't. It felt like a betrayal.

But then again, all of this felt like a betrayal. I was betraying Shea by not only being unable to prove Selesia's innocence but also actively hunting down proof that she was the killer. I was betraying Sam by pointing the finger at his sister and, possibly, his nephew. And I was betraying myself, betraying who I thought I was. Was I really someone who put the importance of keeping my job above the people I cared about deeply? Had Jack been right all along?

"Kate? Earth to Kate?"

Dougie stood in front of me, tapping the face of his watch. "We're going live in a few minutes. I've got everything set up." He glanced over to where Ben was readying the bingo ball cage. "Are you guys ready to go?"

I paused as a thought struck me. "Dougie, do you do any landscaping work over at the Glass House?"

"Yeah, why?"

No hesitation or concern. That's a good sign.

"You acted like Rosalie was a stranger at the studio. Like you'd never met her before."

"I hadn't. I'd only met Scott, her assistant. He's the one who hired me to cut their lawn."

Of course! Another theory dashed. But just to make sure, I had one further question.

"I saw you've got a new truck. Scott must be paying you well."

He smiled and glanced proudly out the front door to where his sparkling clean truck sat in the parking lot. "Like I could make that kind of money cutting grass! No, my great-aunt passed on. Left me a nice little nest egg, so I decided to invest in a new truck. I'm getting my business name put on the side sometime next month."

"That's what I thought." I tapped a few keys on my laptop before looking back up. "I'm ready. Are you ready, Ben?"

"As ready as I'll ever be."

"Good. Okay, Dougie, count us in at the top of the hour."

Dougie rushed back to the camera, glancing at his watch as he did so. "Okay. Five, four, three, two," And with a silent one, he waved his hand in my direction and pushed the start button on the camera.

"Good evening, Wynter Island, and all of you outside of Wynter Island for joining us tonight. As many of you know, a tragic event at our station forced us to cancel our programming. But we are back tonight and ready to play Fish Bingo!"

My cell phone rang. I glanced down at the number. It was Phil. Of course, it was Phil. That was the last thing I needed right now: a drunken fisherman going on about the unfairness of a stupid bingo game. I paused as a thought struck me.

Who caught the salmon for the prize this evening?

Had it been Phil? Or Brad? Brad had said he would get it to me if Phil was unable to, but how could he catch a salmon if Phil was out of commission? Brad couldn't just throw out a line from the Hope Bay dock and hope for the best! He would need a boat, a commercial fishing license, all the equipment, as well as the skills to do it. All things he didn't have.

What on earth is going on with those two?

But I couldn't figure that out while I was live on-air. I sent Phil's call to voicemail and turned back to the camera.

Chapter Twenty-Two

F ew things in life instantly ruin your day like seeing the face of Jack
Donahue.

As I walked out of the General Store in Harrow Village, my mail
in one hand and my P.O. Box key in the other, a sudden flurry of movement
caught my attention. Before I knew it, Jack Donahue and a young man—a
film student, I'm guessing—blocked my path. Jack held a hand mic, the cord
trailing back to the small camcorder the young man carried on his shoulder.

*Really? Ambushed? They're going to ambush me? Who do they think I am,
Angelina Jolie?*

"Kate Thomas, I'm Jack Donahue reporting for CGN-Online Entertainment News. I have a few questions for you."

I glanced from Jack's earnest, angry face to the perplexed young man
holding the camera. "Are you serious?"

His eyes glimmered with pleasure. "Yes, I am deadly serious. As are our
viewers."

"What, two elderly women in the Poconos and that shut-in in Florida?"

I tried to push past him, but he blocked my path.

"Your disdain for regular, hard-working people doesn't cast you in a
particularly attractive light, Ms. Thomas."

"I don't need to worry about *my light*, Jack, because I am no longer working
in mainstream media. Get out of my way, please."

I gained a few inches of ground and had almost passed him when he spoke
again.

"No, a small community TV station isn't mainstream; that's true. But I

135

would say that Rosalie Morgann qualified as mainstream media."

I paused. "You want to ask me questions about Rosalie Morgann's murder, is that it?"

"Yes, and not just her murder, but the shocking trail of murders that seem to follow in your wake. First, your translator in Afghanistan, then your boyfriend here on Wynter Island, and finally, Rosalie Morgann, one of Hollywood's brightest stars."

"Spare me your hyperbole, Jack. As you know, I have already stated the station's perspective on Rosalie's tragic passing. We are deeply sorry for the suffering of her fans and family, but all further questions about her murder should be directed to the Wynter Island RCMP."

"Does your employer know about 'your history' with murders, Kate?"

I swiveled back to him, my face most likely expressing the fury bubbling inside me. The young cameraman took a wary step away from me, pulling the cord connecting him to Jack's microphone taut.

"Where are you going with this, Jack?" I rumbled out with a dangerous softness.

I spotted Betty Wu out of the corner of my eye, walking up the hill towards us, her rapid steps moving with a jerky agitation.

"Where I'm going, Kate, is this: did you have anything to do with the death of Rosalie Morgann? There is a great old saying. Once is a chance, twice is a coincidence, but three times is a pattern."

Without even considering the foolishness of giving him such dramatic footage, my arm instinctively drew back, my hand clenching into a fist. Before I made another move, a hand grabbed my arm from behind, pinning it back down to my side. My head swiveled around to see Bob standing there, Doreen a few feet behind him.

"Get out of here!" he bellowed at Jack and the cameraman. "I said scram! Now!"

Irritated by Bob's interruption, Jack snapped back in a holier-than-thou tone. "I represent CGN. I have the right to be here."

Bob released my arm and took a few steps towards him. "I don't care if you represent the bloody Queen! You are on private property. I told you to leave, so get out of here! Capisce?" He turned back towards Doreen. "Go inside and get the cell phone, Doreen. I'm going to call the police."

"Okay, okay." Jack held up his hands in mock surrender. "We'll go. But I'm not leaving this island or..." his eyes narrowed in on me, "...this story. Brandon, stop filming." He handed the relieved young man the microphone and turned to walk back up the street to his car.

"Sorry," the young man whispered and clunkily ran after him with their camera gear.

Betty Wu strode up to us, pausing for a few moments to catch her breath. "What on earth was all of that? I thought I would have a peaceful walk around the harbor, not witness a brawl!"

I don't know which stunned me more, the fact that a film crew had just ambushed me or that Bob Corker, of all people, had saved me.

"Bob, thank you. Thank you for stopping me from doing something stupid."

He waved Doreen back towards the hotel. "Didn't want the hotel getting any bad publicity," he muttered and followed her inside.

Is it possible that Bob Corker has a heart, after all?

"His name is Jack Donahue," I said to Betty.

"Oh, I know, dearie, I know."

"You do?"

"Come with me," she motioned toward Annie's Bakery. "Let's have a cup of tea. There are some things we need to discuss."

In shock, I followed her to the bakery, grabbing a mug of tea, before heading to a table.

Things were getting curiouser and curiouser. Betty Wu had inside information on Jack Donahue? What next? Would Fisherman Phil turn out to be best buds with the Prime Minister?

"Betty," I asked after taking a sip of my hot, milky tea, "How do you know Jack Donahue?"

"Oh, I don't know him personally. My daughter Caroline is the one who knows him."

"Your daughter, Caroline?"

"Oh yes." She pulled her cell phone out of her purse and thumbed through the photos before handing it to me. "That's Caroline, right there. She's with her husband, Mark."

A tall, willowy woman, her sleek black hair hanging like a silky curtain alongside her face, stood next to an equally attractive man while a crowd of black tie-clad people bobbed around them. She wore a white column-style gown, tastefully decorated with only a slight pearl embellishment on one shoulder. She was stunning.

"This is your daughter?"

"Yes," Betty nodded. "I think it was the Hospital Foundation Gala at the Hotel Vancouver last year."

"She is beautiful."

I couldn't keep the astonishment out of my voice. In her knit sweater and corduroys, Betty appeared like a sweet Asian grandmother, not the mother of this stunning apparition.

"Yes, she is, isn't she." Betty beamed and took the phone back. "She started modeling in high school and then started her own modeling agency with her husband. They live in Point Grey with their two kids."

Point Grey was synonymous with big money. The modeling agency must be doing well.

"My other daughter, Karen, lives in Burnaby. She is an elementary teacher. Married with one daughter."

"How does Caroline know Jack Donahue?"

Betty took a long sip of her tea. "I was talking on the phone with her after Rosalie died, telling her about the press blocking our road with their TV trucks. Luckily—well, not luckily for him—that movie star ODed, and most of them headed off to cover that story. She asked if I'd seen a particular journalist. She described Jack Donahue, and I said yes, I'd seen someone like that. She told me to stay as far away from him as possible."

"Why?"

"Because he's a trashy tabloid hack. She'd had a run-in with him over one of her up-and-coming models. He insisted the girl was going to do Paris Fashion Week because she was having an affair with a pop star on a

European tour. It was all garbage, Caroline said, but he refused to listen to her and ran it anyway."

"That doesn't surprise me."

"Well, what surprised me is what she said next: that there was a connection between him and Rosalie."

"Our Rosalie?"

"The same."

"What kind of connection?"

"She said he had interviewed Rosalie in his previous job as an entertainment reporter. Unfortunately, he showed up to the interview as high as a kite."

It was difficult to match this slimy individual with the quiet but oh-so-forgettable young man I knew in school. How had he gone from forgettable to a train wreck? It couldn't be because of me, could it?

"It wasn't just that he was on drugs. He made a very ham-handed pass at Rosalie, and she complained to the TV station. He was fired and then relocated to Vancouver."

"So that's how he ended up at CGN-Online Entertainment News," I murmured.

"Yes," Betty replied. "So I knew who he was when I spotted him and that young man attacking you in front of the General Store."

"Attacking is a pretty strong term, Betty. Ambushing is more accurate."

"Well, ambushing doesn't sound much better."

"So he has another connection to Wynter Island. That's very interesting."

"What's this other connection to Wynter Island?"

"I went to university with him, Betty. Twelve years ago. In Toronto. And I'm afraid he doesn't like me very much."

"Well, that just proves he's a fool, doesn't it?" she replied succinctly and took a sip of her tea.

I smiled. There was something heartwarming about Betty that made me want to hug her. "Hold on a second. You said you saw him walking along your street. When was that?"

Betty paused and appeared to be counting dates in her head. "I'm not sure. It was a couple of times. I know he was part of that mob of reporters and trucks parked in front of her house. But there was a time before that, I think."

"Before? Before Rosalie's death?" A red-hot shock zinged through me.

"Yes, it must have been. There were no other reporters around. He was walking down the road to her house in his black leather jacket. A few days before she died, I think."

Snap! That meant Jack had been on Wynter Island before the poisoning. Unless he was now billing himself as a psychic journalist, I had a new suspect. Was Jack Donahue our killer?

Chapter Twenty-Three

The amber light streaming through the windows of the Legion bar hazily cut through the nighttime fog of rain that had settled over Wynter Island. I glanced at my watch: seven-thirty. That was enough time for everyone to have finished Friday night dinner, and returned to the bar.

I had made the difficult decision not to attend the weekly Legion dinners. A whole roast dinner with dessert and drinks every week may have been delicious, but my waistline couldn't take it. I needed to be able to fit into my jeans in the morning.

"Kate!" a voice hailed me from across the room.

Ian was sitting at a small table with Shea and Lesley. As I pushed through the crowd of after-dinner drinkers, I could tell neither Shea nor Lesley looked to be in the best of moods. Ian, sitting in between them, gazed at me with a tremulous smile of desperation.

"Hi, Kate. Have a seat." He gestured to the last seat at the table.

I sat down, placing my bag on the floor. "Hi. How's everyone doing tonight?"

Shea glanced up from her glass of wine with a look that said quite clearly: *How the hell do you think we're doing?* Lesley just kept her eyes stubbornly fixed on her rum and coke.

"Okay, great," I muttered and looked at Ian. "How are you doing, Ian?"

"Busy. Working away on the Rosalie Morgann case."

"I don't think we should talk shop," Lesley said with a prim set to her lips.

"Well, what would you like to talk about?" Shea clapped back. "Where you were last night?"

Lesley looked up from her drink, her lips tilting into a small, sad smile. "Shea is upset because she doesn't believe I was at Crafting with Cocktails last night."

"Or last Sunday afternoon," Shea spat out.

"Shea, why can't you just trust me on this?"

"There's a difference between trusting someone and being made a fool of, Les. And I feel more like the latter than the former."

"Kate," Ian pushed his chair back and grabbed his tin of Coca-Cola, "let's go and get you a drink."

With unseemly haste, I grabbed my bag and said a quick goodbye to Shea and Lesley. Neither said anything, too entangled in their private misery to care whether we left.

"I thought I was going to be stuck there for the rest of the evening," he whispered as we made our way to the polished wood bar.

"I know." I took a stool at the bar, and Ian followed suit. There's nothing more uncomfortable than getting caught in someone else's crossfire."

"Either verbally or physically." Ian smiled and took a long sip of his soda.

Harald walked over to us. He had lost some weight, I noticed, and his skin looked paler than usual, contrasting sharply with the cranberry-colored birthmark on one side of his face. Dark shadows dragged his eyes downward.

"Hi, Kate. Staff Sergeant Singh. What can I get for you?"

"I'll have a Carlsberg, please," I said. "How are you doing, Harald? I haven't seen either you or Kurt since I got home from my trip back east."

Harald busied himself with grabbing a glass and a chilled bottle of Carlsberg from the fridge. He placed them on the bar in front of me.

"Well, we've been busy with a lot of paperwork. You know, related to the Immigration Canada case. I hired an immigration lawyer in Victoria to help us go through it."

I glanced over at Ian's face. He was staring somberly at his sweating soda tin, no doubt remembering his part in uncovering Harald's fraudulent immigration paperwork while investigating Daniel's death.

"I don't blame you, Staff Sergeant Singh," Harald said unexpectedly. "It was my fault. I shouldn't have done something so stupid."

Ian said nothing, just nodded sadly.

"How is Kurt doing?" I asked.

A lengthy sigh. "He's trying to … move on. We both are."

With a silent nod goodbye, Harald headed down the bar to serve another customer.

"Is it something in the water?" Ian asked as I poured a long stream of golden lager into my glass. "I can't turn around without coming face to face with domestic strife on Wynter Island."

"It's pretty amazing when you think about it. The butterfly effect. How a single action ripples through a community. If Daniel hadn't been murdered, no one would be any the wiser about Harald fibbing on his immigration paperwork. Or about Anna's affair with her co-worker."

He nodded. "That's true."

"And Daniel would have found me, explained everything, and—"

"And?"

I hesitated. "I don't know."

"Would you have returned to the States with him?"

"Probably." I took a long sip of my beer.

"Well, I'm glad you're still here."

I glanced up from my drink, aware of a sudden shift in the tone of our conversation. No, not Ian. Not more romance. I had enough on my plate with Ben and Michael. I needed to nip this in the bud. Now.

"You've never told me anything about your private life, Ian. Married? Girlfriend?"

He shook his head. "Neither. My mother says I'm married to my job."

"Where'd you grow up?"

"South Vancouver, Fraserview area."

"You must miss your family now that you've moved to Victoria."

"Yes, I do miss them. But I needed to make my own way in the world." He gestured to his short military haircut. "I chose to cut my hair and not wear a turban when I left high school. It was upsetting for them, but I didn't want to live in the past. I wanted to be my own person."

"And they weren't keen on that?"

He smiled. "No, they weren't. I also got sick of the whole arranged marriage thing. I couldn't visit my mom without being presented with a who's who of available Sikh women."

"Does that mean I'm not allowed to keep an eye out for a single, attractive lady for you?"

He examined my face for a moment before his lips creased into a sad smile. *Yes, Houston, he has received my unspoken message.*

"No, you can pass along anyone that you find."

"Good." I hadn't realized until that moment that our relationship had moved from purely police work to a kind of friendship. A friendship that mattered to me. I didn't want it ruined by romance. "Changing the subject, how's the investigation going?"

"I'm assuming you heard about the robbery attempt?"

I nodded. "Yes, Jason got hurt, and the thief escaped, apparently without finding what he was looking for. Her autobiography, I'm guessing."

He shrugged. "Perhaps, we don't know."

"What does it mean?"

"It means that unless Jason and Scott are part of a larger conspiracy, neither of them is our murderer."

"You never thought Scott was the murderer, did you?"

"Not once we reviewed the evidence. His alibi is rock solid. We have CCTV video of him at different locales in Sidney and Victoria in the days before Rosalie's death. When Jason called him with the news about Rosalie, he caught the next ferry home."

"Perhaps he poisoned her drink beforehand?"

"Nope. He was off the island for a couple of days before the murder. There's no way he could have tampered with Rosalie's drink."

"And Jason?"

"Her murder and that robbery are most likely connected in some way. They must be. It's the only thing that makes sense. And if they are, Jason is no longer a viable suspect."

"I don't like the direction this is taking."

Ian shrugged. "I don't have the luxury of liking everything I do, Kate. I just have to do it."

Neither of us had the heart to say her name. It just hung in the air between us, unspoken.

"I've met Selesia several times," he finally said. "She is quite a," he hesitated to think of the right word, "force of nature."

"That's true. But that doesn't make her guilty."

"No," he shook his head, "but saying things like I'm going to kill Rosalie if she comes back to Wynter Island doesn't make her look good."

"I know of one suspect you might not have considered yet."

He looked up quickly from his coke. "Who?"

I filled him in on my run-in with Jack Donahue at Harrow Village as well as Betty's surprising findings.

"So he was seen on Wynter Island before Rosalie was murdered?"

"Betty is pretty sure of it. The day before her death. And he has a motive for wanting to hurt Rosalie. She cost him his job at a news station, forcing him to relocate to Vancouver and work for an online gossip site."

"Maybe I'll have a little chat with both of them."

"Good," I replied, glad to have taken at least a fraction of the heat off of Selesia for a moment. "Ian, you know how you asked me if I would have returned to the States with Daniel? If things had gone differently that day?"

He nodded.

"I want to change my answer. Maybe I wouldn't have left. Maybe I would've tried to convince Daniel to stay here on the island with me."

"Two world class journalists on a small island in the Pacific Northwest? Don't think there'd be much work for you both."

"Probably not, but we could have tried. This place was, after all, my second chance."

"Second chance?"

"Yes," I took another sip from my glass. "my second chance to build a new career, a new life, after everything that happened in Afghanistan."

"Yes, I see."

My eyes traveled over the stony faces of Lesley and Shea sitting silently opposite one another. Harald was pulling a pint of Guinness for a customer at the far end of the bar. Kurt was nowhere to be seen. In fact, I hadn't seen him since he retrieved Harald from the Victoria jail all those months ago.

"I just hope it can offer a second chance to them," I tipped my head towards Shea and Lesley and then Harald. "Because God knows they need one."

Chapter Twenty-Four

The rain pelted through the thick darkness at the top of Wynter Mountain as I pulled into a parking space in front of Gwen's farmhouse. I was a little buzzed from my Carlsberg but still sober enough to drive. My knock on the side door was greeted by the sound of slow, laborious movement from inside. Gwen appeared to be having some difficulty getting to the door.

She finally opened it to show Betty, Doreen, and Vera seated around the kitchen table.

"Kate, this is a surprise."

Gwen's cheeks were a brilliant Rudolph's nose red, and as she spoke, a healthy gust of alcohol fumes rushed towards my face. If I had lit a match at that precise moment, the place would have burst into flames.

"Hi, ladies."

"Hi, Kate," Betty said. Her face was also rosy, so much so that I could have warmed my hands by her flushed cheeks.

"Kate, come in and have a drink," Doreen offered, shakily getting to her feet. Once standing, she swayed back and forth for a moment before gesturing to a large pitcher on the counter. "It's a Bama Slamma."

"She means Alabama Slammer," Vera replied. "These women cannot handle their alcohol."

I stepped into the kitchen. The pitcher was filled, with a rich amber-colored liquid, vibrant enough to be a child's soda or cough syrup. "What's in it?"

Doreen, listing a bit to one side, grabbed an empty cocktail glass. "It's got

Southern Comfort, Amaretto, Gin, and a mixture of orange and pineapple juice. It's delish."

It sounded more devilish than delish. "Well, it's certainly got enough booze in it. I'll try a bit." Doreen started to slosh some into the glass, but I took the pitcher out of her hand. "Just let me do it, Doreen. It's safer that way."

I filled the glass half full and took a sip of the ruby-colored liquid. The sticky sweetness of orange juice and southern comfort overwhelmed almost everything else, with a kick of almond at the end from the amaretto. This wasn't a beverage for a women's craft get-together. This stuff was meant for a toga party.

"Whoa! Who made this?"

Doreen nodded. "I did. I found the recipe on the internet. We take turns bringing a different cocktail each week."

"Please tell me that none of you are driving!" I asked, pushing my glass to the back edge of the counter. "That stuff is powerful enough to put all of you over the legal limit."

"Dougie is bussssy tonight," Betty's words slurred out, "so Gordon is coming to get us."

"Good! What are you all doing here?"

"It's our Crafting with Cocktails get-together," Doreen answered.

"I thought you met once a week."

"Yes. Yes, we do," Gwen replied.

"But I just saw Lesley at the Legion. She said your meeting was last night."

Gwen hesitated, glancing at Vera for guidance.

"It was," Vera supplied hurriedly. "But we decided to have an impromptu meeting tonight."

"Without Lesley?"

"Yes, she can't always make the meetings anyway. You know, her work schedule."

"So, at the last minute, you decide to get together, get drunk, and ..."

"Decoupage," Doreen threw in, gesturing towards the table full of photos.

The photos were spread haphazardly over its surface and appeared to be of different people and places on the island. As I stepped forward to get a closer look, Vera quickly picked a few large cardboard sheets off the table and placed them face-down on the floor.

"It's for Shea," Doreen blurted out. The other three women looked at her in horror. "No, No, I don't mean that. I mean…"

"She means we're doing a photo collage for the island's centennial," Vera cut in quickly. "It's the library that's getting it, Doreen." Her voice sliced across Doreen's name with a crisp and pointed anger. "Not Shea."

"Yes, yes, that's right," Doreen agreed, her words tumbling out in a drunken rush.

"Perhaps you've had enough to drink, Doreen," Vera continued, an uncomfortable silence settling over the room.

"Yes, of course. Too much slamma in my Alabama. I don't know what I'm saying."

"Why are you here, Kate?" Gwen said, clumsily changing the subject.

"I was over at the Legion and thought I'd stop by on my way home. See if there's been any news from the benefactor. Any hints about what he's thinking as far as the station's funding is concerned?"

"Nope," Gwen shook her head from side to side with dizzying force. She paused to get her bearings again. "I haven't heard a peep. And you know what they say: no newsh is good newsh."

I hadn't realized, that news had an h at the end.

"Well, I have news. Betty and I were talking about that reporter who's been snooping around the island, Jack Donahue. I found out some interesting things about him."

"Such as?" Vera took a long sip of her drink before replacing it on the table. She looked as sober as a judge at a temperance rally.

"Why aren't you drunk, Vera?"

Vera smiled. "Unlike these ladies, I really enjoyed the sixties."

"That means she took a lot of illegal subshtances," Gwen filled in for me.

"Yeah, I figured that out, Gwen."

"Drugs have been a constant in both my personal and professional life," Vera stated.

Pharmacist by day, flower child at night.

"I discovered, that Jack had a beef with Rosalie," I continued on.

"Andddddd," Betty butted in before I could continue, "he was here on Wynter Island before," she paused dramatically, "Rosalie died."

"Oh, that is suspicious," Vera said.

"Yes. I talked to Ian, Staff Sargent Singh, about it tonight at the Legion."

"Ian?" Betty's brows lifted.

"Yes, Ian. But not like that, Betty. I'm helping him find a girlfriend."

"Matchmaking. I enjoy that, too."

"He's going to look into Jack and see if he has an alibi for the time of the murder. That will mean he'll be dropping by to interview you, too, Betty."

"That's fine. It will give me a chance to find out what he's looking for in a girlfriend."

I had the feeling that my impromptu offer of matchmaking had been wrested from my grasp. Betty now had a hold of it. I was merely a diminishing figure in her rearview mirror.

"Anyway, I'll leave you ladies to your crafting. Unless you need some help?"

"No!," four voices stated at the exact same time.

"Okay, you don't have to be quite so definite about it."

"No, Kate, it's not you. It's something else. We ran out of," Vera's mind appeared to be running over all of the possibilities, "decoupage glue. Doreen will have to pick up some next week when she goes to Victoria. So, no more crafting for us this evening."

"Yes," the remaining ladies agreed, again in near-perfect unison.

"Just drinking?"

"That's right."

"Alright then, I'll see everyone at the station next week."

I could taste the desperation in the air as I said my goodbyes and stepped back out onto the front porch. They wanted me gone. Now. *Immediatmente.* And it had nothing to do with either collages or glue.

What the hell are they up to?

Chapter Twenty-Five

"Dougie, it's okay. Most people's first attempts at editing aren't usually that great."

Dougie's first try at editing was, however, worse than most. The quick flashes of abrupt cuts and rollicking dramatic music were jarring and in no way projected a peaceful image of the island to viewers.

"I did say let's aim for something nice and pastoral to advertise the channel, Dougie. Not James Bond."

"Jason Bourne, not James Bond," he replied rather indignantly. "No one wants peaceful shots of the marina or orca swimming by, Kate. If we want to promote the station, the island, we need some action, adventure."

"Well, it's not an action/adventure piece, Dougie. Wynter Island is not the streets of Marseilles during a full-speed car chase."

"All the footage I used was taken on the island."

"It may have been, but Nate driving at full speed past all of the local sites defeats the purpose of this video. We want people to see the beaches and the Lind hotel, not make it appear that life on Wynter Island is like living in the middle of some cop show."

"But people love cop shows." He paused and sighed. "If I'd had the camera with me this morning, I could have gotten some great footage of all the RCMP vehicles out on Rte. 97."

The sound of the Beatles' "Hello, Goodbye" blasted from where my phone sat on the edge of the editing bay.

I punched a finger at the screen and held the phone up to my ear. "Hello?"

"Kate? It's Shea. Can you please come to the Reserve? Right now?" Shea's voice, high-pitched and frantic, pummeled my eardrums.

"What the hell is going on, Shea?"

"Someone called the Crimestoppers line in the middle of the night with an anonymous tip about Rosalie's murder. They said Selesia is the killer, and the RCMP would find proof of it on the Reserve."

"I'm on my way."

* * *

At eleven a.m. on a cloudy Thursday morning, traffic was pretty light. Traffic was always pretty light on Wynter Island, the only exception being summer weekends when the roads filled with vacationers and day trippers. Sadly, there were no such crowds to worry about this summer.

A beaten-up cream-colored Chevy flashed by me as I turned onto Rte. 97. One black leather-clad arm hung out of the window. It looked like Brad Sixto. Where the hell was he going at that speed?

It didn't take long to get to Selesia's house. Two RCMP vehicles occupied all of the space in the driveway. Bodies were moving around inside. I jumped out of the truck and headed to the open front door.

"Hello?" I called out.

Ian's head popped out from the kitchen. "Kate? What are you doing here?" He stopped and shook his head. "Foolish question. Someone called you and told you we were here."

"Yeah, Shea did. What's going on?"

"That's none of your business, Kate," Stewart said as he emerged from the hall that adjoined the small front foyer. "You're butting into a police investigation."

"This is serious, Kate," Ian added. "You're going to have to leave. This is no place for an amateur detective."

"You're kicking me out?" I laughed, trying to keep things light, but the heaviness of the atmosphere in the tidy split-level squashed that.

Lesley walked out of the kitchen, her hands encased in latex gloves. "Yes, we are." Her brown eyes were troubled but firm. This was serious, they seemed to say, and there was no point in pretending otherwise. Her eyes mirrored the pain she knew she was inflicting on Shea. "Shea is down at Sam's with Selesia."

"Okay, I'll head down there then."

Before the words were even out of my mouth, they had turned back to their investigation.

* * *

Shea's blue SUV was parked in front of Sam's rancher. He had the best patch of land in the entire Reserve, his modest brown house facing out onto a shore of beach grass and granite that fell away to a stunning view of the Salish Sea.

Sam's front door was cracked open. I stepped a few feet into the front hall and called, "Hello? Anyone here?"

Toenails scratched frantically over the wood floor as Jojo, Sam's black lab, raced out to greet me.

"Kate? Is that you? We're in the kitchen," Sam's rich baritone floated out from the back of the house.

"C'mon Jojo," I bent over to allow her to lick my face before heading into the kitchen, "Let's go and see everybody."

The kitchen resembled a wake. Selesia, Shea, and Sam were seated around the small wooden kitchen table, three full cups of coffee sitting ignored in front of them.

"Hey," I nodded, pushing Jojo down from jumping on me. "I guess there's no point in asking how everyone is doing."

Shea's desperate eyes connected with mine. "Thanks for coming, Kate."

I pulled out a chair and sat down, waving away Sam's offer of tepid coffee. "I'm not sure what you expect me to do."

Sam said, "I'm sorry we had to take you away from work, but—"

"We need fresh eyes on the situation here," Shea finished for him. "Someone who's had a decent night's sleep and can see things clearly."

I glanced over at Selesia. She was still as a statue, her angular face carved out of marble, her long black hair pulled back into a loose ponytail. Her eyes never lifted from her untouched coffee cup.

"It's okay. I left Dougie to watch the station. He's editing footage. Thinks he's the new Michael Bay. Anyway, what happened?"

Sam sighed. "The three of them showed up at Selesia's house. Someone called in an anonymous Crimestoppers tip saying that Selesia had killed Rose and they would find evidence on the Reserve."

Selesia's head jerked up, her dark pupils connecting with mine, but she said nothing.

"So the three of them have been ransacking her house ever since," Shea finished. "Selesia called me, and I met her here at Sam's."

"Where's Brad?"

Shea shrugged her shoulders. "I don't know. He was already gone by the time I got here."

"He headed out as soon as he saw them," Selesia replied. "I've no idea where he is. Like usual."

That's interesting. Why did he need to leave as soon as the police arrived?

"Well, I saw him heading south on Rte. 97 about ten minutes ago. He's roaming around the island somewhere. Did Ian say anything to you?"

Selesia snorted a derisive, angry sound. "They didn't need to. It's pretty obvious what they're thinking. What everyone on the island is thinking."

"Selesia, that's not fair," Sam started, but she cut him off with the swiftness of a fox biting the head off a chicken.

"It is fair. And I don't care what anyone thinks. Rose got what she deserved. She ruined people's lives and didn't give a damn about it."

"She was a child," Sam offered.

"Child or not," Selesia continued, "she knew what she was doing and, ultimately, paid the price."

Selesia's words hung dangerously in the still air of the kitchen. Even Jojo seemed cowed by their fury as she headed into the living room to curl up on her dog bed.

"Don't say such things, Selesia," Shea warned.

"Why not? What's it going to do? I'm going to be heading off to prison anyway."

"Don't say that!" Sam barked, startling all of us. "Do you hear me? You're not going to prison!"

In the silence after Sam's angry outburst, we could hear footsteps crunching up the front path toward the house.

"Excuse me," Ian called through the partially open front door, "RCMP here."

No shit, Ian. Really?

"We're in the kitchen," Sam replied.

Jojo's toenails clattered on the floor as she danced joyfully at the appearance of even more people. The three officers made their way into the kitchen.

I could tell instantly that it was terrible news. Melancholy leached off the three of them like water spilling into wine. Lesley could not even look at Shea.

"Selesia Sixto?" Ian said in his deep, magisterial voice.

"Yes?" Her face tilted towards them, anger and pride written across her sharply cut features.

"We found this in your backyard, mixed with the ashes in your fire pit."

He held up a clear bag that held a smoke-tinged, melted piece of glass. I leaned forward to read its label but couldn't make out anything.

"It appears to be some kind of medicinal bottle. We're not sure where from yet. Most of the label is gone. But we've got a pretty good guess at what was in it: lily of the valley tincture."

Before Selesia could say a word, Sam pushed his chair back and stood up, one hand trembling as he gripped the back of the chair.

"It's mine," he said, his voice clear and decisive, "not Selesia's. I'm the one you should be arresting. I killed Rosalie Morgann, not her."

Chapter Twenty-Six

Chaos ensued. Everyone shouted simultaneously. Selesia screamed at Sam not to be such a fool; Shea shouted at Selesia to shut up before she said something stupid, and Jojo yapped at everyone from the living room as she sensed the sudden emotional shift.

"Enough! Enough!" Ian's full volume bellow drew everyone to a halt. "Sam Hanks," The sudden silence in the room was jarring. Sam's breath wheezed in and out in rapid gusts. "Are you confessing to the murder of Rosalie Morgann?"

He nodded his head. Selesia opened her mouth to say something, but Stewart's hand rose to stop her.

"I need to hear you say it, Sam," Ian continued.

He swallowed twice. "I killed Rosalie Morgann."

"No!" Selesia screamed. "He's lying! Don't listen to him!"

"Sam Hanks, I am placing you under arrest for the murder of Rosalie Morgann." Ian reached into his back pocket to retrieve a pair of handcuffs.

"Do we have to, Ian?" Lesley asked, her quiet question barely audible against Jojo's barking. "It's not like he's fighting us or anything."

Ian gave her a stern glance before turning back to Sam. " You do not need to say anything. Anything you do say may be used as evidence against you in court. You have the right to retain and instruct counsel. If you cannot afford this, counsel will be retained free of charge through the Provincial Legal Aid System."

Sam held his hands silently in front of him so that Ian could put on the cuffs. Jojo stopped barking, and in the sudden silence, we could hear them click shut around his wrists. We, three, stood there frozen: Selesia's hysteria silenced; Shea looking sick with concern; and me, unbelieving of what was happening in front of me.

The sound of a sharp knock on the front door brought us all back to our senses.

"Hello? Anyone here?" Gwen's voice called out in the silent house.

"No, Gwen. Don't come in," Sam shouted, but it was too late. She was already in the open doorway to the kitchen, staring aghast at the scene in front of her.

"What the hell is going on?"

She looked from Ian to Stewart and then Lesley before settling, bewildered, on me. I walked over and took her arm.

"Gwen, we need to talk." I tried to pull her from the kitchen, but she shook my hand off.

"What do you mean we need to talk? I need to find out what the hell is going on here!"

Sam looked up from the floor, his eyes connecting with hers. "I killed Rose."

Gwen laughed, her disbelief slipping into horror. "Don't be ridiculous. Stewart, what's going on here?" She turned to him, her eyes desperate for a saner explanation.

"It's true, Gwen. He's being arrested for the murder of Rosalie Morgann," Stewart said.

"Let's get a move on," Ian said as he began to lead Sam from the kitchen.

"No." Selesia and Gwen's shouts were simultaneous, echoing back at us from the kitchen walls.

Before Selesia could move, Gwen grabbed Sam's other elbow, yanking him to a stop.

"I don't know what you think you're doing, Sam, but this is too much."

His eyes, so sad and tired, suddenly lifted for a moment. "Remember when we were young, Gwen? When we'd sneak away to the beach?"

Her expression shifted from fury to confusion. "What?"

"When we were at UBC. We'd sneak down to the beach on a sunny weekday when it was empty."

Her eyes shifted from confusion to clarity. "Yes, but what does that have to do with any of this?"

He continued as if she hadn't said anything. "We'd bring down a beach towel and sunbathe. Remember?"

The clarity shifted to sadness. "Yes, but why are we talking about this, Sam?"

"And I would tell you how much I loved you." He gazed deeply into her eyes, unable with his cuffed hands to touch hers. "I still do, Gwen. I always have."

"Sam!" She started in shock, but Ian pulled his arm free of her hand and began to walk him toward the front door. "Sam!"

He glanced over his shoulder, smiling at each of us before settling on Gwen's stricken face. "I just wanted you to know."

And with that, Ian led him outside to the patrol car with Stewart and Lesley on their heels. Jojo tried to run after him, but I grabbed her collar to keep her back. She whined and pulled, looking back at me in confusion when I wouldn't allow her to follow her master.

I bent down, burying my face in her short, black fur. "You can't go with him, Jojo," I whispered. "None of us can."

* * *

The single cell in the basement of the Wynter Island RCMP detachment looked as if it hadn't been used in years. It was clean but had the dusty smell of an old storage cupboard. Sam was seated on a fold-down cot that doubled as a bench. In one corner, an aluminum toilet sat against the concrete floor.

"Kate's come to see you." Lesley coughed into her hand, causing him to look up. She pulled a key out of her pocket and jiggled it in the lock before pulling the steel door open.

Sam smiled as I walked into the cell, looking over at Lesley as she clanged the door shut and relocked it. "Is this typical RCMP policy, Lesley?"

She smiled sadly. "No, it most definitely isn't. But Kate's convinced me she can wrangle the truth out of you. You know, being a seasoned journalist and all. You've got fifteen minutes, Kate. That's it."

She turned and headed back up the stairs.

"Thanks, Lesley. I appreciate it." I sat down on the rough blanket and sheet that covered the cot. "I love what you've done with the place, Sam." I glanced around the chilly, spartan cell. "Interesting decorating choices."

His broad smile cracked across his seamed face. "You can talk your way into just about anywhere, can't you, girl?"

"Yup, pretty much. Although talking my way into jail is a new one for me."

He sighed and looked away. "I'm afraid it probably wasn't worth the effort."

"I disagree. I know you didn't kill Rose Morgan, Sam, so don't bother trying to deny it." I raised my hand in the air. "You think you're protecting Selesia, but you're not."

"Oh, and why would that be?"

"Because Selesia didn't kill Rose."

He said nothing.

"I know the melted apothecary bottle looks bad, but there could be several different explanations for how it ended up there. Not just that Selesia was trying to burn evidence in her fire pit."

"Is that so, Sherlock Holmes?"

I was not going to be distracted. "Yes, it is. She needs you, Sam."

"Yes, I know. That's why I'm here."

"So you're admitting you lied to stop the police from arresting Selesia?"

"I'm not admitting shit, Kate."

"Sam, I'm trying to find the killer. You throwing yourself on your proverbial sword is not helping anything."

"Really?" He looked around the empty cell in mock surprise. "I don't see anyone else in here with me."

"No, that's right. Selesia is at home with Shea now, heartbroken. Heartbroken because she believes her brother thinks she is capable of murder."

"She'll get over it."

"I don't think so."

159

He stared stolidly ahead at the cement wall. "I'm in here because I poisoned Rose Morgan."

I threw my hands up in the air. "You're determined to destroy your life, aren't you? Your martyr act is just a diversion, Sam, and one that won't buy very much time. The police will figure out the truth eventually."

"What are you talking about, Kate?"

"You confessed because you wanted to protect Selesia. What if she's innocent, Sam?"

His brow furrowed in confusion. "Then, just for the sake of argument, who burned the apothecary bottle in her fire pit? Or did it just magically arrive there?"

My mind flashed back to the image looping in my memory for the past hour: the black leather sleeve hanging out the open window of a beaten-up Chevy. What if Betty Wu was mistaken? What if Jack Donahue had not arrived on Wynter Island before Rosalie's death? What if the young man she had seen was instead Sam's nephew, Brad Sixto? Could there be a nefarious reason why he was headed towards Rosalie's house in the days before her murder? Perhaps doing some reconnaissance?

"What if Brad put it there."

He jumped to his feet in shock. "What the hell are you saying, Kate?"

"I'm saying that there is another person on the Reserve that people have been ignoring as a possible suspect: Brad. He could have been attempting to destroy evidence in Selesia's fire pit. No one would have thought anything of it."

"That's ridiculous!" He stamped to the other side of the cell.

"Is it, Sam? A young man, angry with a world that doesn't want him, alone for the first time without the steady presence of his older brother?" I stood up and walked over to his side. "Is it so crazy to imagine that Brad might have done something terrible to protect his mother from more pain? To choose to act like the man of the house for the first time in his life? Even if it was in an horrific, twisted manner?"

He stomped away from me. "That's just lies. Fantasies. You're not going to talk me out of this, Kate."

"It's not lies, Sam. I can't prove that he did it. Yet. But I have my suspicions."

"And so you want me to walk out of here because you have suspicions? So that my spot can be taken by who? My nephew?"

"Yes, I do. Because at least a few of my suspicions are rooted in fact, like Brad being seen near Rose's home before she was murdered."

Silence.

"However hard you try to lie your way into prison, Sam, they will figure out that you are just trying to draw them away from the real criminal. And if that is Brad, Selesia is going to need you right by her side. Because she won't survive a blow like that without you."

Chapter Twenty-Seven

I headed directly from the detachment to the Reserve, the station pick-up engine whining as my foot pressed down on the accelerator. Lettucetown flew past me in a pastiche of pale lime greenhouses. I skidded to a halt at the stop sign before swinging left toward Selesia's house.

The front door was open again. Or perhaps it had never been closed? Was it only that morning I had turned down this same road to see police cars in Selesia's driveway and officers swarming through her house?

I parked the truck and headed inside at a trot. Shea's stressed voice pierced through the bowels of the house to greet me at the front door.

"Selesia! You can't do this! You can't confess to the murder of Rosalie Morgann! For Christ's sake, what is this? Everybody Confess to a Murder Day?"

There was the sound of someone moving things around. "Yes, I can, Shea, and I will. Can you get out of my way so I can get this laundry out of the dryer?"

"Who cares about the fucking laundry!"

"I do. You know as well as I do that the boys aren't going to do anything around the house if I'm not here."

"Because you'll be in jail? Perhaps that's why you shouldn't be wasting your time cleaning now, Selesia."

"Shea, I just want to get the house sorted, okay? It may seem stupid, but I want to get something settled in my life." Her voice had risen to a sob, and the shuffling sounds ceased.

I headed down the hallway to find them standing by the washer/dryer in the bathroom. Shea had wrapped her arms around Selesia, Selesia's angular face buried in Shea's fine blonde hair.

"Hey," I said quietly, trying not to startle them.

They pulled apart, Selesia rubbing a hand over her eyes. "Hi, Kate. How did it go with Sam?"

I leaned against the bathroom door frame. Jojo was pacing in the barricaded living room, stopping to stare out the front window every few moments.

"Okay, I guess."

"Is he going to reconsider this craziness?" Selesia picked up a sheet, trapping it under her chin as she folded it into an even square.

"I don't know. Maybe."

"Well, that's something," she muttered and picked up another sheet to fold.

"Even if he recants, Selesia," Shea begged, "that doesn't mean you have to confess. It's not a one-in-one-out kind of situation."

Selesia's smile was a bitter line drawn across her face. "You mean it's not 'I trade you one of mine for one of yours?' What do they call that in a war?"

"Prisoner swap," I answered.

"That's it. A prisoner swap."

"That isn't funny," Shea said.

Selesia chuckled sadly and placed the folded sheet on a neat pile of laundry. "Believe me, I don't think it's funny."

"Where's Brad?" I asked.

"God only knows," Selesia snipped the words out angrily, but I could hear the deep seam of worry in her voice. "He's not answering his cell, but that could be because he doesn't have a signal. I tried calling Phil after Shea told me he might be there, but no answer. What on earth would he be doing over at Phil's?"

"He's been helping him out," I replied. "Phil was pretty broken up about Rose's death. Brad made sure he was eating and didn't get a DUI driving himself to the liquor store."

"But why Phil?" Shea asked.

"I don't know. Is your family close to him, Selesia?"

Her black eyebrows shot up. "No. He's Sam's age, but I don't think they were ever great friends. I don't remember seeing them together. It was always Sam and Gwen."

"Sam and Gwen," Shea murmured. "That was something this morning, wasn't it?"

"Yes, it was," Selesia replied.

"You knew, didn't you?" I asked.

Selesia nodded. "Yup, although he made quite the effort to hide it. I even thought he might get married a couple of times, but it never panned out. No one could ever hold a candle to Gwen."

"Do you think she knew?" Shea asked.

I shook my head. "No. I think she was as stunned as everyone else this morning."

"I wonder," Shea started, but I waved her to a stop.

"Don't. We've got to focus on getting Sam out of jail right now. Not get distracted by a love story."

The phone's ring cut through the air, drawing Selesia down the hallway at a run.

She picked up the receiver. "Hello? Will? Is that you?"

An incoherent male voice rumbled through the receiver. "Yes, you need to come home, Will. Right now."

Another pause.

"Yes, Uncle Sam has been arrested. For murder."

The mumble on the other end of the line rose in pitch and got louder.

"Yes, for the murder of Rose Morgan. You won't know her. She and I were," Selesia paused, "friends a long time ago."

Another pause.

"Yes, the TV star. I'm sorry you've got to leave your job early, sweetheart, but I need you at home. We both do. Brad especially."

Another burble of sound.

"No, I don't have a lawyer for Uncle Sam yet," she hesitated, "I'm hoping he won't need one. It looks like there may be another lead in the case."

Another lead in the case. So she wasn't going to tell Will what she was about to do.

"No, don't head out tonight. It'll be a long drive for you, and it's better that you're well-rested. Get a good night's sleep first. Yes, babe, I love you, too. See you soon."

Selesia paused, holding the handset mid-air before replacing it on the phone.

"You didn't tell him," I stated.

"No," she shook her head, "he's got enough to deal with now, processing the news about Sam."

"But," Shea started.

"But nothing. By the time he gets here, it will be done."

"What will be done?" We had been so engrossed in Selesia's call with Will that we had neglected to notice Brad standing in the open doorway. "And why is Jojo barricaded in the living room?"

He took a few steps up, leaning a hand over the half wall to pet her.

"It's because." Selesia cleared her throat. It's because we have to, had to." Her eyes swam in confusion for a moment as she tried to put the words together: "Look after her for Uncle Sam."

"Why?"

"It's a long story. C'mon, let's go sit down."

The anger in Brad's voice sliced across the room toward her. "I don't need to sit down, Mom. What's going on?"

Selesia sighed. "They arrested your uncle for the murder of Rose Morgan."

His eyes fluttered like a man awakening suddenly from a deep sleep. "What?"

"He's being held in the Wynter Island jail."

"What the hell?" Brad bounded up the last few steps to come level with his mother. "Uncle Sam's in jail?"

"Yes, he is. For now. C'mon, why can't we just sit down for a moment and talk?"

"For now? What does that mean?"

Brad's eyes frantically turned to look at both Shea and me.

"Your mother," Shea started, "is planning on turning herself in to the police."

"What? Why?"

Selesia took a deep breath. "Because I'm the one who killed her, Brad."

In the sudden silence, Jojo whimpered from the living room.

"No!" Brad took a step back, half stumbling at the top of the stairs. "What are you talking about?"

"You're going to be fine. Uncle Sam will come back to look after you. And Will is coming home from his job. He should be here in the next couple of days. Just—"

"No! You're lying!" Brad screamed, turned, and ran down the stairs and out the front door. His car door slammed shut, followed almost immediately by the screaming of tires spinning on the gravel driveway. He disappeared down the road in a cloud of dust.

Selesia sank down to the floor. Shea plunked down beside her. I couldn't make out what she was saying due to Selesia's crying and Jojo's frantic barking.

I had seen something on Brad's face just before he raced out the door. Something that made my breath catch in my throat. Although his shout had sounded like nothing more than an emotional outburst, what if it had been a statement of fact? That he knew his mom *was* lying and sacrificing herself for someone? For someone other than Sam.

For him.

Chapter Twenty-Eight

Two days passed, and I was ensconced at an editing bay trying to remedy Dougie's artistic masterpiece when a high-pitched shrill squawk erupted from my phone. Jupiter raised his head from his dog bed and looked straight at me, as if he knew something was wrong.

I picked up my phone and looked down at the text. My heart sank. It was the Island Emergency Alert System saying there was an Amber Alert out for Brad Sixto.

Brad Sixto has not been seen for 48 hrs. All available adults, please report to the Wynter Island RCMP detachment ASAP.

I placed the phone back down on the editing bay with a clatter.

"C'mon, Jupe. We've got someone we need to find."

* * *

The parking lot in front of the RCMP detachment was filled with an eclectic assortment of trucks, SUVs, and electric cars. I pulled in and jumped out with Jupiter on my heels. The islanders grouped in the parking lot were a microcosm of island society: farmers, fishermen, retirees, and Gen X entrepreneurs who had stepped away from their online ETSY businesses so that they could help with the search. I spotted Michael in his black GORE-TEX jacket and headed toward him.

"Hey, Michael," I said.

"Kate, good to see you," He smiled down at Jupiter. "You too, Jupiter. Perhaps your nose can come in handy today."

Our conversation was cut short by Stewart's appearance at the front door of the police station.

"Okay, everyone, thank you for coming today. As the text stated, Brad Sixto has been missing for 48 hours. Phil and the Wet Witch are also missing, which may be a coincidence or might tell us something about where Brad is. We did find his car parked down by the marina." He paused to catch his breath. "Unfortunately, the Wet Witch is not responding to any Coast Guard radio calls, and Brad's cellphone is going directly to voicemail. As most of you are aware, his mother was arrested two days ago, and the last time he was seen, he was extremely agitated. We need to find him. If you can pair up amongst yourselves, great. If not, I can put together search groups. Those with surnames A to M, please focus on the north of the island. Those with surnames N to Z, please focus your search on the southern part of the island."

"Well, I'm an R and you're a T, so I guess we're in the same group," Michael said. "You want to take your truck or the Subaru?"

"The Subaru."

"Great. Let's go."

We headed south from the RCMP detachment, stopping at Steeltun Bay.

"I know this isn't your favorite place, but we still need to see if he's here," Michael stated.

We parked the car and got out. The ocean was green, the color of malachite, darkened with flashes of black. It swooshed in angry waves against the beach, the icy tendrils of white foam washing up toward us to pull at our boots. It looked as cold, no colder, than when I had last been in it. I tried to push those memories away, but they clawed their way back into my consciousness. The sudden shock of cold, then the panic of fighting, sputtering, drowning, followed by that trickle of warmth that could mean only one thing: hypothermia and then death. I kept walking around the beach, head down, pushing the memories away.

Focus on Brad. Keep looking for Brad.

Michael was combing the opposite side of the bay while Jupiter snuffled noisily in amongst the grass and rocks, most likely on the trail of a squirrel.

"What are we looking for, Michael?" I shouted across to him. I hated to say it, but the question needed to be asked. "Are we looking for Brad or a body?"

He sighed as we rejoined our paths and headed back to his Subaru. "I don't know. I don't think anyone knows. We just have to try and find any clues we can."

We drove around Wynter Mountain, slowing down to examine any isolated chunks of waterfront where a body might have washed up, before turning down 97 toward Harrow Village.

"There's his car," Michael said, pointing to the beige Chevy parked near the dock. "He must have gotten on the Wet Witch with Phil."

"But then why aren't they answering any of the Coast Guard's calls?"

"That's the 64,000 dollar question, isn't it?"

The windscreen began to fog up from our combined breath, so Michael rubbed it clear with his coat sleeve.

"Holy shit, Kate! Is that who I think it is!"

I peered through the steamy glass. Sure enough, a small, ugly fishing trawler was chugging into the harbor. I watched as it moved closer, its rusty metal sides vibrating in displeasure. I sat up taller in my seat.

"You're right, Michael! It's the Wet Witch!" I shouted, drawing Jupiter to his feet with a confused bark. "That must be them!"

Michael and I were out of the truck and running down to the docks before I had time to think.

They're back!

I scrambled down the neon green mossy dock while Brad readied a rope to throw out onto a pier.

"Brad! Brad!" He looked up in concern as we skidded to a stop beside him. "Where the fuck have you been!"

"Hey, that's not very ladylike language," Phil said as he stepped out from the ship's cabin.

"Ladylike language or not, Phil," Michael said, "where the fuck have you been?"

"Up the western side of Vancouver Island. Over towards Ucluelet. What's the problem?"

"The problem is," I said in an exasperated tone, "that you haven't been answering your radio."

Phil stood a little straighter in his dark green rubber overalls, attempting and failing to project a sense of righteous indignation. "It died soon after we left port. And why is everyone shouting at me, for Christ's Sake!"

I took a deep breath to calm myself down. "We've been looking for you, Brad. A lot of people have been looking for you."

"Why?" He paused, his brows drawing together in concern. "Did something else happen to Mom?"

Is he that good an actor, or does he honestly have no idea what I'm talking about?

"Because you disappeared when you heard your mother was turning herself in to the police. The last anyone saw of you, you were pretty upset."

"Yeah, but I didn't do anything stupid, if that's what you're thinking. I went to see Phil, and he suggested we get away on the boat for a few days. You know, just to give me a chance to chill and process everything. I left a message on Uncle Sam's cellphone telling him."

"Your uncle didn't get the message."

"I don't know why. Perhaps the signal cut out or something. I did try."

"Well then," The anger left my body like air whooshing out of a deflated balloon. "We need to let everyone know you're home and safe. The RCMP and half the island have been out looking for you."

"Talk about making a mountain out of a molehill," Phil grumbled as he picked up a plastic bag and stepped over the side of the trawler onto the dock.

"It was not a molehill," Michael replied in irritation. "Wouldn't you hope someone would hunt for you if you went missing, Phil?"

"Harumph," was the only answer he gave. "C'mon, Brad. Grab the cooler. We've got to get these fish into the fridge at the cottage."

They started down the dock as if we weren't even there. We scampered to keep up with them.

"I need to talk to both of you. Now!" I said.

"Well, then, you'd better come with us to the cottage," Phil said over his shoulder as he and Brad set off up the hill.

We stopped briefly to allow Michael to call Ian and Sam and let them know that both Brad and Phil were safe. He convinced them we would return Brad to the Reserve ourselves, so there was no need for the cavalry to descend on Harrow Village.

By the time he finished the second call, Phil and Brad had made it to the small tumbledown house. The front door was ajar, so we stepped inside with Jupiter.

"Phil? Brad?"

"We're in here," Brad shouted from what I assumed to be the kitchen.

It was as dated and pokey as the rest of the house, stuck in 1969 alongside the Royal Doulton figurines and the glass-encased China cabinet in the corner.

"Brad, put the kettle on and make us some tea," Phil asked as he stacked the fresh fish in newspaper on the lower shelves of the fridge. "Kate, you get the mugs out of the cupboard. Michael, here's the milk." He handed him a plastic jug with the ubiquitous bag of milk in it, the scent of fresh fish blood clinging disgustingly to the plastic handle.

"I told the police I would take you back to the Reserve, Brad," Michael said. "ASAP."

Brad pulled a brown betty teapot off the shelf and threw in a couple of Red Rose tea bags. He placed it on the table as the simmering tea kettle whistled.

"Fine, whatever," Phil said, standing up and closing the fridge door before collapsing onto a seat at the kitchen table. "But I need a cup of tea before anyone goes anywhere."

"Alright, alright, one cup," I muttered as we all pulled out a seat.

"Brad, the cookies are in the cupboard."

Brad placed a bag of Peek Freans Fruit Cremes on the table before filling each mug with the amber liquid.

"Milk for me," Phil ordered.

"None for me," Michael said.

I placed a dribble in Phil's cup and my own before adding a teaspoonful of sugar.

"God, that taste's good," Phil said as he took a long sip, smacking his lips in contentment. "So what is all this fussin' about?"

I took a sip from my mug. "I already told you, Phil. The Wet Witch was gone, and no one was answering any of the radio calls from the Coast Guard. Brad was missing, and we didn't know what the hell was going on."

Phil snorted and rummaged in the bag for a cookie. "It's not my fault the radio cut out. It's finicky like that.

"You mean old," I murmured quietly before raising my voice a bit louder. "Well, the RCMP thought Brad might have done something stupid."

"Like what?" Brad rummaged one hand in the half-empty cookie bag. He pulled out a biscuit and took a bite.

I studied his face. Yes, he was calm now, but I could tell from the dark shadows beneath his eyes that he hadn't slept well. Worrying about his mother, most likely.

"I don't know, stolen the boat, run away."

"But why would I do that?"

Michael sighed. "A lot of people have been worried about you this summer, Brad. Your mom, your uncle, a lot of us."

"I don't understand why."

"Because you've been struggling," I finished for Michael. "You keep disappearing. Nobody knows where you go or what you're doing. And with Will gone and your mom under suspicion after the death of Rosalie, people began to get ideas."

Brad took another bite out of his cookie, staring into the middle distance. "So by ideas, you mean people thought I was doing drugs or stealing."

"Yeah, I guess," I said. "Or something worse."

His eyes narrowed in to focus on my face. "Worse? What could be worse than that? You mean that I may have killed Rose?"

We stared at each other for a lengthy moment before I curtly nodded.

Phil slammed his mug down on the table. "What in the name of all that's holy are you talking about, Kate?" he shouted. "Are you saying that you think Brad had somethin' to do with Rose's death!"

Rather than the shock or anger I expected, Brad's head fell backward, and a roar of incredulous laughter spat out of his mouth. He half sputtered out his remaining cookie, wiping his mouth with one hand before rattling to a stop. 'I don't know why I'm laughing. It's not funny. None of this is funny. I guess it's just so crazy, I can't help but laugh."

"Crazy is one word for it," Phil barked out. "Bloody stupid is another!"

Unlike Brad, Phil did not find anything funny in this, his grey brows dropping so low that they formed bushy arches just above his eyelids.

"Why would anyone think I would want to hurt Rose?" Brad asked.

Michael shrugged. "Your family has a long, and not particularly happy, history with her. She hurt your mother terribly and ultimately played a role in your parents' divorce."

He nodded. "Yes," he said with a matter of fact tone that surprised me. "That's true. She told me all about it."

"Your mom?" I asked.

"Oh no." He shook his head and drained the last tea from his mug before looking me straight in the eye. "Rose did."

Chapter Twenty-Nine

My heart stopped for a moment in my chest. Beat. Pause. Beat. "She what?"

"Rose told me all about it. All of it."

"When?"

"When she'd stop by to visit me, for Christ's sake," Phil said. "I don't know what's so hard for you to understand about all of this, Kate."

"But what were you doing here, Brad? I mean, at Phil's house before Rosalie died? I know you came to help him afterward, but…"

Brad and Phil shared a long look before Phil curtly nodded his head. "Go ahead and tell her," he said. "It's going to come out now anyways."

"What's going to come out?" Michael asked, his eyes moving back and forth between the two.

"I've been working with Phil all summer."

"All summer?" My voice rose in surprise. "Doing what?"

"I've been teaching the boy, alright? Teaching him how to fish," Phil said, pointing in my direction. "And you can wipe that shocked expression off your face. You think I'd been teaching him how to rob banks the way you two are looking at me."

"You have been teaching Brad how to fish," I repeated, my mind trying to make sense of this unexpected turn of events. "Why?"

"Because I want him to become a chartered accountant, that's why." He snorted. "Why do you think? So that he can become a commercial salmon fisherman when he graduates from high school."

"Become a commercial salmon fisherman?"

174

"Yes," Brad picked up the narrative. "I don't want to go to college. I don't want to work in an office. I know that's what Will wants, but it's not for me. I want to be outdoors, doing something with my hands."

"Fishing," I repeated, still in shock.

"Yes, fishing. One day, I was sitting down at the docks when Phil came in with the Wet Witch. He asked if I'd help him get the catch out of the hold. And that was the start of it."

"He started showing up all the time," Phil continued. "I just gave in and began to teach him."

"And I knew it was the right thing for me," Brad's broad, genuine smile pushed against the outer reaches of his cheeks. "It was something I enjoyed doing that didn't involve reading a book or writing something down."

"But why all the skullduggery?" Michael asked, taking another sip of his tea. "Why not just tell your mother you'd decided to become a commercial fisherman?"

Brad shook his head. "My mom went to college, Uncle Sam went to college, and now Will is off to college. She wanted me to make something more of myself. More than just being a fisherman."

"Surely she'd accept your decision?" I asked.

Brad shrugged. "That's what I've been battling with all summer. I wanted to tell her, but I knew she'd be so pissed off with me. I just kept avoiding it. And her."

"No wonder she thought you were in trouble, Brad. You wouldn't talk to her and kept disappearing at all hours. I'd have thought the same thing if I was your mother. And it was all because of...fishing."

"Yes, at least until Rose died. Then I had to look after Phil."

"And he's been a good boy," Phil said with a gentle gruffness I had never heard from him before. "Kept me going in those first weeks."

"But you said you'd talked to Rose," I continued. "That she told you about what happened between her and your parents."

"Yes, she'd stop by the Wet Witch or visit the cottage to see Phil. That's how I met her. And when she found out who I was, she wanted to know everything about my family. And she wanted to talk to me about why she returned to Wynter Island."

"To work on her autobiography."

Phil snorted. "Bah, that was just a time filler for her. That's not why she came back."

"What?" I repeated in confusion.

"She was a Buddhist," Brad started.

"Yes, I know. I went to her funeral."

Brad nodded. "She believed in all that Buddhist stuff. That she needed to make peace with her past so she could 'adjust her karma for her future existences.'"

"A smart girl, but what a load of rubbish," Phil grumbled.

"Well, it wasn't to her," Brad continued. "She believed that every person has the power to change their destiny."

"Still not getting where this is going," Michael said.

"She said she had been hurt a lot as a kid. When she got older, she turned that pain into a weapon she could use to hurt others. Other people like my mom."

"Are you saying she came to Wynter Island to apologize to everyone? To ask for forgiveness?" I couldn't keep the shock from my voice.

"In a way."

Michael sighed. "That was a bit overly optimistic of her."

"She realized that, but she had to try. It wasn't as important for them to forgive her as it was for her to admit she was sorry for all the pain she had caused. That's why she wanted to do the thing with mom."

A sudden zing of realization shot from the top of my skull to the tip of my toes. "You mean the TV show?"

"Yes. I told her there was no way Mom would willingly sit down and talk with her, even if I asked her to. She has a temper and a bad habit of," he hesitated, "holding a grudge."

"So Rosalie insisted on doing the talk show because it was the only way she could force your mother to sit down and listen to her."

Brad nodded. "Yes. And at the same time, have a chance to apologize to the entire island. But she never got the chance."

I pondered this for a moment. "Brad, did you ever go and see her by yourself? At the Glass House?"

He hesitated, surprised. "Yeah, a few days before she died. How did you know that?"

"I have my spies. Why? Why were you going to visit her?"

"She asked me to stop by. To park the car at the end of the road in case Scott and Jason returned home early. She wasn't ready to talk about her plans with them yet."

"Talk about what plans?"

Brad's eyes locked with Phil's again.

Phil finally spoke. "I was close to Rose's dad, Bill. Her mother, Nancy—I always fancied her, you know. Rose got her good looks from her mom. And then, when Nancy died so young," His eyes filled with unshed tears, "Bill fell apart. And Rose was just left to look after herself. I didn't know how to fix things. And I was grieving Nancy myself. I should have done more," he hesitated, "but I didn't."

"I'm sure you tried your best, Phil."

He waved his hand in the air, brushing away my platitudes. "Rose wrote to me occasionally from California, so I was able to contact her when her father died. She didn't want to come back for the funeral, so I handled everything. And then, out of nowhere, she wrote to me a few months ago to tell me she was returning to Wynter Island. To live here."

"You must have been as shocked as everyone else," Michael said.

He shrugged. "She bought the old Wintford place, and her boyfriend and that other guy moved in along with her. Before long, she started dropping by the cottage for tea. That's how she met Brad and came up with her crazy plan."

"What plan?" I repeated.

"Rose asked me to come to the Glass House so we could talk," Brad said and paused. "She said she'd made a lot of money in Hollywood and wanted to pay Phil back for his kindness to her and her father. She wanted to buy the Wet Witch so that he would have enough money to retire and...."

Phil continued for him. "And then she would sign the boat over to Brad so he could start his career as a fisherman debt-free."

"What the hell!"

Phil looked over at me, his mouth pursing with a touch of puritanism. "Your language today, Kate. Really."

"So what happened?"

"What happened," Brad continued, "was that she was murdered. Before she could do any of that."

I paused as the numbers in the slot machine in my head spun around and then skidded to a stop. "Which means you had nothing to gain from her death," I said.

"Yes," Brad nodded, "and everything to lose."

Chapter Thirty

I pulled into the drive of the familiar log farmhouse and idled to a stop. In the numerous pens, an assortment of injured and abandoned animals that had come to call Shea and Lesley's farmhouse their temporary or, for many of them, permanent home were resting. There was the llama, Hercules, so named because he believed he was the strongest creature on earth. He was surrendered to Shea when his owners could no longer handle his escape attempts. In another, a small clutch of barn owls hopped around their enclosure. Their mother had been hit by a car, and it had fallen to Shea to hand-rear them until she could transfer them to a permanent wildlife center.

Shea had the kindest heart of anyone I knew. But could I count on that kindness once she heard what I had to say to her today? That I didn't know.

I pulled the keys out of the ignition and stepped out of the truck.

I knocked on the thick, hand-hewn front door. I knew she was home. Her blue Toyota Highlander was parked outside. Finally, I heard footsteps coming toward the front door. The door opened to show Shea, but a very different-looking Shea than I was used to.

Her shoulder-length blonde hair, thin to the point of wispiness, had been crushed into a messy bun on the back of her head. Violet half-moons hung suspended beneath her blue eyes. Eyes that usually held joy and curiosity were now dull and leaden.

"Hi, Shea. Sorry to pop in without warning. I wondered if we could talk?"

She said nothing, merely opened the front door wider and gestured me inside.

The interior of the house was an odd mixture of old and new. It had been one of the original settler's homes on Wynter Island, still evident in its thick log walls and the massive pine beams supporting its dark wood ceiling. Electrified oil lamps swung from those beams, making the house hazardous for anyone over 5' 8". Luckily for them, both Lesley and Shea were shorter than that. I, on the other hand, had to make sure to duck or find myself clobbered by the base of one of the swinging lamps.

I sat on the sofa, moving one of her rescue cats, an orange tabby named Oskar, to another cushion. Shea sat down in a rocking chair opposite me.

"What's up?" she eventually asked as she rocked back and forth with a metronomic rhythm.

"I wanted to check in on you. See how you're doing."

Shea waggled her head indecisively as if she lacked the strength to hold it steady.

"About what you'd expect. Selesia is in Victoria jail awaiting her bail hearing. Lesley will be going over to help with that." She ground the last words out through her teeth.

"Lesley is just doing her job, Shea."

A spark illuminated her dull eyes, adding a sudden flush of crimson to her pallid face. "I don't want to talk about Lesley."

Oh boy. She's in worse shape than I thought.

"Okay. Did you hear about Brad? That Michael and I found him and Phil yesterday? They were fishing up by Ucluelet. Apparently, Phil's radio broke down."

She nodded. "Yeah, I heard. Thank goodness he's okay. That was the last thing Selesia, " she stuttered on the name, "needed to be worrying about right now. And Sam, too."

"I heard Rick arrived from Prince George."

"Yeah. He's staying at Selesia's with the boys for the time being. Brad is adamant that he won't return with him to Prince George, so he may stay here, under Sam's care. After all, it's not like he's a toddler. He'll be eighteen in four months."

I hesitated. "I found out some other stuff, too, Shea."

Her eyes focused on my face. "What stuff?"

"About what Brad has been up to this summer."

"Ohh." One eyebrow raised with only mild interest. "It seems such a trivial thing to have been worried about after everything that's happened. What was he doing? Hanging out with friends? Drinking?"

"No. He was with Phil."

"Yeah, I know he was with Phil. You already told me that."

"No, I mean he's been with Phil all summer. Even before Rosalie died."

"Really?" Shea said, confused. "What were they doing?"

"Fishing."

Oskar butted my arm out of the way with his thick orange head so he could crawl into my lap.

"Fishing? You mean salmon fishing? On the Wet Witch?"

I nodded. "Yes. Phil has been teaching him the ropes to become a commercial fisherman. That's what Brad has decided he wants to do for a career. Fish."

Shea was temporarily dumbfounded. "Selesia never mentioned anything about this to me."

"She didn't know. That's why he was skulking around the island. He didn't want his mom to find out what he was doing."

"Why?"

"Because he knew it would make her mad. She wanted him to attend college like Will or, at the very least, get training in something."

Shea nodded. "Yes, he's right about that. She had high hopes for both boys."

"That's not all of it, Shea."

Her eyebrows rose. "This is quite the information dump. What else is there?"

"He met Rosalie."

Shea sat quietly for a moment, letting that soak in. "I'm not surprised he didn't tell his mom about that. Selesia would have been livid."

"Rosalie visited Phil a lot. She got to know Brad pretty well. They talked about his hopes and dreams..."

181

"And?"

"And about what happened between her and his parents."

Shock stilled all movement in Shea's face. "So she was trying to rewrite history. To make herself look better."

"No, not at all. Quite the opposite."

"What did she say?"

I stroked one hand down the white speckled stripe that ran along Oskar's spine, his head tipping up to stare dreamily at my face.

"That it was her fault. All of it."

"You're kidding."

"No. She said she had taken the pain and abandonment she felt as a child and turned that into a weapon to use against the other islanders. And that Selesia was one of the people she had hurt."

"I'm stunned. Then why did she come back to Wynter?"

"To make amends."

"Amends? Like in Alcoholics Anonymous?"

"Yes, but based on Buddhist philosophy. She needed to atone for the suffering she had caused, so she returned to the island to accept responsibility for what she had done. To try and change her karma."

"Did Selesia know about this?"

"No. That's why Rosalie insisted on being a guest on Vox Pop. She realized that Selesia would have no choice but to be in the same room as her."

"Which would then give her an opportunity to apologize to Selesia," Shea murmured.

"Exactly."

"Well, that's a turn-up for the books. Except for her reconnecting with Phil, which I expected. He always saw the good in her."

"And she loved him for it. I think, in many ways, he became her surrogate father. He tried to be there as much as a grumpy, bad-tempered bachelor fisherman can be for a teenage girl."

Shea nodded. "Yes, I think so."

"But that's still not all of it, Shea."

"What else?"

"In the days before her death, Rosalie devised a plan to repay Phil for his kindness and do something for Brad."

"What?"

"She was going to buy the Wet Witch," I paused, "and give it to Brad."

"You're kidding! It may be a rusty old tub, but it's still a functioning commercial trawler. It must be worth thousands!"

"Many thousands. Enough thousands that Phil would be able to retire on the nest egg, and Brad would be able to start his salmon fishing career without any debt."

"Holy shit. I did not see that coming."

"Neither did I. It also made something else abundantly clear."

"What?"

I hesitated. This was going to be the tricky bit. The rubber hitting the road bit. A truth that I didn't want to say, and I knew Shea did not want to hear.

"It means that Brad had plenty of reasons to want to keep Rosalie alive." Her eyes connected with mine, but she stayed silent. "Which means that Brad gets taken off the suspect list." Still nothing, just two blue eyes staring steelily at me. "And that leaves only one name left on the list. I'm sorry, Shea, but we have to accept the fact that Selesia probably murdered Rosalie Morgann."

I don't know what I expected: anger, screaming, tears, or all of the above. But Shea did none of it. She closed her eyes for a moment and then stood up.

"I think you should go, Kate."

"Shea, I'm sorry. I wish I didn't have to tell you this."

She snapped back at me with an intensity I hadn't expected. "But you didn't have to tell me this, did you? What happened to the promise you made to me? That you would help me prove Selesia was innocent? Did it just vanish into thin air because things became difficult? Because you heard Lesley's plan to lock her away and agreed that was for the best?"

"C'mon Shea. I know you love Selesia like a sister, but you've got to face facts!"

Her eyes turned to me, blazingly angry. "You mean face facts like I did with you? When I believed and supported you when you said you hadn't murdered Daniel? Even when all the evidence pointed straight at you?"

My breath caught suffocatingly in my throat.

"That's what friendship is, Kate. Being there for the other person. Believing in them even when no one else will."

She turned on her heel and stormed out of the living room, her bedroom door slamming shut behind her.

I sat on the sofa, stunned, as Oskar rolled onto his back in a futile effort to get me to rub his belly.

Chapter Thirty-One

The next morning was misty and cool rather than frigid and raining, so I decided to humor Jupiter with a walk. I needed to get outside and give myself time to think about what had transpired over the previous seventy-two hours. Sam's confession, followed by Selesia's, then Brad's disappearance and the uncovering of his big secret. Then came the worst part: telling Shea. I had known she would be hurt but was stunned at the level of betrayal she felt. Who was right in this situation? Me for being practical, or her for being loyal to her friend? I had a terrible feeling that I would not win that equation. My decision was practical, but Shea's came from her heart. My attempts to reach out to her had been stymied by Lesley, who eventually had to ask me to stop calling.

"Shea needs time, Kate," she had said sadly, "to forgive both of us."

I parked the truck near the headland on the north of the island. It was a small patch of land abutting the W'en'e'win Provincial Park at the end of Millionaire's Row. The drop from the nearby mansions to the beach was gradual, but once you passed Betty and Gordon Wu's house, the headland rose to tower above the ocean below, giving walkers stunning views of the other Gulf Islands.

Jupiter bounded out the driver's side door of the truck as I opened it, propelling himself in rabbit-like bounds out onto the open stretch of woodland.

"Okay, don't go crazy, Jupiter. I know it's been a while since we've had much of a walk, but it's still pretty mucky out here. I don't want to return to the station with a different colored dog."

In the silence after I spoke, I heard a distinct cracking noise in front of me. Jupiter did as well, his bounds of joy immediately switching to a tense, rock-steady stillness. As we waited, a man emerged from the trees, dressed in a rust-colored anorak and holding a sturdy walking stick in one hand.

"Hi, Kate. Sorry. I didn't mean to startle you," Scott said, hesitating nervously at the sight of Jupiter crouched, waiting on the path in front of him. He looked well turned out in an LL Bean catalog way, as if he chose each day's wardrobe according to the activity he would be undertaking. What did theater- types call preparing a stage set? Dressing? Yes, that was an entirely appropriate term for Scott.

"It's okay, Scott." I whistled softly to Jupiter. "Come here, boy. Everything's fine."

But Jupiter refused to move, intently watching Scott walk towards me. He shakily extended one hand toward him, but Jupiter refused to be tempted. He, instead, stared with a searing intensity as Scott continued down the path toward me.

"He's a good guard dog, isn't he?" Scott said with a bright smile that couldn't entirely hide the shakiness in his voice.

"Yes, he's a rescue. They tend to be protective of the people who adopt them."

"Ahh, gratitude."

"Yeah, I guess. Something like that. I'm surprised to see you out here, Scott."

He shrugged and glanced over at the ocean. "I don't know why. It's so close to the house. I would be out here daily if we could get some decent weather."

"I know. It hardly feels like summer. You must miss the sunshine of California."

"Yes, I do, but it won't be long now."

"Oh, you're heading home to California?"

"No," he shook his head, "Vegas."

"That's right. I forgot that's where you and Jason are from originally."

"Yes. I don't know when or if Jason's going to return. He's still trying to decide whether to sell and get off the island or take some time to come to terms with everything first."

I nodded. "That makes sense. But you've decided it's time to go."

He hesitated, smiling nervously. "Yes. It was a mutual decision. After all, my work here is done."

The stark reality of this statement would have chilled me if not for the fact that his whole manner exuded an aura of peace and acceptance. Yes, it was true. His work here was done.

"That's right."

Jupiter had sidled beside me and lain down, his eyes watching Scott's every movement.

"I worked for Rosalie, not Jason. He has been good enough to let me stay these past few weeks, but it's time to move on with my life. For both of us to move on with our lives." He paused and glanced around the misty gloom. "I wish I'd gotten to see the Wynter Island she told me about. It sounded beautiful."

"Perhaps you could come back when this weather passes," I hesitated, "if it ever passes."

"No," he shook his head, "I don't think so."

"With someone in custody now for Rosalie's murder, that ties up the last loose end for you and Jason."

"Yes, I suppose."

"You suppose?" I couldn't keep the surprise from my voice.

He seemed startled by it, nodding aggressively, "Yes, no, of course."

"Which is it? Yes, or no?"

His round face blushed with a hint of cranberry across his cheeks. "It's," he paused, flustered, "well, it's yes, of course. They've got that last knot nicely tied."

"You seem doubtful, Scott."

He glanced away to look at the murky greenish-black sea, occasionally glimpsed through a semi-transparent coat of white mist. "I trust that the police know what they're doing."

"Well, it's pretty obvious, isn't it? I mean, Selesia confessed."

He said nothing, just nodded slowly.

"And even if she hadn't, no other suspects are left."

More nodding and silence.

"You don't think she did it, do you?" I couldn't keep the incredulity from my voice.

His nodding stopped, but he didn't return his gaze from the ocean. "I trust that the police know what they're doing."

"That's the second time you've said that. What do you know, Scott?"

He turned to look at me, an odd mixture of fear and exhilaration in his eyes. "I don't know anything, Kate."

"Well, then, what do you suspect?"

"Suspect?"

"Yes, suspect, Scott."

"That's an interesting word. Both the verb and the noun. You can *suspect* someone of something, thus making them a *suspect*."

I didn't say anything, just kept my eyes trained on his face.

"I, I'm not sure I agree with what you said. That there aren't any other suspects left."

"But everyone else has an iron-clad alibi: Doreen is allergic to the poison; Brad had every reason to keep Rosalie alive; and the killer injured Jason, so he couldn't possibly be the…." My voice trailed off as I noticed the musculature in his face stiffening. "You know something about Jason, don't you?"

Once again, he shook his head, glancing behind me, perhaps to see how easy it would be to escape my questioning.

"You were there the night the Glass House was burgled. You're the one who found Jason on the floor with a nasty blow to his head."

"True," he said and then stopped.

"But what?"

"I don't want to discuss this, Kate." He stepped to one side of the path to go around me, but I brazenly stepped the same way to block him.

"A good woman is sitting in jail charged with the murder of Rosalie Morgann. If there is something else you know, remember, whatever, you have to tell me."

"I, I," he paused to catch his breath. "It's hard to remember every detail from that night, Kate."

"But you told the police that you heard a shout and came running downstairs to find Jason injured on the floor, a burglar speeding away in a zodiac."

"No, I didn't. Well, I mean, I did. Kind of."

"Kind of isn't good enough, Scott. What did you actually see?"

He looked into the distance, his eyes clouded as they slipped back to remember that distant night.

"I heard Jason's shouts and ran downstairs. I found him on the floor, blood everywhere, and the sliding door from Rosalie's office to the back deck wide open. Jason was screaming at someone, telling me to run after him."

"You mean, run after the thief?"

"Yes."

"The one you heard pull away from the beach in a zodiac."

Silence. Scott's eyes met mine, but he said nothing.

"You didn't see him pull away from the beach in a zodiac, did you?"

Still silence.

"It was Jason who said that, wasn't it? That's what Jason told the police, not you."

"I couldn't hear anything because he was shouting. And it was pitch black outside. The burglar could have been leaving in a zodiac. I just couldn't...see or hear him."

I stepped out of Scott's way, opening a path for him back to the road. He lunged past me but hesitated before continuing. "Jason has been good to me since Rosalie passed. I don't want to get him in any trouble, Kate."

"Even if he killed your soulmate?"

His brows drew together in fear and consternation before he turned away abruptly and started down the path back to the Glass House.

* * *

"Knock, knock," I said through the open door of the Wynter Island RCMP

Detachment. "There are two of us here. One with four legs. Is it okay for us to come in?"

A chair scraped across the floor, followed by the clattering, tinny sounds of a dog crate door being opened and then shut.

"Okay, Kate. You two can come in. Billy is in the crate."

"Great."

The station was a one-room-fits-all place, with a couple of desks pushed up beside a wall covered in the latest local announcements. A large coffee/interview room was the only segregated space besides the washroom. Billy pressed his snuffly French bulldog snout up against the steel frame of his dog crate and whimpered softly.

I bent down to scratch his forehead in between the bars. "I know, Billy. I'm sorry, but you and Jupiter don't always get along."

Jupiter, staring in disgust at the sight of me comforting another dog, sat stolidly in the middle of the room. Was there a slight hint of superiority in his posture? Just a touch of *I'm free, haha, and you're not*?

"Have a seat," Stewart gestured to the wooden chair in front of his desk. I sat down, noticing it was unchanged since the last time I had been there, down to the Wayne Gretzky bobblehead sitting on one corner. "What's up?"

"What's up is that I wanted to talk to you about Rosalie's murder. And Selesia."

His eyes widened, and he leaned back in his chair to get more comfortable. "I'm afraid I can't get you into the Victoria jail to chat with Selesia if that's what you're thinking about. Lesley shouldn't have even let you into our cell here to talk to Sam."

I shook my head. "No. It's something else. I found something out this morning when Jupiter and I walked along the headland near W'en'e'win."

He sat back up in his seat. "What?"

I glanced around the empty room. "Where are Ian and Lesley?"

"Lesley is running a speed trap near the ferry, and Ian is off doing something with his realtor."

"His realtor? Did he find a property that he liked?"

"Yeah," Stewart nodded. "A little cottage not far from the Reserve. I think

190

he's signing the paperwork today. He'll be heading back to Victoria soon."

Of course, the sight of Ian around the island had become so commonplace that I had forgotten he wasn't a permanent member of the Wynter Island force. He had a home and another life awaiting him back at his new job in Victoria.

"I ran into Scott this morning. Scott Quillimento. Rosalie's assistant."

"Yes," he smiled, "I know who you're talking about."

"He said that he," I hesitated, trying to figure out the best way to put it, "wasn't sure about what he saw the night of the burglary."

"What do you mean?"

"He isn't positive he saw the thief. He ran downstairs, found Jason injured and screaming at someone, but never actually heard or saw the intruder himself."

"That's not what he told us."

"Yes, I know. I think it's more that he believes he saw the same thing as Jason without considering the details."

"Lying to the police is a crime," he stated.

"I don't think it was with intent, Stewart. More, that he was swept up in Jason's version of things."

Stewart mulled this over for a moment. "What are you expecting me to do with this information, Kate?"

"I don't know." I shrugged. "Go out and talk to him again?"

"Why? We have a suspect in custody who confessed to the crime. A crime for which there is motive, evidence, and witnesses to support her confession. There is no point in wasting police time going back over old ground." I started to say something, but he cut me off. "I understand you don't want to believe that Selesia did it. Both you and Shea and, well, many of us don't want to believe it." He glanced over at Lesley's empty desk, which displayed a photo of Shea on a beach holiday. "But that doesn't change the reality of the situation. It's finished, Kate. It's over. You need to accept that."

"But..."

"No," he said firmly, "It's over."

Chapter Thirty-Two

I was helping Gordon Wu learn how to use the studio camera when I was accosted—accosted is the only possible term to use here—by his wife, Betty, and her new BFF, Vera.

"No, Gordon. You have to consider it a single shot rather than an unending video stream. No one wants to watch a single camera follow anything for longer than a few minutes. That's why we do two or three camera shots. You will get your shot, say a close-up, while the other cameras offer different perspectives that the director cuts into a single episode."

"Kate, Kate," I felt a hand pulling at my sweatshirt sleeve. I looked behind me to see Betty and Vera. "We need to talk."

"Hi, sweetie," Betty reached forward to give Gordon a peck on the cheek, rubbing away the tiny smear of red lipstick with her thumb.

"What are you two doing here? I'm in the middle of a training session. We are working here. Didn't you see that the red light was on at the studio door?"

"Is that what that was?" Vera asked, surprised. "I thought you were just being festive."

"Festive? In August?"

She shrugged. "Who knows. I celebrate all religious festivals without prejudice."

"As long as they come with cake," Betty added with a wide grin.

"But that's not the point," Vera continued. "We found something last night at Crafting with Cocktails. Something you need to see. Now."

"It's alright, Kate. Go find out what they're going on about." Gordon waved me toward the studio door. "I'm just going to familiarize myself with this camera for a bit."

We exited out the closed studio door, the red light still brightly warning everyone that work was in progress.

"Festive, my foot," I grumbled as we sat down around a table.

"Okay, Vera. What's going on?"

She reached into a reusable grocery bag and pulled out a stack of photos. "This is what's going on." She placed the images on the table, equidistant between the three of us, tapping the top one with a knobby forefinger. "We found this last night."

"We were looking for, " Betty said, "some party photos. We needed party photos for the Centennial display we're making for the library."

She was lying; that was as obvious as the nose on her face. In fact, the whole squad of them was lying about Crafting with Cocktails.

Sure, Centennial display for the library. I'll bite.

"Okay, so you found a photo. Not that shocking since that's what you ladies have been busy doing. That and consuming alcoholic beverages."

"But this isn't just any photo, Kate. Look."

Vera stabbed her forefinger, on the top photo again. I pulled it closer to examine it.

It was a crowd scene from Harrow Village. Perhaps a July 1st Canada Day party, with red maple leaf bunting draped around the exterior of the Lind Hotel. People congregated on the sidewalk, the hotel patio crammed with tourists enjoying an alfresco lunch.

"It's Canada Day, I guess. A party in Harrow Village?"

"Yes, that's where our annual Canada Day parade finishes up. Everyone gets something to eat at the Lind or brings a picnic to the Village Green."

"Okay. When was this taken?"

"1996."

"How can you be so sure, Vera?"

"Bob didn't paint the patio floor another color until the spring of '97. This was the last shade before he chose that hideous eggplant. It's July of '96."

"Okay."

"Look there, in the corner. Just at the edge of the hotel. Right in that gap leading to the back entrance." Vera imperiously tapped the photo again.

I leaned closer, this time picking it up. Yes, she was right. Two people stood in the corner of the frame: a man and a young woman. It looked like he had just pulled her into the privacy of the gap, his arms draped possessively around her waist. She was smiling up at him. Her thick golden hair was falling forward, concealing a portion of her face.

Golden hair.

"That's Rosalie!"

Betty nodded. "Yes, it is. I pulled it from the stack to show Vera. I thought it was just a sweet photo of a young couple in love."

"Well," Vera corrected briskly, "at least one of them was young."

"Who is he then?" I asked.

"Frederic Stern."

"The pulp and paper billionaire?"

"Yes. The significantly older, married, pulp and paper billionaire."

"I read in the Vancouver Sun that his youngest daughter is being married this Fall," Betty said, "to the son of that television conglomerate owner, Simmons, or something like that."

"How appropriate. Old money marrying new money."

"His eldest isn't that much younger than Rose," Vera continued with distaste. "You'd think men would realize that running after young girls only makes them look sad and foolish."

"It's in their DNA," Betty offered. "The need to procreate with the most viable females available."

"Betty, you sound like Richard Attenborough," I laughed. "Like Frederic Stern is a rare buffalo breed in some nature program."

Betty smiled and shrugged. "In some ways, he is."

"Yes," Vera added, "but buffalos don't have the smackeroos to wine and dine their conquests and then take them on luxurious shopping trips."

"So that means Frederic Stern is the mystery lover."

"Yes," Vera said. "that's what it looks like."

"Okay," I placed the photo back down on the table. "It's interesting to have that little mystery about her sugar daddy solved, but what do you want me to do? The case is closed. Selesia is under arrest for Rosalie's murder. It's finished."

I pushed the thought of Scott's doubts to the back of my mind.

"Not exactly," Vera spoke slowly, allowing each vowel to lengthen.

"Not exactly how?"

Betty and Vera looked at one another. Betty spoke first. "Well, what if we found someone else with a significant motive for Rose's murder? Someone the police haven't considered yet."

"Okay. Who? Frederic Stern? But why?"

Betty glanced down at the photo. "Vera believes Rose was about 15 in this picture."

I looked at it again. It was hard to tell. "Okay."

"Only fifteen. Standing there with her incredibly wealthy, older," Betty paused and enunciated the last word, "*lover*."

I felt a hot flush of anger rush to my cheeks. Fifteen? Below the age of consent? That meant this was....

"Statutory rape," I murmured aloud.

"Yes," Vera agreed. "If this got out, it wouldn't just ruin him professionally and personally. He could end up doing some serious jail time."

"But why would it become an issue now?" I hesitated and then answered my own question. "Rosalie's autobiography. He didn't know whether she'd included anything about their relationship in her manuscript."

Vera and Betty nodded in smug unison. "Yes, but there's more. When Gwen saw this photo, she knew she couldn't hide the station benefactor's identity any longer."

I didn't even pause to think. "It's Frederic Stern, isn't it? That's why he threatened to shut us down! He couldn't take the risk of someone connecting his name with Rosalie's. Either in the past or in the present."

"Yes," Vera replied. "And I think that's a pretty good motive for murder, don't you?"

"Yes, I do."

I glanced down at my watch. It said 10:25. When was the next seaplane to

Vancouver? 11:30. If I hurried, I could just make it.

I grabbed the photo and shoved it into my hoodie pocket. "Vera, can you check on Jupiter for me? Let him out and give him some kibble at around five? The house key is under the white painted stone by the front door."

"Where are you going?" Betty asked as I prepared to dash back into the studio to apologize to Gordon for the abrupt end to his training session.

"Coal Harbor. Vancouver. I need to speak with Frederic Stern."

* * *

When I pulled up, the Salish Air seaplane was already at the dock of the aerodrome at Coho Bay marina. A frantic telephone call to their Vancouver airport base had let me book the last seat. I grabbed my bag, tossed in a couple of granola bars to tide me over, and jumped out onto the gravel parking lot. The last figure handed his small overnight bag to the pilot to stow before he climbed awkwardly up the steps and into the cramped interior.

"Dave!" I shouted, "I'm coming, too."

Dave frequently flew the route from Wynter Island to the mainland. Although pricey, the seaplane was the quickest and easiest way to get to the city. From take-off to landing, it took approximately 45 minutes. I would arrive in downtown Vancouver with plenty of time to hunt down Mr. Frederic Stern.

"Yeah, I got the text from Robert at the office. You're cutting it pretty close with this one," he said as I skidded to a stop beside him on the mildew-stained wooden dock.

"I know, but I made it."

"No bags?"

I shook my head. "Nope. I'm coming home, on the eight o'clock this evening."

"Oh, a fast trip then. Doing some shopping?"

He slammed the metal cargo door closed as I shifted my bag on my shoulder and stepped up on the small metal tread hanging off the left pontoon.

"Kind of," I answered. "A very particular kind of shopping."

I tucked my head to squeeze in through the back door. The DeHavilland Beaver sat six, with one passenger lucky enough to get the shotgun position beside the pilot. But it was a cramped six. A chance to get cozy with your fellow islanders.

"Kate? You're going into the city?"

I recognized the voice instantly. I forced a smile on my face and lifted my head. Ian was sitting next to the last empty seat, looking crisp and handsome in his neatly pressed RCMP uniform. After half an hour in these cramped conditions, he wouldn't look nearly as tidy when we landed in Vancouver.

"Hi, Ian. What a surprise!" I plunked down beside him and buckled my seatbelt. "You're going to Vancouver, not Victoria?"

"Yes, some police business downtown tomorrow, and then I'm going to take a couple of days to visit with my family."

"Oh, that's nice."

"And you? I noticed you didn't have any bags. Or," he glanced quickly up and down at my disheveled red hoodie and jeans, "um, a change of clothes. An unexpected trip?"

Dave had clambered into the pilot's seat, adjusting his headphones and buckling himself in. "Yeah, she cut it pretty close this time," he commented. "Got the last seat with only 15 minutes to spare."

Ian's black eyebrows arched in surprise, and I was afraid, suspicion. "So a very unexpected trip then."

"Yes." I tried to quickly come up with some acceptable reason for my last-minute trip. "Shopping. The Bay is having a big sale today."

"Really? I didn't take you for a shopaholic."

"Oh no," My mouth was beginning to run away with itself, but I couldn't stop it. "I love a good sale! Shopping? Fantastic!"

I slapped my lips closed and glanced up at his questioning hazel eyes. Nope, he wasn't buying any of this.

"What's going on, Kate?"

"Going on? Nothing. Nothing is going on..."

"Kate?" he cut me off. "We are going to be stuck together for the next forty-five minutes, with barely an inch to spare between us. Do you honestly believe you're going to be able to maintain this act for that long?"

I sighed. "No."

"Me neither. Tell me what's going on."

Chapter Thirty-Three

I n the brief silence, before the propeller engine started up, I told Ian about the photo of Frederic Stern and a young Rosalie canoodling in the shelter of the Lind Hotel.

When the plane engine sputtered to life, the roar made talking impossible. We switched to writing details in the Notes app on my phone, swapping the cell back and forth between us like a shuttlecock. By the time we glided onto the harbor with the skyscrapers of Vancouver looking down on us, Ian knew precisely why I had dashed to get on this flight. He had also informed me, with a solemn expression that would brook no disagreement, that he would be tagging along on my visit with Frederic Stern.

The Stern and Sons building, a twenty-story cement and glass monolith, was only a five-minute walk from the dock. The central rotating door spat dark-suited business persons out onto the rush of West Hastings St. Once inside, the space opened into a multi-level atrium with a twenty-foot statue of a bronze fir tree occupying pride of place.

"I think they're in the forestry business," I murmured in an aside to Ian, who was already drawing curious stares. He cut a dramatic figure walking across the lobby, his tall, slim build carrying his wrinkled uniform with authoritative aplomb.

"Yes, I think so," he murmured as I stepped up to the main desk.

A young woman, black hair coiled neatly behind her head in a low-slung bun, smiled perfunctorily at me. She gave Ian an extra second of attention.

"Good afternoon. What can I help you with?"

"We're here to speak with Frederic Stern," I said.

She glanced at her computer screen. "Your name, please?"

"Kate Thomas. I'm afraid we don't have an appointment."

The smile turned slightly condescending. "Mr. Stern is a very busy man. I'm afraid you'll have to make an appointment. Perhaps you could call his assistant? I have the number here if you need it."

Ian leaned closer to the receptionist. "Ms. Thomas, in her street clothes." They both gave my hoodie and jeans a quick up and down glance, "may give you the impression that this is a social call. It is not." He pulled his wallet from his pocket, brandishing his RCMP ID. "I'm sure Mr. Stern can find a few moments to talk with us."

The condescension slipped from her face to reveal a wary concern. "Of course," she leaned forward to read his name off the card, "Staff Sargent Singh. Please have a seat. Someone will be down to speak with you in a moment."

Remarkably quickly, a young man dressed in a blue three-piece suit walked across the marble floor to where we were sitting.

"Staff Sargent Singh and...?"

"Kate Thomas."

"Lovely. Please follow me."

He led us to an elevator, gesturing us inside before pushing the number for the top floor.

"Mr. Stern can give you fifteen minutes, but that's all. He has several important meetings today."

We stepped off the elevator into the hush of a wood-paneled office. The young man knocked on a closed door, and a deep voice called us in.

Frederic Stern sat behind a massive mahogany desk, its intricately carved edges and frontispiece a marvel of Victorian craftsmanship.

It must have been his grandfather's. A family heirloom.

"Hello," he said in a warm baritone.

He looked distinguished in an American capitalist kind of way, backed by a wall of windows showcasing a spectacular view of the North Shore mountains across Burrard Inlet. His grey hair was thick, brushing back off his forehead in a smooth wave. His face was shaved with sparkling precision, almost as if his personal barber had just left the room. I could smell the subtle, tangy aroma of expensive men's cologne. His grey suit jacket, lined with black pin-striped silk, hung open over his crisp white oxford shirt.

Thomas Pink, I'm sure.

"Good afternoon, Mr. Stern. My name is Kate Thomas, and this is Staff Sargent Singh of the RCMP."

"So I was told. And your reason for being here with Staff Sargent Singh is...?"

Before I could say anything, Ian spoke. "Ms. Thomas has been assisting the RCMP with our investigation."

His greying eyebrows lifted a millimeter. "Investigation? Investigation into what?"

"The death of Rosalie Morgann."

He showed no emotion, the slight tensing of the lines bracketing his mouth the only sign of concern.

"Mr. Stern," I started, "I'm the manager of CWYN, the community television station on Wynter Island."

He relaxed slightly. "Okay."

"You know CWYN, don't you?"

"Yes," he said but offered nothing further.

"I know Gwen Wynter contacted you a couple of years ago and convinced you to donate to the non-profit she was starting. You provided funds for the creation and the upkeep of the station."

He said nothing.

"That was extremely generous of you."

He raised his hands in a loose gesture of acceptance of my compliment.

"I believe your family has a long history with the island. They've owned a summer home there for quite some time. And you've spent a lot of summers on the island?"

"That's correct."

Boy, he isn't giving me anything. I'm going to have to pull it out of him bit by bit.

"We have a photo of one of those summers." I pulled out the snapshot and placed it on the desk before him. "We think this was the summer of 1996. A Canada Day party at Harrow Village."

He picked up the photo and glanced at it before placing it back down on his desk. "If you say so."

I tapped where he and Rosalie could be seen kissing in the gap beside the hotel. "And this is you with your arms around a woman named Rose Morgan. A very young Rose Morgan. She would go on to become the well-known Hollywood actress Rosalie Morgann."

The smile straightened out into a solid line of disapproval. "What are you trying to say, Ms. Thomas?"

I took a deep breath. "You were in a romantic relationship with Rose Morgan. In fact, you are the so-called 'mystery lover' the islanders talk about, the man who paid for lavish trips and secret romantic rendezvous with her."

He glanced down at the photo again for several moments. "If that is true— and I am not saying it is—wouldn't that be something between myself and Miss Morgan? It's not a matter for the police."

"It becomes a matter for the police when someone is murdered," Ian said. "Especially someone writing an autobiography that may detail their relationship with a certain wealthy businessman."

"A wealthy, *married* businessman," I added.

His smile shifted from warmth to an icy condescension. "Infidelity is not illegal. Or at least it wasn't the last time I checked."

"That's true," I said, "but it can create a lot of messy headlines, can't it? You threatened to pull CWYN's funding if we didn't tamp down the press attention regarding the station and Rosalie's death. And you have a big family event this Fall: your daughter's wedding to the heir of the Simmons television empire. It would be a shame to have that marred by some nasty personal stories in the press."

"That is why morals clauses exist, Ms. Thomas. To protect the reputation of associated businesses or individuals."

"Well, you certainly seem to have been worried about the effect Rosalie might have on your business."

"You mean the effect her *death* may have on my business. Death leaves a nasty odor. Most businesses try to avoid any contact with it."

"Statutory rape charges can cause more than a nasty smell, Mr. Stern," Ian said. "Not only can it destroy someone's reputation, but it often comes with a hefty prison sentence."

"Are you accusing me of statutory rape, Staff Sargent?" The calm exterior cracked, anger seeping through to spill across his face. But was it righteous indignation or outright fear? I couldn't tell. "You had better be certain of your facts before you do."

"We are not accusing you of anything, Mr. Stern. Merely trying to gather information." Ian's small smile showed that he, too, realized he had struck a nerve. "There is also the matter of an attempted robbery at Rosalie's house after her death. We believe it may have been someone attempting to get a copy of her autobiography. Would you happen to know anything about that?"

A spasm of something—anger, frustration, fear, fury—pulled his skin taut around his lips. Frederic pressed a button underneath his desk and rose to his feet. "This discussion is over. If you want to speak with me again, it will be under the supervision of my lawyer."

Before either of us could say another word, the door opened, and his assistant stepped inside.

"Please see them out, Pierre," he stated. "Out of the building."

With swift efficiency, Ian and I found ourselves hustled back to the elevator by two burly security guards and out to the main floor. They bookended us and marched us out the rotating door.

"I don't think he liked us, Ian."

"The feeling is mutual."

"He's slick, smart, and incredibly wealthy," I said as we were catapulted back onto the street. "Almost above the law."

Ian turned to look down traffic-clogged West Hastings St. "The key word there is almost. No one is above the law in this country."

"Except for the Queen."

"Are we going to debate the monarchy now? Or go and find ourselves some lunch?" A smile cracked across his face.

"I vote for lunch."

He pointed to a small restaurant tucked in beside another skyscraper. "Me, too. Let's try that Thai place over there. While we eat, I can get someone to check out some things about Mr. Stern for me."

"For us," I reminded him as we waited for the light to change.

"Sure, Kate. You believe whatever you want."

Chapter Thirty-Four

We were finishing up lunch when Ian's cell phone rang. Most of the tables surrounding us were unoccupied, but that didn't mean the restaurant wasn't busy. The telephone rang steadily, and we could hear the ding of texts from the kitchen. The staff was busy preparing food or handing over deliveries to a steady stream of *Uber Eats* drivers.

"Yup, got it. Yeah, what time do they want to meet?" A pause. "Yes, I can do 10:30. Thanks, Chris."

He placed the phone down on the table and leaned toward me. "We have information."

"Good. What is it?" I wiped my mouth with a napkin and leaned back to finish my beer.

"First, Mr. Frederic Stern may be a very successful businessman, but he appears to be a lousy husband."

I nodded. "Rosalie wasn't his only affair."

"No, not by a long shot. He's lucky he has such an understanding wife."

"But he was right when he said infidelity isn't a crime."

"That's true. He has no criminal record, only a handful of speeding and parking tickets. Other than that, he is pristine: a pillar of the community, a philanthropist to numerous local arts organizations, and a doting father to three daughters."

"Just a shitty husband."

"That's right."

"Not murderer material. Although, the threat of prison could make a murderer out of even the most unlikely killer."

"Yes, well, there's something on that, too. They checked Rosalie's info. Her birthday was in May. May 19th, to be exact. So that would make her ..."

"Sixteen in that photo. Unseemly but not illegal."

"Yes, which pretty much nips that whole statutory rape/murder theory in the bud. If they were intimate before that, we don't have any proof of it. I asked Chris to double-check the manuscript. There's nothing in there about Stern. She kept his secret to the grave."

"Damnit! I thought I had something! Something that might get Selesia out of jail!"

"There has been one interesting development."

"What?"

"As soon as we left the office, Stern must have been on the phone with his lawyer. The lawyer's already been on to the brass at HQ, throwing around claims of harassment, etc."

"Really?"

"Yes. But, rather unexpectedly, they want a meeting. Wednesday morning."

"Just you?"

He smiled. "Yes, just me. You don't get to be involved in every aspect of my investigations."

"But won't that bite into your time off? I mean, that's two days away."

He shrugged. "It's just one morning. I'll still have lots of time to see my family."

"Why do they want to meet with you?"

He drained the last of his beer from the bottle. "I've no idea. It will be Stern, his attorney, and the assistant, Pierre Hâvre."

"The assistant?"

"Yup."

"Huh," I gazed out the window at the rush of cars and the blur of office workers racing by on their lunch breaks. "There goes another theory."

He nodded, taking a last slurp of his lunch. "I know you think Selesia is innocent, but you've got to face facts, Kate. All the evidence points to her."

"I know. The problem is that I don't want to believe it."

"I understand. I would prefer it wasn't true, but there's nothing we can do about it."

"Why? Why do you care if Selesia is guilty or innocent?" I turned back from the front window to look at his face.

"Well," he took a long pull from his beer bottle, "I found a property on the island."

"I heard that from Stewart. Congratulations."

"Thanks. It's a cottage close to the Sydney Cliffs."

"A water view?"

"No," he shook his head sadly. I'm afraid I don't make enough to afford one of those. But it's a nice half-acre of land with a vegetable garden and flowers. And it's an easy walk to the Cliffs or a bike ride to the beach."

"Or the Reserve?" I asked.

He smiled. "Yes, it's not far from the Reserve. I had a chat with Selesia about it. I spotted her in the village one day and asked if she would be willing to answer some questions I had about the property, seeing as how she'd lived on Wynter Island her whole life."

"Was this before or after she became a suspect?"

"Well, it was before she became our primary suspect."

"That sounds like you're on shaky ground, Ian."

His face split into a wide grin. "Are you going to turn me in, Kate?"

I pretended to think about it for a moment. "This is your lucky day. I'll let you off."

"Thank you so much," he said with sarcastic flourish.

"What did Selesia have to say?"

"That she knew the property. It had been owned by an elderly couple who were moving into Assisted Living in Victoria. She said they'd taken good care of it and didn't know of any reason I shouldn't make an offer."

"And...?"

"And we had a nice chat about that side of the island. Things to see and do, you know."

"Or perhaps people to visit?" I asked.

His smile spread and then slowly slipped from his face. "That would have been nice. But I guess it wasn't meant to be."

"I'm sorry, Ian."

He shrugged. "It's okay. More fish in the sea, you know. How about you, Kate? Any romantic leads?"

I stared down at my dirty plate. What to say? Yes, Ian, as a matter of fact, there is a man I am madly in love with who barely knows that I exist—other than as a friend. Oh, and he's in the middle of a marital crisis that may take him away from both the island and me—forever.

"I've been seeing a bit of Ben Navaerez," I said.

"The vet?"

I nodded. "Yeah. He's a nice guy."

"Just a nice guy? Not something more?"

I thought about that for a moment. Was Ben ever going to be something more?

"I don't know. We'll have to wait and see."

Chapter Thirty-Five

"Hello? Anyone here?"

Jupiter and I were alone in the studio rearranging the set when a voice echoed from the office. An icy tendril of fear slipped down my spine. After all, this was the same place where a young woman had been murdered only a few weeks previously.

Jupiter raised himself from the ground and moved stealthily to my side.

No, how foolish of me. I'm not alone. I have Jupiter.

"It's okay, Jupe. Let's go see who it is," I said.

He was tight by my side as I opened the heavy studio door, my own protective shadow. Where I saw people, he saw threats. Perhaps that's what love was to him: a constant effort to protect his human.

Scott stood by the front door, dressed as immaculately as ever in grey khakis and a crimson polo shirt. He smiled at me before turning a quick, worried glance at Jupiter.

"Hi, Scott. This is an unexpected visit."

"Yes. I hope you don't mind me dropping by?"

"No, of course not. What can I help you with?"

He glanced towards the sofa seating area. "I was wondering if you had a few minutes to talk?"

"Sure." I waved him toward the sofa before pulling a chair from a neighboring table. Jupiter lay down beside me. "What's up? I know you're not here to volunteer for the station. After all, you're going to be headed south soon.".

His smile widened. "Yes, that's right. I'm booked to fly out this weekend.

Victoria to Vegas, non-stop."

"Great. You'll escape our omnipresent rain."

He nodded. "It'll be nice to wear shorts for the first time in months." He hesitated. "I wanted to talk to you about what you said the last time we met."

"You mean out on the headland?"

"Yes, that's right."

"I suppose I should apologize for blocking you on that path."

"No, no," He waved a hand to brush away my apology. "I needed someone to smack me across the face and wake me up. When I heard they'd made an arrest, I felt an immense wave of relief. It was over. All of this horror was over."

"You mean the murder and all the difficulties with the islanders."

"Yes, everything. Even all the fuss that occurred before that."

I paused to let that settle in. "So there were problems before the three of you left Los Angeles?"

He nodded. "Rosalie kept Jason and me in the dark about her plans for months. Her lawyer even bought the house here before we knew anything about it."

"Really?"

"Yes. When she finally told us, Jason was livid. He couldn't believe she'd snuck around behind his back and bought another house."

I shrugged. "I think that's a justifiable reason to feel angry."

"Yes, but it was more than just that she hadn't consulted him."

"Yes?"

Scott hesitated, weighing up his words carefully. "Her retirement affected a lot of things, more than just us leaving Los Angeles."

"No more money coming in," I stated.

"Yes. She was our Queen Bee. If she quit, how would we all survive? Our only jobs were to help her maintain production."

"Surely, she'd made enough money so that she and Jason could retire comfortably?"

He shrugged. "Yes, in real-people money. But not in Hollywood-star money. Hollywood-star money wants private planes and luxurious vacations. I don't think they had enough cash squirreled away to maintain that kind of lifestyle for the next forty years."

"Did Rosalie know this?" I asked.

"I think, as part of her Buddhist studies, she had started to move away from material stuff. She said she didn't need three cars anymore. One would do. And that life here on Wynter Island would be quiet and less expensive."

"Yes, that's true. As long as you're smart with your money."

He sighed. "But I don't think Jason wanted to give up that lifestyle."

Really? What would he have been willing to do to preserve it?

"What did Rosalie think about that?"

"She knew neither of us would be happy with her choice, but felt she had to do it."

"So you were unhappy as well?'

"Yes," he sighed. "Rosalie and I had a big fight about it. For a while there, I thought I wouldn't be joining them here."

"But the two of you were so close."

He nodded. "Yes, but we had diametrically opposed opinions on this issue. I thought it was a serious mistake for her to retire."

"Why?"

He considered that for a moment. "Hollywood is a cruel place, especially to older women. As long as they retain the illusion of youthful beauty, they're golden. But once that passes…."

"Then they're kicked to the curb."

"Correct. The smart ones retire to a low-key life, leaving behind only the flickering images of themselves in their prime. The not-so-bright ones end up doing bit parts on cop shows."

"There must be some middle ground."

"Yes. Someone with Rosalie's natural beauty could have easily worked for another ten years. But she wanted to retire and felt she could return if she changed her mind."

"And you felt she couldn't."

"No," He shook his head. "Rosalie was a beauty, not an award-winning actress. Once that beauty faded, she would be nothing to Hollywood but a familiar face who could sell Depends undergarments on late night TV."

"That's pretty harsh."

"But true," he stated forcibly. "That's why we had such a huge blow-up. I just …" The shaky passion in his voice was so intense, I thought he might cry, "couldn't bear that humiliation for her. But she wouldn't listen to me."

"But you still moved to Wynter Island with her."

"Yes, she needed me to protect her."

"Protect her? That's a strange way of putting it."

"Not protected in the physical sense. More protection in the sense of her heart, her legacy."

"And you felt that Jason wouldn't do that for her?"

"Jason had," he hesitated, "other concerns."

"Like what?"

He slipped into silence, examining the laces of his New Balance sneakers. "It hurt my feelings when you said I didn't care about who killed Rosalie," he said, his eyes connecting with mine. "I care very much. More than you will ever know."

"I wasn't trying to hurt you, Scott. I was just trying to make a point."

"I know," he nodded. "You believe your friend is innocent, don't you? The one who confessed."

I considered this for a few moments. Did I? After all, Shea and I had fought over just that. It wasn't so much that I believed she was innocent as I wanted her to be. I wanted the pain to stop for those I cared about: Shea, Sam, Brad, and Will.

"Why do you ask, Scott?"

Another long pause. "As you know, Jason and I met in Vegas. He got a lucky break and started doing semi-permanent shows at a handful of hotels on the strip. Not the big marquee stuff, but he still pulled in a nice crowd."

"And you?"

"I was more second-tier. Smaller hotels, off the strip. Did private gigs for small conventions and parties and such. An okay living. Everyone knew everyone else. Like all theater folk, there was lots of gossip."

My breath caught briefly in my chest. "You heard something about Jason,"

I stated.

He nodded. "Yeah."

"And you used that to get something from him."

"No, nothing like that. He knew I was a big fan of Rosalie, so he invited me to stop by and meet her when I was in LA."

"Because he wanted to stay in your good books," I added.

"Yes, but there was no quid pro quo. I thought it would just be a quick coffee and an autograph. And then Rosalie and I met, and it was just—"

"Fate."

"Exactly."

"She wanted me to work for her; I wanted to stay, and then—"

"Jason had to live with you in his back garden."

"That's right."

"That must have been tricky."

He shrugged. "We're both magicians. It wasn't that tough for us to make things work."

"But still. Talk about the sword of Damocles. The constant knowledge that he had to keep you happy, or you might spill the beans."

"I never threatened him, Kate. It wasn't that difficult for us to maintain the illusion. After all, that's a magician's stock in trade, isn't it? First, you figure out what you want your audience to believe they're seeing."

"And then work backward from there?"

"Yes. We rarely do anything that complicated in magic. At least nothing as complicated as people think we're doing. It's like David Copperfield and the Statue of Liberty."

"Huh?"

"Haven't you seen that trick? It's his most famous one."

"No, I don't think so."

"Really?" He almost rubbed his hands with glee at the thought of explaining it to me. "It took place at Battery Park, Manhattan, late at night. The audience was seated on an outdoor platform facing the harbor. All they could see was the Statue of Liberty in front of them, lit by massive floodlights. On either side of the stage were two large pillars ready to suspend a curtain to block their view. You got the picture?"

"Yes."

"The curtain goes down, followed by rousing classical music and a lot of magical flimflammery, all building the audience up to a fevered anticipation." He paused, his eyes twinkling. "And then the curtain drops, and, voila! The lights show that the statue has disappeared."

"Thrilling," I said. "How did he do it?"

"I don't know for sure, but I believe he slowly rotated the stage, including the pillars and the curtains."

"Clever."

"It's mainly a distraction, which is the essence of most magic tricks. Look here at this big bright ball of whatever I'm using to distract you so that you can't see my other hand manipulating your world over here in the corner."

"But you still haven't told me Jason's secret."

He hesitated. "Do you really think that they've arrested the wrong person?"

My mind returned to the previous day when I had dashed to Vancouver to interview Frederic Stern. I had been so sure it was him, but then…I didn't know what to believe anymore.

"What's the secret, Scott?"

"Jason has a daughter. She lives with her mother in Vegas. He didn't want to scare Rosalie off, so he didn't say anything about the girl when they first met. And then, before he knew it, it was too late to say anything without looking like a lying bastard. He would lose Rosalie and—"

"The nice house in the Hollywood Hills with the plunge pool and the sports car."

Scott nodded. "The gossip was that he bought the mother off. He pays handsomely for her and the girl's upkeep, and she keeps her mouth shut."

"Until Rosalie decided to quit acting and retire to Wynter Island. Which meant his cash cow would no longer be producing any milk."

"Yes, and what about those monthly payments? If he couldn't pay her anymore, would the mother talk?"

"And if she talked," I continued, "Rosalie would drop him faster than a hot potato. So he had to find a way to either keep the mother quiet or— "

CHAPTER THIRTY-FIVE

"Get Rosalie out of the picture."

Chapter Thirty-Six

For the rest of the day, I mulled over what Scott had said. It was still rumbling around in the back of my mind when I returned to the station the following morning. I turned on the space heater to warm up the office and sat in one of the comfy armchairs. Jupiter settled on another, the padded arm height perfect for resting his chin on.

So, my hunt for Rosalie's killer had brought me a complete 360-degree back to Jason again. Money. It was always about the money. Or power. Some combination of the two. What was it Vera had said weeks ago? That the theatricality of the murder meant there must be great passion involved? She was wrong. No passion here. Just a desperate need for money so that he could keep his boat of lies afloat.

"So now, what do I do, Jupe?" I murmured.

Jupiter's head lifted from the armrest, tilting sharply to one side to see if my words included those oh-so-important phrases, walk or treat. As they did not, he lowered his head and closed his eyes again.

I couldn't go and speak to Ian. He would still be in Vancouver for several more days, meeting with Frederic Stern's lawyer and then visiting his family. I could go to the RCMP detachment and speak to whoever was on duty. Either Lesley or Stewart. And tell them what? That a bit of showbiz gossip that neither Scott nor I could prove meant Jason was the killer? No, that didn't make much sense.

Perhaps there was someone else I should talk to.

I grabbed my bag and a coat, Jupiter leaping hopefully off the chair. "C'mon, Jupe. We need to go talk to Shea. If there's a chance this might prove Selesia's innocence, she needs to hear it."

I jumped in the station truck and headed out of the parking lot, pointing south towards the Wynter Island Public Library. As I pulled to a stop at Rte.97, I heard the discordant wa-wa of an ambulance siren. But not just one. There were several, and they sounded like they were coming from different parts of the island.

"I wonder if there's been an accident, Jupiter?"

A flash of red and white light zipped past me as an ambulance sped north on Rte. 97.

"Yikes. That's the Harrow Village ambulance. Something bad must have happened."

I pulled out onto the road, turning left toward the village. The sound of ambulance sirens screeched into silence. That meant the distance from where the ambulance had passed me to the accident site wasn't that great. Perhaps somewhere in Lettuceville?

We were almost at the library when I saw Shea's familiar Blue Highlander pull out of the gravel parking lot. Her tires skidded on the small stones as she put her foot down on the accelerator, kicking up a cloud of gravel and dust behind her. She passed me, her face pale with shock, her eyes not even registering my presence. I pulled to the side of the road, watching in my rearview mirror as she disappeared down Rte. 97.

Something was wrong. Terribly wrong.

I did a quick U-turn in the direction Shea had gone. It didn't take long to find where she had been headed.

The Legion sits at the end of Harrow Town, off Rte. 97, just as you head into the agricultural area of the island called Lettuceville. Its squat white building was usually quiet during the day. But not today. Both RCMP cruisers were in the lot, along with a gaggle of ambulances. Shea's Highlander and Dougie's tree service truck were also in the parking lot.

Cars had pulled off to the side of Rte. 97, locals getting out to find out what was going on. Dougie stood at the entrance to the lot, blocking everyone from entering.

I pulled in behind one of the cars and jumped out onto the tarmac.

"You stay here, Jupe," I said before running up to the crowd gathering around Dougie.

"What the hell, Dougie? My God. I never thought I'd hear of something like that happening here on Wynter," an older man in a thick flannel shirt and work pants said as I pushed toward the front. "It's a sad day, that's for sure."

"Dougie!" I shouted, drawing everyone's attention to me. "What's going on?"

His pale face, so white that the thin framework of green-blue veins across his forehead was visible, turned anguished eyes to me.

"Kate." He stopped, and for a moment, I thought he might start to cry. "There's been a shooting at the Legion."

"A what?"

I couldn't believe it. A shooting here on Wynter Island? Shootings happened in big cities, not tiny pieces of rock floating in the Pacific!

"Yes," he nodded. "I was here doing some tree trimming for Harald and Kurt. I didn't even see the kid arrive. He must have come on foot."

"What kid?"

"I don't know. I didn't recognize him. He's a teenager, not a local."

"I bet he's with that American sailboat," a middle-aged woman said. "Peter at the marina was telling me about them."

"Who are they?" the man in the flannel shirt asked.

"I'm not sure. They're from the States. Seattle or something."

"Not great weather for a sailing holiday," a voice added from the back of the crowd.

"No. The father told Peter he would be the only one leaving the boat. Peter said he saw a woman and a young man, but neither came ashore. Looked a little fishy to him."

"What happened, Dougie?" I asked.

"I had just gotten the loppers out of the truck when I heard a gunshot from inside the Legion. I ran over and looked in the front window. I saw," Dougie's hand vibrated as he raised it in the air, one finger extended beside his skull, "a kid holding a gun to Kurt's head. Harald was trying to talk to

218

him."

"What did you do?"

"I called 911. They put me right through to Lesley. She said that I wasn't to do anything. Just stay put where I was." He paused, his eyes looking sightlessly past me. "She was here within minutes and tried to sneak inside. The kid must have seen her coming because he shot just as she entered the door. He turned the gun back to Kurt's head and—"

"And what?" I whispered, afraid to say the words aloud.

"Harald threw himself toward the kid. He shot Harald and then raced out the back door."

The deep-throated whoosh-whoosh of a helicopter blade cutting through the air silenced all of us. The white med-flight helicopter with red and blue accents appeared over the trees, hovering above us like an omen of bad things to come. They didn't call in the med-flight unless someone was critical. We watched in silence as they lowered down into the parking lot. As soon as the propeller blades had slowed, two paramedics jumped out; one racing inside the building, while the second brought supplies from the back.

I could see movement inside the Legion, but we were too far away to see anything clearly. We waited, afraid to say anything and break the fragile silence that had settled over us.

Our Father, who art in heaven, hallowed be thy name. Thy Kingdom come, thy will be done, on earth as it is in heaven.

I repeated The Lord's Prayer in my head. I'm not religious, but I found comfort in saying those long-ago memorized words.

Stewart appeared at the front door, holding it open with one hand as a red blanketed basket-style stretcher was carried through. I couldn't tell who it was. Shea stood there, gripping the patient's hand. It must be Lesley. It was impossible to tell what her condition was. The paramedics loaded the stretcher into the helicopter, leaving Shea waiting outside.

Shea! Look at me! Look at me! I silently shouted, willing her to turn her head in my direction. *Please, please, look over here!*

I pushed past Dougie so she could see me better, the sudden movement catching her attention. I raised my hands over my head and framed my fingers into a heart. I wasn't sure if she understood what I was trying to say. A paramedic took her left hand to help her step into the helicopter. She paused and looked directly at me, her right hand resting over her own heart before she disappeared inside.

She saw me. She knows. No matter what happens, she knows I'm here.

The pilot slammed the doors closed and returned to the cockpit as a tear trickled down my cheek.

"But what about Harald?" Someone asked.

As the copter rose vertically and swept off to the west, I realized the obvious: the med flight could take only one patient.

That meant that either Harald was less critical than Shea, or he was....

But there was sudden movement as Stewart came outside to hold the door open again. This time the patient was on a hospital-style gurney. Kurt stood beside the stretcher.

It must be Harald! He survived! Thank God!

Not only had he survived, but his condition must be stable enough for a boat transport to the local Saanich hospital.

Our motley group waited as they loaded him into the ambulance along with Kurt. The ambulance pulled out of the parking lot, pausing beside us before turning right onto Rte. 97. I found myself next to the glass windows at the back door. I pressed my hand against one and saw a hand hover over mine from inside. It was Kurt.

The ambulance turned onto Rte. 97, leaving us behind as it disappeared toward Harrow Village.

Chapter Thirty-Seven

Rather than return to the station, I pointed the truck north toward the Reserve.

"Jupiter, I need to tell Sam what's happened," I said.

Jupiter gave me the stink-eye.

"Yes, I know. Jo-jo will be there. You will survive." I came to a stop at the crossroad just past Lettuceville. "I also need to talk to Sam about ... well, everything."

A shooting on Wynter Island. It was so ridiculous I had to keep repeating it to myself to make it real. And Lesley. Getting the med-flight meant she was in bad shape, but how bad? Survivable bad or...

I couldn't go there. Shea would not be able to recover from something like that. First Selesia and then Lesley...

"I've got to go and talk to Sam about Selesia, Jupe. Selesia and everything else that has happened during this shit storm of a summer."

I turned into the Reserve, noticing a new truck parked in Selesia's driveway. It must be Rick's. He was staying there with the boys while Selesia was in custody.

As it had started raining by the time I reached Sam's bungalow, Jupiter and I dashed to the front door. I knocked twice and waited. There was no sound besides the excited dance of Jo-jo's nails on the linoleum floor of the front hall. I knocked louder. Jo-jo began to whine softly on the other side of the door.

I glanced behind me. Sam's black Honda was sitting in the driveway. He must be there.

I knocked once again as Jo-jo snuffled along the base of the door. No Sam.

Where is he? His car's here, Jo-jo is here. Even if he's having a nap, he would have heard me banging on the door. Could there be something wrong?

I reached forward and twisted the door knob. It swiveled smoothly in my palm. I pushed it open.

"Jo-jo, stay put." I blocked her with my leg from rushing out the door as I stepped in with Jupiter and snicked the door shut behind me.

She spun around in paroxysms of happiness at our arrival.

"Yes, Jo-jo. Hello." I bent down to quickly ruffle her fur before standing back up. "Where's your master, hmm? Has something happened, Jo-jo? Is there something wrong?"

If there was, you couldn't tell from Jo-jo's joy toward her old BFF, Jupiter. She swarmed over him, smelling and licking with lusty abandon. Jupiter shot me a look that said many unspeakable things in dog-speak.

"You're fine, Jupe. I've got bigger problems to deal with."

"Sam? Are you here?" I called out. "It's Kate."

A loud thump came from the area that I assumed was his bedroom. "Sam? Is that you? Is everything okay?"

I headed down the hall towards the closed door. Why wasn't he answering me? Had he had a stroke or something? Or was it possible that someone else was in there? Had the shooter taken Sam hostage?

I was almost at the door when it suddenly opened. Just visible through the overcast morning light streaming through the bedroom window, Sam and Gwen stood, their naked bodies hastily covered with a couple of rumpled bed sheets.

Oh my God.

"Kate," Sam said rather breathlessly and then stopped, unable to say anything further.

I couldn't blame him. After all, what could you say in a situation like this?

"I'm so sorry," I stuttered, hurriedly backing up. My foot connected with Jupiter behind me, and I stumbled, half falling to the ground.

Sam instinctively leaned forward to help me, allowing his bedsheet to gape open in a dangerous manner.

"Sam," Gwen muttered, pulling him back to her with the edge of the sheet. "Be careful."

I stood back up, leaning my burning face against the wall. "I saw that the car and Jo-jo were here," I said to the wall, "and when you didn't come to the door, I thought you might have had a stroke or something," I rambled on in embarrassment. "I didn't mean to intrude."

"It's alright, Kate," Sam said.

"Yes, Kate," Gwen continued. "I hate to break it to you, but senior citizens have a sex life, too."

Sam's shoulders began to shake, and a deep chuckle burst from his mouth. Gwen began to laugh, too, her mouth splitting open as the laughter built until she was struggling to stay upright. I joined in until the three of us were almost hysterical with laughter.

"Gwen, watch your sheet," I managed to get out as our laughter subsided. She pulled it closer to her chin.

Sam smiled. "Take the dogs into the kitchen, Kate, and put the kettle on. We'll be there in a few minutes."

When they entered the kitchen, I poured the freshly boiled water into an old teapot.

"That was quite the wake-up call," Sam said as he grabbed the milk from the fridge and placed it with three mugs on the table.

I placed the teapot down on the table and sat down. "For both of us, Sam," I replied, pouring the steaming amber liquid into everyone's mugs.

"Hopefully, you're not too shocked, Kate," Gwen murmured and took a tentative sip from her mug.

"After what Sam said in this kitchen before they hauled him off to jail, not really." I stirred some milk and sugar into my tea. "Now that I've had some time to think about it, it's quite sweet."

"Sweet?" Sam grimaced, "I never thought my sex life would ever be considered 'sweet.'"

"She's not trying to dent your manhood, Sam. She meant romantic."

"Yes, you're right, Gwen. It's romantic."

Sam shrugged. "Romantic I can live with."

"How long has this," I pointed to the two of them, "been going on?"

Sam glanced toward Gwen with such adoration in his eyes that I felt my heart squeeze painfully with the sheer beauty of it. "All our lives, wouldn't you say, Gwennie?"

"Gwennie? Did you say, Gwennie?" I repeated.

"Yes, that's what I used to call her when we were young," Sam retorted.

"Should I start calling you Gwennie now?" I asked jokingly.

Gwen's expression gave me an immediate answer to that. "No, I don't think so. I'm not even sure how I feel about Sam using it. It's been such a long time since anyone called me Gwennie. But yes, on some level, Sam and I have been together our whole lives." She reached across to grip his hand on the table. "But what brought you over here, Kate? It's pretty early for a social call, isn't it?"

"Oh my God! How could I have forgotten? There's been a shooting at the Legion."

Sam's mug clattered back onto the tabletop. "What? I thought I heard sirens. A shooting! Is everyone okay?"

"No, both Lesley and Harald were shot."

"Oh my God, no," Gwen whispered. "Shea? Does she know?"

I nodded. "Yes, she went on the med-flight helicopter with Lesley to Victoria. Harald is stable enough to be transported via the ambulance zodiac."

"What on earth happened?" Gwen asked.

"We're not sure. It looks like some teenager tried to rob the Legion. Not a local, maybe someone off a sailboat. He shot Lesley as she tried to sneak in, and then, " I hesitated, "he looked like he was going to shoot Kurt in the head."

Gwen gasped.

"But you said it was Harald that was shot?" Sam asked.

"Yes, Harald threw himself at the gunman, and the kid shot him."

"He was willing to die to save Kurt's life," Gwen murmured. "He loves Kurt that much."

"Yes," I nodded. "I don't think anyone can ever call Harald a coward again."

"No," Sam said, "they can't."

"But there's more than that," I said. "I talked to Scott yesterday. Rosalie's assistant."

"I heard something about him heading back to the States," Gwen offered.

"Yes, this coming weekend. To Vegas. Both he and Scott worked there as magicians. That's where Jason met Rosalie at one of his magic shows. When they started to date, he neglected to tell her something important."

"That he was already married?" Sam offered.

"No, but close. He has a daughter with an ex-girlfriend."

"Big deal," Gwen replied. These days a lot of people come into relationships with children."

"I know, but he thought it would scare her off. Perhaps she told him she didn't want children or something. Anyway, when he got up the courage to tell her, it was too late. She wanted him to become her manager and move to LA. He couldn't take the risk of losing her, losing this new life, if she dumped him."

"Secrets," Sam muttered. "They always get you in the end."

"So what did he do?" Gwen asked.

"He cut the girl's mother a deal. He could easily afford to keep them comfortable. But the mom had to promise she wouldn't talk."

"I mean, it won't win him Father of the Year, but I don't see what it has to do with Rosalie's murder?"

"Rosalie hid from Jason and Scott until the last minute that she planned on retiring and moving to Wynter Island. Her retirement meant that, financially, things were going to change for all of them. There would be much less money coming in every month. What if Jason no longer had the funds to pay off the mother? Would she tell Rosalie? And what would Rosalie do then? Dump him? They weren't married. He would literally be out on the street without a pot to piss in."

"I see," said Sam. "So he had to find a way to either shut the mother up, or make sure that Rosalie couldn't kick him out."

"By killing her?" Gwen said. "That seems pretty extreme."

225

"There's more. Scott never saw either the burglar or the zodiac on the night the Glass House was broken into. He came downstairs to find Jason screaming and bloody, with the sliding door wide open. It was Jason who told the police about the thief."

"Thereby creating an alibi for himself by placing suspicion on this imaginary thief/murderer," Sam stated.

"Yes. One that convinced us to look elsewhere for a suspect. Like at Selesia."

"But what about the burned apothecary bottle?" Gwen asked.

"It could have easily been placed in the fire pit by Jason before he called in the tip to the police."

"This is so bloody complicated. I'm getting a headache," Gwen stated. She fumbled around in her pocket before realizing she had placed her reading glasses on the top of her head. She pulled them down onto her face and glanced at her watch. "I'm going to have to get doubles of everything so I can leave one set here, Sam."

"Fine with me."

She plopped her glasses back on the top of her head. "If not, I'm never going to be able to find my glasses when I need them."

Sam took a long sip of his tea. "It sounds like you're moving in, Gwennie. Are you trying to take advantage of my manly charms?"

Gwen stopped and gave him a sarcastic sideways glance. "That's it, Sam. You got it in one."

I took another sip of my tea, pondering a question. "Sam, Gwen's been back on the island for fifteen years. Why did you take so long to tell her how you felt?"

His eyes studied Gwen's face. "Afraid, I guess. Afraid that if I said anything, I might lose her again. I couldn't bear to lose her friendship after not seeing her for twenty-five years. If you're starving, even crumbs are better than nothing."

Even crumbs are better than nothing. That's what I was getting from Michael, the odd crumb of attention, kindness, and friendship. Was I willing to waste the next twenty-five years surviving on just that?

CHAPTER THIRTY-SEVEN

No, I need more sustenance. I want the whole bloody cake.

The image of Ben's handsome face materialized in my mind.

"So what made you take the leap now? Was it because you thought you'd end up in prison for Rosalie's murder?"

"Yes, some, but mainly it was the loons," he replied.

"Loons?"

He nodded. "Yes, the loons. You must hear them over at Steeltun Bay?"

I thought back to those still evenings where, if I was lucky, the loon's haunting call would drift in an open window at the cottage. The Hoooooo-eyyyyy call transmitted a sense of loss and loneliness that was almost visceral.

"Sometimes, if I'm lucky."

"Well, Jo-jo and I were sitting out on the front porch last week, watching as the fog swept in toward the island. And I heard them, a whole family. So close, so clear. Probably a male or female calling out to find their chicks or their mate. It was beautiful."

"So what does that have to do with Gwen?"

He smiled. "Loons are a totem, a spirit being or guardian, that symbolize the reawakening of old hopes and dreams. When you hear a loon, we say the spirit is calling you to pay attention to your dreams, especially ones that have been allowed to sink below the ocean's surface for too long."

"A second chance," Gwen murmured.

He smiled and squeezed her hand. "That's right. A second chance. As they put those handcuffs on me, I realized I might never have another opportunity to tell you the truth."

"So you did." She leaned forward, kissing him softly on the lips.

I pushed my chair back from the table. "Alright, you lovebirds, I'm going to leave you alone. I've seen enough x-rated stuff for one morning."

Chapter Thirty-Eight

Only one RCMP cruiser was still in front of the Legion as I drove past on my way back to the station. It must be Lesley's. Stewart would be on the road with his own vehicle, searching the island to try and find the shooter. The Legion looked exactly the same as it did any other morning, except for the single shattered pane of glass where a bullet had pierced it. Part of me couldn't believe that any of this had actually occurred.

What happens if there's another emergency? It will take time for support to arrive from another RCMP detachment. For right now, the rest of us are on our own.

And not just on our own. Trapped on this small island with whoever shot Harald and Lesley. The ferry service would have been stopped for security reasons, so unless the shooter had a boat of his own, we were all stuck here together.

I pulled into the station, quickly dashing through the rain with Jupiter to get inside.

Who do I call to find out how everyone is doing?

Stewart was, of course, the obvious first choice. But he was occupied with more important things than answering my questions. Shea would be in Victoria with Lesley, as would Kurt with Harald. I couldn't possibly call and bother either of them at a time like this. Ian was in Vancouver, unaware that anything had taken place.

I dropped my bag and pulled a rolling office chair from one of the editing bays. There was nothing for it but to try and distract myself with some work.

I tapped the trackpad and filled in my password. Working amidst all this turmoil seemed silly, but it was better than just pacing the floor.

I scrolled down to see how much editing was waiting to be done when the Google Chrome icon caught my eye. I clicked on it, opening up a new window. I typed YouTube into the address bar and then David Copperfield's Statue of Liberty.

Sure enough, the video was there. The scratchy VHS footage started with clanging, moody classical music as the camera spun around a brightly floodlit Statue of Liberty. Fifteen minutes of stagecraft followed, attempting to impress upon us that something vitally important was about to take place. A curtain was raised to block the statue.

In a 1980s silver bomber jacket, David Copperfield held a finger to his temple and contemplated his magical powers. A dramatic gesture from him, and the curtain fell, revealing the empty floodlit space. A helicopter hovered above as if it had watched the entire thing transpire.

I replayed it, pausing at points to go over the details. Beautiful models with blue eyeshadow and glossy lips did a lot of locking of boxes and dramatic pointing. Copperfield did a great job of appearing deeply serious, concerned at the enormity of what he was about to do. The audience—stooges or not—looked appropriately shocked.

I hadn't noticed the stage moving, but that could be selective editing. Could every single person in the audience be fake? It was possible, but it felt like cheating to me.

So was it as Scott had explained it? The dramatic movement, all the different locks, and boxes to be examined, the stirring music: was that the big, bright ball Copperfield used to distract the audience from the slight but steady movement of the stage?

Yes, it was.

I was suddenly struck by a thought. Had those same techniques been used to distract the police? By Jason?

Look here at the dramatic cut on my head, at the profuse amount of blood on the floor, at the curtains flapping frantically beside the open, sliding door. I have been attacked in my own home!

Was it all a carefully plotted illusion? From the magician living right here on Wynter Island?

My cell phone rang. I looked down at the number. It wasn't a local area code, but I answered anyway.

"Hello."

"Kate, it's Scott. I need your help. Something is up with Jason. I think he's figured out that I talked to you, about him, about his daughter, the other day. I don't know what to do! I don't feel safe."

"Then call 911, Scott. Call the police." The words were out of my mouth before I could even think.

"I've called 911, but they say no one can come to help. That something terrible has happened, and the police can't come and help. What am I supposed to do?"

My stomach plummeted to the floor. "There's been a shooting, Scott. An RCMP constable has been badly wounded and flown to Victoria. We only have one other officer on the island, and he is busy trying to track down the shooter. As crazy as it seems, they're telling you the truth. There are no police officers available on Wynter Island right now."

His voice rose an octave as the fear settled in. "I don't know what to do, Kate. He's in the other room!"

I hesitated. Was this all some kind of trick? Was Jason trying to coax me out alone to the Glass House? But no, Scott would have to be involved then. And the only way Scott would know there were no officers available on the island was if he had called 911. You can't lie about something like that. There would be a record of the call. He must be telling the truth.

"Can you escape? Just try and get out on foot?"

"No, he's sitting in the kitchen. He'd see me heading towards either of the doors."

"Then just make up an excuse. Say that you heard something out front and want to go and check."

"No, he won't fall for that. I know him, Kate. He's clever. He's going to kill me, isn't he? Just like he killed Rosalie!"

"No, Scott. Just calm down and let me think for a second."

But his words were already tripping frantically out of his mouth. "Can you come, Kate? If you ring the doorbell, I'll have an excuse to run to open the door, and then I can escape in your truck. Please! You've got to help me!"

I looked into the rain, suddenly wishing I was anywhere but Wynter Island. "Yes, Scott, I'll come. I'll leave Jupiter here at the studio. I'll be there in about twenty minutes."

* * *

The island was strangely quiet. Everyone had sensibly hunkered down as Stewart hunted through the rain and mist for the young man who had shot Lesley and Harald. I was not sensibly hunkered down. I was driving along, talking angrily to myself.

"Why am I doing this? This is crazy! Who does this? Goes out in the middle of an emergency situation to try and help a stranger? I don't owe Scott anything. What if I stumble across the shooter while I'm out here in the mist trying to find my way to the Glass House?"

I turned right at the crossroad and headed northeast toward the isolated part of the island that held Millionaire's Row.

"Just calm down. Scott is probably just panicking. And you don't know for sure that Jason is the murderer."

My mind traveled back to the YouTube video of David Copperfield's illusion. It was interesting to finally see it and understand what Scott had tried to explain to me: that magicians trade on the audience's unconscious assumptions. It reminded me of what Ian had said about the police: the most obvious explanation was usually correct. The difference was that in magic, the hoofbeats were always the unexpected: zebras, not horses.

What's the zebra, and what's the horse then in David Copperfield's Statue of Liberty trick?

That was easy. The horse was the audience's assumption that they had been sitting in their seats, immobile, the entire time. The zebra was the imperceptible movement of the stage, unfelt and totally unexpected.

231

Could Jason have applied the same techniques to Rosalie's murder? Manipulated the assumptions of the police to try and cover his tracks? Was there a horse and a zebra in her murder? But if there was, what were they?

I turned the truck onto Millionaire's Row, slowing down as my mind worked through the puzzle. I pulled off to the side, put the truck into park, and turned the engine off. I needed a few moments to think.

Well, the horse would be that she had been poisoned by her drink. It's the obvious choice. Then what's the zebra? That she had been poisoned in some other way? If that were true, why were there traces of poison found on the bottle?

I thought about it. Technically, no bottle was left, only the shards covered in 'bodily fluids.' Could they have been contaminated after she was poisoned by the vomit and blood rather than before? But then, how was she poisoned in the first place?

An image of her reapplying her lipstick after arriving at the station floated into my memory. Why had she done that? It hadn't been long since she'd applied her makeup at the Glass House. Was it because she had rubbed some off on the lip of the bottle? And then consumed it?

A chill washed over me.

Big, bright ball. That's what Scott had said. Look at this big, bright ball so that you can't see my other hand manipulating your world over here in the corner.

My breath caught in my throat as the domino pieces began to fall forward, each triggering the next.

Was that what this was? Were all of the clues nothing but distractions?

Look here! Look at this bottle! The drink must have been poisoned! Why else would someone go to the bother of cutting the power to the General Store CCTV, except to conceal the killer tampering with the bottle? It must be the drink. Follow its path to the killer!

But that path wouldn't lead to the killer, because the poison had never been in the bottle in the first place.

It had been in her lipstick. In the tube she had used while doing her makeup at home, not the one that Stewart had immediately taken as evidence at the station. She didn't need to bring the other lipstick, because Jason said she had a copy of her favorite color in every bag. The lipstick at home could then have been easily removed and replaced, leaving no trace of poison anywhere in the home.

But that still left me with one major question: who had exchanged the poisoned lipstick for her regular one and then removed it after her death? It must be Jason. He was the only one with something to gain by Rosalie's death. Scott's assumption was correct. Jason *was* the killer.

What am I doing here? Am I crazy? I can't do this on my own. I need to find someone, anyone, and get some help for Scott, and try and get Jason into custody.

I reached down to turn the key in the ignition when a sharp tap sounded on the driver's side window.

I raised my eyes to see Scott standing there, smiling. His gaze followed my hand to the keys, and he raised a gun on the other side of the glass level with my head.

"I don't think so, Kate. After all, you've driven all the way over here. Don't you think we should have a little visit first?"

Chapter Thirty-Nine

My hand hovered halfway toward the ignition. If I moved quickly enough, could I get the truck started and moving before he could do anything?

Another tap on the window, this time with the gun barrel.

"I wouldn't do that if I were you, Kate. You'll be dead before you can put it into Drive."

I retracted my hand slowly to my lap and turned to face him.

"Smart move." He opened the driver's side door and motioned me to the passenger seat. "It's better if I drive."

He started the truck and then headed back toward the Glass House.

"I couldn't understand what was taking you so long, so I decided to head out and have a look. I was worried that the shooter might have found you." His smile was an odd mixture of concern and malice. "And then I spotted the truck parked down here."

"You never called 911, did you?" I tried to keep my voice as steady as possible. No use in letting him see how scared I was. This was a high-stakes poker game for the biggest pot imaginable: my life.

"Afraid not."

"Then how did you know about the shooting? That we were down to only one RCMP officer?"

"Through social media, of course! How else does one find out anything these days?"

To my surprise, he drove past the Glass House and Betty and Gordon Wu's oceanfront home.

"Rose's drink was never poisoned, was it, Scott? You put the poison in something else, something you could conceal from the police."

He smiled but said nothing.

"So when you cut the power to the security system at the General Store, you weren't trying to hide footage of someone placing a poisoned bottle in the cooler. You only wanted to make it appear that way."

He nodded. "It's all part of the trick, Kate. The rats gnawing at the wiring was an unexpected bonus. It added a nice touch." He pulled into the makeshift parking area at the end of the street abutting the walking paths at the W'en'e'win Provincial Park. "Out we get."

"Here? The park?"

"Yes, and there's no point in screaming or trying to get anyone's attention. The only people who could hear you would be the Wu's, and they've already headed out to do their weekly shopping."

"And Jason?"

"Well, Jason is a bit busy with other things at the moment. C'mon, out you get."

He nudged my shoulder with the barrel of the gun. I opened the passenger door and clambered out, my heart beating a frantic tattoo in my chest.

Run! Now!

But where? Scott would have a clear shot at me no matter which direction I headed.

Stay calm. Play the long game. Stay alive as long as you can. Buy time. Something, someone, may come. There was still Jason. Where was he?

"Off you go," Scott gestured toward the forest with his gun, and I started walking.

"You had me fooled, Scott. I thought it was Jason. But that's what you wanted, wasn't it?"

"Pretty much. Take the path to the right, Kate."

We headed deeper into the woods, the path muddy from so much rain. It was silent, not a bird singing or animal rustling, and certainly no other people. Just silence and that thick coating of damp mist that smothered all sound.

"Where are we going, Scott?"

"You'll see soon enough."

We continued deeper into the forest. I couldn't figure out our direction because the bloody sun wasn't shining. Would I ever see the sun again?

And then, the trees began to thin a bit, and I could hear the ocean's thrumming. We must be getting close to the shore. We stepped into a small clearing, and any hopes I had that Jason might save me shriveled up and died.

He was lying on the forest floor, his mouth gagged and his hands tied behind his back. I thought he was already dead until his head lifted slightly, his bleary hazel eyes gazing at me with a mixture of confusion and fear.

"Go and sit beside him, Kate."

I sat down on the mucky leaves and branches that carpeted the forest floor. I reached forward and pulled the gag out of Jason's mouth.

"Hey, I didn't say you could do that," Scott snapped at me.

"Who's going to hear him, Scott? You said that no one would hear me if I cried out. What difference does it make?"

Scott weighed that up for a few moments before curtly nodding his head. "Fine. He gets the chance to say something if he wants to. Not like it's going to do him any good."

"What are you planning?" I asked.

He smiled, a self-satisfied smirk. "It's pretty simple, really. You confronted Jason with your suspicions, which I'm guessing you've already shared with others on the island?"

I immediately thought of what I'd said to Gwen and Sam that morning. *Damnit!*

When I said nothing, he nodded. "Just as I thought. When he realizes that you've figured everything out, he shoots you in a panic and then, realizing he has no way to escape, kills himself."

"With rope burns on his wrists and cuts on his face?" I asked.

"You're quite observant, Kate. But once again, it's all about appearances. Your body will be found here. Jason's will be found, eventually, in the ocean. That's what happens when you kill yourself on a beach. You get washed out

236

to sea."

"But why kill me? Wouldn't I have been more useful to you alive, telling the police that Jason was the murderer?"

He waggled his head from side to side, as if weighing up some trivial decision. "I did consider it. That you'd be so desperate to get your friend out of jail, you'd believe anything I'd say about Jason. But I realized you're too much of a risk. You might have supported my story, or you might have stumbled on to the truth. I couldn't be sure. You see, you are the worst kind of audience member."

"Lovely. A last insult before I die."

"The best audience members want to believe. They want you to shock and awe them, to convince them that the impossible is truly possible. They're quite easy to pick out of a crowd, actually. They have a malleable, almost childlike, quality to them."

"It's been a long time since anyone called me childlike."

"Exactly. You're the audience member who steadfastly refuses to believe. Even if you want the trick to be true, you can't let it go until reason has won out. You're a journalist and an investigator, digging and digging until you get the whole story. So, I had to make sure you didn't somehow throw a wrench into the works. After all, once you've killed one person, the total number no longer matters."

"You bastard!" The words croaked from Jason's mouth. The red gashes in the corners of his mouth, from where the gag had cut in, dripping blood onto his chin.

"I'm the bastard? Really? You let Rosalie come here. This was all your fault."

"Jason let Rosalie come here?" I repeated. "I thought both of you wanted her to stay in LA?"

Jason shook his head, the effort causing his head to drop back onto the forest floor.

"No," he croaked out. "Scott didn't want her to come. He was the one who tried to convince her, to convince both of us, to stay in LA. He wanted the..." he coughed, "...money."

Scott stepped closer, his outstretched arm shaking with rage as he pointed the gun at Jason's head. "It was never about the money!" His finger hovered over the trigger, trembling so badly I thought he might accidentally shoot Jason.

"Calm down, Scott," I whispered. "What was it about then? What was all of this about?'

"It was always about Rosalie," he stated, his shaking hand still pointing the gun toward Jason. "Always about her."

"I don't understand," I said, glancing around to try and get some sense of where we were in the park. It looked like we were near the headland on the island's northern side. Besides the few residents of Millionaire's Row, there were no homes or people for miles. But there were still lots of trees, trees that might provide me a little cover if I wanted to attempt an escape.

Just keep him calm and talking for as long as you can.

"He wouldn't listen to me when I told him what retirement would do to Rosalie. He said he wanted to keep her happy now, not think about the future." Scott laughed derisively. "As if he would ever think about the future. That was my job. To be the adult in this group, the practical one."

"Adult," Jason whispered hoarsely, "More like an asshole."

"I'm still not getting it," I cut in, determined to try and keep Jason alive, even if he no longer seemed to care. "So you were being the practical one in the group."

"Yes. Like I told you, they'd have run out of money within a decade. Would he have earned any? As a washed-up magician? I don't think so. He'd force Rosalie back to Hollywood to try and raise some cash."

"And you felt she would be humiliated, a has-been," I said.

"Yes. I had to stop that, stop them. For Rosalie's sake."

"And so you killed her? That doesn't make any sense, Scott. I thought you loved her?"

The gun shifted toward me, the butt of it waving madly in the air. "I did love her. I do love her. That's why I did what I did."

"You poisoned her live on television."

"I gave her immortality. Rosalie will never age, will never become

238

irrelevant or a joke. She will always be remembered as a beautiful star, preserved in amber like Marilyn or Diana. Forever thirty-six and stunning. An icon."

"Holy shit," I whispered, "you honestly believe that, don't you?"

"Yes, I do. Because it's the truth. She didn't die in some trailer park at 70, washed up, forgotten, alone. She died on camera for the world to see. So that everyone would remember Rosalie Morgann."

"You mean Rose Morgan."

"No, that was the girl from Wynter Island. She disappeared a long time ago. I mean Rosalie Morgann, the star."

I glanced around at the still forest surrounding us. No, that wasn't true. She had wanted to return to Wynter Island for many reasons, none of which had anything to do with her being a star. She wanted to ask forgiveness for her past transgressions, repay Phil for his kindness toward her, and try to find the young girl whose life suddenly stopped on the day of her mother's death.

She wanted to find Rose Morgan, not Rosalie Morgann.

I stood up suddenly, Scott's gun following me. "You're wrong, Scott. You're wrong about everything!" My voice rose to a hysterical screech as I tried to look as unhinged as possible. I could see out of the corner of my eye that Jason was struggling to sit up. "How could you do that to her? That wasn't love! You didn't love her! You killed her!"

I slammed my hand against a tree in anger, trying to spot the best path toward the shore as I did so. I knew there was a drop-off to the beach below, but I wasn't sure how far the drop was. I stamped a few feet closer, still keeping eye contact with Scott. I had to get him over there, to the edge. It was the only hope I had other than running, and my luck wouldn't last long enough for me to get out of the park alive.

Look at me, Scott. Don't look at where I'm going. Don't think about what I may be doing. Look at this big, bright ball so that you can't see my other hand manipulating your world over here in the corner.

"You ruined everything! She would have had a new start and a new life here, but you wouldn't let her, would you? No, you knew better than everyone else, didn't you?" I stumbled backward towards another tree, grabbing its branches in a frenzy. "And in the process, you destroyed the station. The station I worked so hard to get running. And you ruined Selesia's life. You didn't care about anyone but yourself!"

I took another step backward, praying I didn't stumble over a fallen log. The only way this would work was if it looked utterly unplanned, unscripted.

Scott took one step and then another, unconsciously following me, his brow furrowing as he tried to comprehend what I was shouting at him.

"Stop it! That's not true!"

I took a massive step backward, feeling my sneaker land solidly on flat soil. I raised my voice even louder, its sharp edges scratching against the silence of the sky. "It is true, Scott. You cared about what Rosalie's reputation meant to you, not what might happen to her. This is all about you, isn't it? You couldn't make it in Vegas, so you decided to attach yourself to her success and bask in her reflected glory."

"You bitch!" Scott shouted, beginning to run toward me with the gun outstretched. "How dare you say that! Those are lies! Lies! I loved Rosalie!"

I glanced over my shoulder. I was still a good twelve feet from the edge. Not close enough to accomplish anything. Scott ran toward me, his face lit with a brutal, unforgiving wrath.

My trick hadn't worked. I had pushed too far and now had to pay the price. I closed my eyes. I didn't want to see the bullet coming. Just blackness and then nothing.

I felt him stop beside me, the smell of sweat creeping from his body to envelop mine. "You bitch," he whispered in my ear as the sound of a gun being cocked clicked beside my head.

I took a deep breath.

It'll just be a moment. Just a moment, and then it will all be over.

Daniel's face and then Michael's washed before me as a single tear trickled down my cheek.

I will miss you, Jupiter.

A pause, and then I felt a rush of wind, of motion, sweep beside me. I opened my eyes, swiveling on my feet to catch the briefest instant of Jason barrelling straight towards the edge like a steam train, pushing Scott forward with the force of his body. There was a sudden whoosh of dirt, water, and stones cascading away as the sodden ground collapsed beneath their feet, plummeting them down toward the ocean.

Chapter Forty

Screams filled the air as they fell, stopping abruptly as their bodies smashed onto the beach below. Then silence. I stood for a moment, unable to move, my limbs vibrating with delayed shock.

I'm alive. I'm still alive.

I slowly made my way to the crumbling headland, taking care to hold on to the trunk of a tree as I peered over the edge. Approximately twenty feet below, two bodies lay spread-eagled on the rocky shore. Jason was face down, a growing pool of crimson spreading over the mossy stones beside his head. He had landed face first, unable to break his fall because his hands were still tied behind his back. He was dead. I was sure of it.

Scott, lying on his back beside him, suddenly moved, one hand clawing at the stones where his gun had landed. His other hand held a ripped-out tree root, most likely grabbed on his way down to slow his fall. It must have worked because his eyes flickered and then opened. He was alive.

A wave of fury engulfed me.

He's alive! He killed Rosalie and Jason, and he survived!

A groan escaped his lips and traveled up to where I was standing. Was he trying to talk?

"Kate."

Can he see me? Does he realize I'm here? Does he expect my help after all that he's done?

"Kate." Again, the single word hung in the air.

"You bastard!" I suddenly screamed, "Jason's dead! Rosalie's dead! All because of you and your delusions of grandeur! I should just leave you here to die on the beach!"

The words were out of my mouth before I could even process what I was saying. Did I mean it? Could I just walk away and allow him to bleed out on this isolated beach? No one would ever need to know.

"Kate."

"You don't deserve my compassion!"

My shout echoed through the forest.

"You're right," he said weakly. "Go."

My breath came in deep gusts of anger mixed with shock and adrenalin. There, he had said it. Go. Leave him there to die. I couldn't be held responsible. That's what he wanted.

And yet I didn't move. I shifted one foot, and a stone rolled down the headland towards the beach.

"Are you still there?"

Go! Just go! He deserves it! Leave him to die!

And still, I didn't move. I stepped back from the edge, swallowing a few times to try and calm myself.

He may deserve to die, but I don't deserve to carry the burden of that decision with me for the rest of my life.

"I'm going for help, Scott."

* * *

I made it to Betty and Gordon's house, managing to bang on the front door before collapsing on their porch. Betty's round face blanched as she opened the door and saw me on the ground. She shouted something in Cantonese, and Gordon came running. I babbled out that Jason was dead and Scott badly injured, that the edge of the headland had given way beneath them. Gordon gasped and ran toward the beach.

Within twenty minutes, an RCMP cruiser, lights, and sirens going, tore down the street and pulled into Betty's driveway. A constable I didn't recognize clambered out and walked over to us. Gordon must have called 911 from his cell phone.

"Are you Kate Thomas?"

I nodded. He reached into his back pocket to pull out his portable radio. "Yes, I've got her." He glanced over at me before continuing to speak into the handheld radio. "She appears to be alright. Upset but alright. Yes, yes, I'll hand her the radio." He thrust the radio out to me. I took it and gingerly brought it up to my face.

"Kate? Kate, is that you?"

It was Ian's voice.

"Yes, Ian. It's me," Exhaustion and grief bubbled up in my throat. "I'm okay. But Jason is dead. And Scott is badly injured. Scott killed Rosalie, Ian. He's the murderer. He poisoned her with her lipstick, I think. I'm not sure."

"I'm sorry I wasn't there, Kate. I've been busy with Frederic Stern."

"Frederic Stern?"

"It's too long a story to go into now, but his assistant confessed that he set up the burglary at the Glass House. He wanted to get a copy of the autobiography to see how damaging it might be to Stern."

"You mean Stern asked him to do that."

"No, he's taking the fall for his boss. Probably for a nice chunk of change and a light tap on the wrist sentencing-wise."

"So someone did break into the Glass House and hit Jason over the head."

"Exactly. We can talk it all over when I get there. I'm catching the three p.m. flight. I'll meet you at the detachment."

"Okay. But Ian, how is Lesley doing?"

Static came over the radio for a moment before he spoke. "She's still in surgery. Internal bleeding. We won't know anything until she's out of the OR."

"Oh, okay. Bye."

I handed the radio back to the constable as Betty wrapped her arms around me.

* * *

Betty accompanied me to the station after calling Gwen and Vera and telling them to meet us there. Vera brought some food and an herbal tea that was supposed to treat shock. It tasted like boiled grass.

At the station, we were able to get some news from the scurrying ant-like troop of RCMP officers who had descended on the island. Stewart had caught the shooter near Hope Bay. A gun still clenched in his hands as he tried to untie and steal a sailboat from the dock. It turned out that he was the teenage son of a Seattle couple who had dragged him onto their boat in an attempt to detox him in the middle of the Pacific.

The kid had burned through rehab program after rehab program, leaving his parents feeling they had no other choice to save his life. After making sure to dose his parents' evening drinks with a sleeping pill, he had woken early that morning, stolen his father's gun, and headed on shore to try and find some money and a way off the island. His first stop had been the Legion.

The shooter had, apparently, been taken by helicopter to Victoria directly after his arrest. They didn't even allow Stewart to book and jail him. I shouldn't have been surprised. The young man had shot and critically injured an RCMP constable. They were not going to mess around with that one.

The minister had started a prayer circle on the island's Facebook page. The four of us made a rather unusual group as we closed our eyes and held hands around the coffee table in the station interview room. I'm sure the RCMP officers walking by were perplexed as to whether we were praying or holding a séance. Perhaps it was a bit of both.

Stewart finally stumbled into the station with Ian beside him. Ian's lanky body tensed as if awaiting Stewart's collapse at any moment. Stewart's face was haggard, dirt and dried blood staining his uniform. I ran out of the interview room, stopping him with one hand.

"Stewart, are you okay?"

He paused to look over at me, his brow crinkling in confusion. It was as if he didn't understand the question or know what okay meant anymore.

"He's fine, Kate. Just exhausted. Let's get him to a seat."

I held his other arm and helped him over to his desk. He sat down with a slow thud of bone-weary exhaustion.

"Is there any news?" I asked, afraid of what the answer might be. Was it bad news? Was that the reason for Stewart's demeanor? Had he already heard how Lesley's surgery had turned out?

Oh no, not Lesley. Please, not Lesley.

Ian glanced over at me, his sharp eyes assessing, most likely correctly, what was racing through my mind. He cracked a small smile.

"Lesley's out of surgery. It looks like she's going to make it."

* * *

I parked the truck in front of the small row of A-frame vacation cottages on the island's eastern side. They looked like they had been built sometime in the seventies, with their weathered cedar siding, but had been well-maintained over the years. They had a lovely ocean view, a fantastic advertising point in typical summer weather. Unfortunately, this morning they were adorned in a cloak of fog.

The previous evening, utterly exhausted, I had texted Dougie before going to bed. I needed him to find out something for me: where Jack Donahue was staying on Wynter Island. It had not taken him long to track down the address for me.

I started up the driveway, spotting an older Hyundai with a license plate that read GSP RUS.

"Christ almighty," I muttered, stopping at the front door.

It had been a difficult twenty-four hours. I had only gotten a few hours of scattered sleep as my mind replayed everything that had transpired. Sensing my restlessness, Jupiter had curled up beside me. I turned on one side and spooned against him, my head resting on his furry spine as I finally slept.

"Here goes nothing," I murmured and knocked on the door.

The silence was followed by the rustling of footsteps headed toward the door. The weathered door opened a crack, Jack's unshaven face peering out at me. He opened the door wider, his face split in an unwelcoming grimace.

"What are you doing here?"

"May I come in?" I asked.

He hesitated. I knew he wanted to slam the door in my face, but I could tell he also wanted to know what had brought me there. He finally opened the door wider, and I stepped in.

The room had the funk of a teenage boy's bedroom. Warm, fetid with the orange cheesiness of day-old Cheetos, dirty clothes heaped onto a small chair, ready to be washed. He brushed the clothes off the chair and gestured me toward it.

"No, thanks. I'll stand."

"Okay." His forehead bunched up in confusion. "What are you doing here? Come to crow about the fact you helped find Rosalie's murderer?"

I examined his face for a moment. It still had some of the soft edges of youth but had corroded and aged, probably due to his smoking and drug use. I could only faintly see the John Donahue I had known in college. The John Donahue I had unknowingly, unthinkingly, hurt.

"No, I haven't, and I'm not going to waste time explaining to you again that I am not the monster you've made me out to be."

"Huh," he sneered and started to speak, but I cut him off with a wave of one hand.

"No, it's time for you to listen to me." I reached into my coat pocket and pulled out the folded piece of paper I had printed just before leaving the cottage that morning. I handed it to him, and he took it carefully, as if poison might somehow leach off it onto his skin. "That is a signed statement from me detailing what happened yesterday, including Scott's confession. The whole story. There are two copies: one for you, the other has been emailed to a CBC Vancouver reporter, Cindy Hu. I will be releasing a full statement to the media tomorrow morning. For the next 24 hours, this will be yours and Cindy's exclusive."

He unfolded the paper and scanned the text I had written. He looked back up, directly into my eyes. The anger in his eyes quickly dashed any faint hope I had that he might be pleased.

"So you think this will buy me off? Is that it?"

I shook my head. "No. In fact, how you feel about it isn't the point. I hate to break it to you, Jack, but not everything is about you."

He snorted but said nothing.

"I can't control what you do, how you feel, whether you want to forgive me or hold a grudge. All I can control is what I do, what choices I make."

"Like the choice you made ten years ago?"

I sighed. "Yes, like the choice I made ten years ago. I was wrong. I should have taken the time to find out where that story came from, and I'm sorry about that. But all I can do now is try and make amends."

I thought of Rosalie. She must have known that it would be a long and challenging path back to forgiveness from the islanders. Over time, some may have understood that she had grown and changed. But for many, it may have been too little, too late. And yet she still returned. Because, as I now understood, forgiveness wasn't necessarily her destination. Understanding her own failings and accepting responsibility for any harm she'd done was the point.

"So, as far as I'm concerned, we're even."

He laughed out loud, a horrible, brittle sound. "Really?"

I didn't join in. "Yes, really. In my heart, it's over. What you choose to believe is up to you." I turned and headed for the door. I stopped as my hand reached the knob and turned to look back at him in his filthy t-shirt and wrinkled jeans. "Can you hear the loons here, Jack?"

"The loons? You mean, the birds?'

"Yes, the birds."

"What the hell does that have to do with anything?"

I smiled. "You've just been given a second chance, Jack, to move past your anger and get to a better place in your life. Take that exclusive and run with it. Use it to get the attention of a bigger, better employer. But know that whatever you choose, it's on your shoulders now."

I stepped outside, pulling the door shut behind me. I could hear muffled swearing as he gasped with anger. I didn't care.

The fog appeared to be thinning. As I headed to the truck, I realized the fog's edge burned, almost shimmered, with a golden light. I stopped in astonishment as a ray broke through, like the finger of God, to dab the ocean with a single pool of light. Was it the sun?

Yes, it's the sun.

Epilogue

4 weeks later, Lions Club Fall Salmon BBQ

The school playing fields smelled like salmon. Barbequed salmon, to be precise. Islanders in yellow Lions Club t-shirts manned two makeshift trough BBQs, the first sizzling rosy-pink slabs of salmon over the coals. The next held what looked to be hamburgers and hot dogs, unopened plastic bags of hot dog and hamburger buns stacked into teetering piles waiting to be filled. A long folding table covered with a white cloth was placed beside them, a mix of salads laid out in a mismatched assortment of Tupperware and mixing bowls, along with paper plates and plastic cutlery.

"Hey, Kate," Kurt called out, waving me towards a table with the Legion banner hanging above it.

"Kurt, how are you doing?" I asked. "How's Harald?"

"He's doing okay. He's resting now. He'll be over later for some food."

"How's his shoulder healing?"

The bullet the drug addict had shot that day had luckily missed Harald's head and instead sliced into his upper arm. The resulting fracture had needed surgery to screw the bones together as well as remove the bullet, but he was going to be okay.

"It's doing better. He's getting physio to try and help him get some movement back. Because the bone was shattered, his right arm will always be weaker than his left."

I nodded. It was a big price to pay, especially for someone who was right-handed, but one I knew Harald wouldn't regret. Kurt was alive. He didn't need anything more than that.

"Would you like a cold drink? With your BBQ ticket, you get a Coke or a Sprite. We also have cold beer for an extra donation."

"I'll have a Sprite, I think, Kurt." He handed me the dripping tin, and I popped it open with a low hiss. "I'll stop by and see you again when Harald arrives, okay?"

He nodded. "Sure. Sounds good to me."

Gwen and Sam were standing hand in hand, chatting within a group. I could see Selesia, Brad, and Phil there. Also, Ian dressed casually in jeans and a t-shirt.

Oh, that's nice. I'm glad he was able to make it.

"Hi, everyone," I said as I walked up to them.

"Hi Kate," numerous voices replied.

"We were just talking to Phil about what he's going to do with all his money," Gwen said.

We had all been stunned to find out in those first horrible days after Jason's death that Rosalie had placed an unusual covenant in her will. For her succession requirement, she had specified that the beneficiary must survive until the process was completed to receive the estate. As Jason died before that happened, the estate was to have been split between Scott and Phil. As Scott had pleaded guilty to Rosalie's death, he was banned from inheriting anything from her estate. That meant everything, including the Glass House, had been passed down to Phil. Fisherman Phil was now the wealthiest individual living on Wynter Island.

"Oh, is he giving some to the TV station?" I asked teasingly. As Phil's brows furrowed in consternation, I quickly added. "That's just a joke, Phil. Don't get upset."

"Well, you know, it's not as if I don't already have my own charity case over here." He nudged Brad playfully with his elbow. "He's getting a commercial fishing trawler for nothing."

"Yes, I heard that you're busy getting ready to take over the Wet Witch, Brad."

He nodded happily. "Yeah, lots of paperwork and paying for my commercial fishing license is all that's left. Then I should be ready to go."

"I'll crew for him the first year, just to keep an eye on things," Phil added, his face splitting into a wide smile.

This was a new Phil, one whose cares seemed to have lifted off his gnarled frame. It was nice to see. Perhaps he had found in Brad what he had lost in Rose.

"Hi everyone," Shea walked up to join us. "Has anyone seen Lesley?"

Gwen dropped Sam's hand and glanced hurriedly at her wristwatch. "Oh, that reminds me of something. I'll be right back," and she dashed over to where the school band was setting up.

"Well, that was sudden," Shea said. "I still don't know where Lesley is."

Shea looked almost back to her old self, although she still needed to regain some of the weight she'd lost during that first stressful week Lesley was in hospital. Lesley was still on medical leave. One bullet had entered her abdomen, hitting her liver and causing internal bleeding. The other had hit her in the right thigh, causing some vascular problems and a broken thigh bone. But she was home and able, in a wheelchair, to get around the farmhouse and out into the community.

"I don't know how I lost her. I mean, she's in a wheelchair. It's not like she's incredibly mobile."

"I'm sure she's around here somewhere," I answered.

"Oh, there she is," Shea said, pointing to where Lesley was being wheeled into the middle of the field. "She's with Vera. Oh, and Betty, Doreen, and Gwen."

Vera was handling the wheelchair while Doreen, Betty, and Gwen walked alongside, holding three large white sheets of cardboard.

"What the hell?" Shea murmured and started toward them when Sam firmly but kindly pulled her back.

"You just need to wait here for a second," he said with a twinkle in his eye.

"What?" Shea looked over at me.

I shrugged. I was as confused as she was.

Suddenly, the rag tag school band, made up of a kid with a trumpet, one

252

on drums, and a young man with a small electronic piano, started playing. A young girl, maybe 13 or so, stepped out on to the field holding a wireless microphone in one hand and began to sing

"It had to be you, it had to be you
I wandered around, and finally found, somebody who
Could make me be true, could make me be blue
And even be glad just to be sad, thinking of you..."

As the first verses drifted off on the ocean air, first Betty, then Gwen, and Doreen flipped over their pieces of cardboard. On the first, the word *Will* had been decoupaged on the cardboard, with what appeared to be photos of Wynter Island.

Of course! That's what Crafting with Cocktails has been working on!

The second had the word *You*, and then the third and final photo montage said, *Marry Me?*

"Some others I've seen might never be mean
Might never be cross or try to be boss
But they wouldn't do..."

Shea didn't move. One hand covered her mouth, which was agape in shock. Sam leaned forward and gave her a gentle push.

"Out you go. You can't expect her to come to you now, can you?"

"For nobody else gave me a thrill
With all your faults, I love you still
It had to be you, wonderful you, it had to be you..."

I watched, my heart filled with joy for them, as Shea unsteadily walked out on to the field, stopping to kneel beside Lesley's wheelchair. There was a moment of silence. And then they embraced and kissed, Shea being careful not to re-injure Lesley. Lesley produced a small box from the side of the wheelchair and removed a ring which she placed on Shea's finger.

"Yes!" The shouts rang out across the school field, drawing the Lions Club volunteers away from their cooking stations. "Yay! Three Cheers for Lesley and Shea! Hip Hip Hooray! Hip Hip Hooray! Hip Hip Hooray!"

I could see Kurt a few feet down from me, wiping a tear from his cheek. After this difficult summer, this moment held a special meaning for so many of us.

"It's a handmade ring designed by Lesley," Sam said to me. "Made by that artist out on the eastern side of the island. Gretchen Steubbs is her name, I think."

I smiled and nodded. Yes, the infamous Gretchen Steubbs. Not woman-stealer, but instead artisan engagement ring-maker.

A few feet down in the other direction, I spotted Michael and Anna, swept up in the romance of the moment, kissing.

I guess they're going to give it another try.

My heart squeezed painfully in my chest. Michael and Anna were still together. I had to accept that and move on.

"Kate?"

I felt a hand on my shoulder and turned to see Ben standing beside me, one hand holding Lucy on a long lead. His smile as he gazed down at me was so warm, so sweet, that I reached both hands around his neck and kissed him. Not a little peck, but a real honest to goodness kiss. He returned it, dropping Lucy's lead to wrap his arms around my waist.

"Hey, get a room," Brad teased as we stepped back from each other's embrace.

"Hi," he said somewhat breathlessly. "It's nice to see you."

I stared into his eyes for a moment and then picked up Lucy's lead with one hand and took his hand with my other.

"Hi, Ben. It's nice to see you, too."

Acknowledgements

I would like to first thank my editors at Level Best Books, Harriette Wasserman Sackler and Verena Main Rose. They, and the mystery-writing community, have been a great support to me as I wrote this book. My husband, Stuart, two sons, and three dogs also deserve my thanks. Depending on the day, they can be equal parts helpful or distracting, but I still love them. The Reserve on Wynter Island—and the island itself—are make-believe, but the Tsawout First Nation is not. They are one of five W̱SÁNEĆ Communities on Southern Vancouver Island that constitute the Saanich nation. I hope I have done justice in these pages to their Indigenous history and continued fight against systemic racism.

About the Author

Kim worked as a journalist in Canada for many years, with experience in both print and broadcast journalism. Her book, Gelato with the Pope, highlights her time as a syndicated travel columnist in the Nineties.

In addition to her syndicated travel column, she has written feature articles for various publications, edited a monthly children's publication in British Columbia, and had her poetry published in Do Whales Jump At Night: A Canadian Anthology of Children's Poetry. She won a Microsoft web design award for Footloose, one of the first digital e-zines on the internet.

The Loon's Song is the second book in her mystery series, The Wynter Island Mysteries. It is based in the Gulf Islands of British Columbia and follows a journalist seeking a new life as manager of a small community tv station.

Kim is a board member of Sisters in Crime New England as well as their Director of Public Relations.

She lives in New Hampshire with her husband, two sons, and three dogs.

SOCIAL MEDIA HANDLES:
www.facebook.com/kim.h.shapiro

instagram: @kimhshapiro
tiktok: @kim.h.shapiro

AUTHOR WEBSITE: kimhshapiro.com

Also by Kim Herdman Shapiro

Do Whales Jump at Night: Poems for Kids, Groundwood Books, Toronto, 1990

Gelato with the Pope: and other adventures of a travel writer in Europe, Bamberry Cove Books, Vancouver, BC, 1997

The Raven's Cry, Level Best Books, 2023

www.ingramcontent.com/pod-product-compliance
Lightning Source LLC
Chambersburg PA
CBHW050153120726
47903CB00002B/602